MARIGOLD

A NOVEL

MARIGOLD

A NOVEL

LORI WAGNER

Marigold
Book 3 of *The Briar Hollow Series*
Copyright © 2015 by Lori Wagner

Design and layout by Laura Merchant
Cover model, Elisabeth Cayten

ISBN: 978-0-9897373-2-6

Library of Congress Control Number: 2015920728

Scripture quotations are from the King James Version.

Requests for information should be addressed to:
Affirming Faith
8900 Ortonville Road
Clarkston, MI 48348
loriwagner@affirmingfaith.com
www.affirmingfaith.com

Printed in the United States of America.

DEDICATION

There was never a question to whom this third book of The Briar Hollow Series would be dedicated. God gave me my own "Marigold." Her name is Hope Wagner, my treasured youngest daughter.

Like the character in the series, Hope is a vibrant young lady who loves the outdoors and animals and spurns ruffles and lace. You never know what might be in her hand when you hear her calling from outside, "Mom, look at this? Can I keep it?"

Also like Marigold, Hope has a discerning, loving heart of compassion. When she was younger, her favorite bedtime Scripture was found in 1 Thessalonians 5:16-17, "Rejoice evermore. Pray without ceasing." In recent years, she has favored Psalm 8:1, "O LORD our Lord, how excellent is thy name in all the earth! Who has set thy glory above the heavens." Both reveal her love for life, concern for others, and appreciation for God and His beautiful creation.

Hope, Mom loves you very much!

I also want to remember my dear friend, Dr. Elizabeth McGhee, who passed this year in an airplane accident. As you read, you will find a character, Fred McGhee, to be one of the "bad guys." While Elizabeth was certainly one of the "good guys" in the years I knew her, I am sure she would delight in being remembered in this small way.

For Lori Wagner's speaking schedule,
booking information, and additional resources,
see the Affirming Faith website at
www.affirmingfaith.com

$\mathcal{A}$CKNOWLEDGMENTS

Special thanks to:

My husband Bill and our children, Charles and Hope, for their loving and patient support as I disappeared in "Briar Hollow" for untold hours.

Kathy Bouren for editing assistance.

CHAPTER 1

"Would you stop smiling like that?" Marigold shook her golden braids, a stern look on her freckled face.

"Like what?" Pansy Joy grinned and adjusted the ribbons of her poke bonnet. "Isn't it a perfectly beautiful day? The sun is shining, the sky is clear, and . . . what's that?"

"What's what?" Marigold scrunched her brows and tried to follow her sister's intense study of the scenery along the roadside. The two had walked the same path only an hour before with nothing notable to see.

Pansy Joy closed her eyes and sniffed. "Yes, I am quite certain," she said. "I do believe I smell something."

Marigold sniffed and paused, and then sniffed again. "I don't smell anything out of the ordinary."

"Oh, yes," Pansy Joy drew in a deep breath, "there is definitely love in the air."

"What?" Marigold threw a sideways glance at her sister and stomped a booted foot on the old buffalo trace that was now the main road to town. "Oh, bosh! You don't know what you are talking about."

"You know Eli is sweet on you," said Pansy Joy, matter-of-factly.

"I don't know any such thing." Marigold pulled her hands from her hips and resumed walking. Her pace was slower than usual, and she walked in silence for a ways.

Pansy Joy held her peace.

"Even if he was," said Marigold, "you know what his ma would say."

"Oy vey," both girls answered in unison.

Pansy Joy gave a hearty laugh, and Marigold snickered. "Who needs a man anyway?" Marigold raised her hands, palms up, and shrugged her shoulders.

"It is not always a question of need, you know," said Pansy Joy.

"I know what you are saying," said Marigold, "but I am not sure I want to be tied down to any fella, no matter how handsome he is."

Pansy Joy noticed Marigold's blush—a nonverbal acknowledgement of Eli Thalman's dark good looks.

"Sure," said Marigold, "a fella might act sweeter than maple syrup during courting days, but what if he changes after the deed is done, and then a girl gets stuck for life with a hard case?"

"I like being stuck with Garth just fine," said Pansy Joy.

Warmth filled Pansy Joy's big brown eyes. "Yes, I like being stuck with Garth just fine." She twisted a curl between petite fingers. "I can't imagine life without him or our little ones."

"Well, that is you and Garth." Marigold clipped her words and picked up her pace to a march of decisive steps.

"And Zion and Rosalie. And Logan and Penny. And the Erlangers. And . . . ."

"Those are all country folk," said Marigold, "did you notice?"

"That is true," said Pansy Joy. "Don't you think any city folks have happy marriages?"

Marigold tucked her chin in her hand. "Honestly, I am not so sure about that."

"It doesn't seem to me you would be thinking about such a thing at all if you were not interested in a city boy."

Marigold pursed her lips and shook her head. "I am not interested in anything but switching out the queens in my hives."

"You mean you did not notice Eli's tender looks your way?"

Color flushed over Marigold's features. She could not deny the pointed question. For the first time in her life, Marigold Johnson felt unsure of herself. Images of Eli flashed in her mind. There was no mistaking the change in his countenance each time they met. There was also no doubt, in Marigold's mind, they were completely unsuited for a match.

Marigold was a boisterous tomboy, still wearing braids hanging down her back, long past the time respectable young ladies pinned their hair up in neat, grown-uppish coiffures. She would have been happy to walk to town barefoot if Pa allowed. Marigold was a country girl, through and through—and not a frilly, dainty one either, like her sisters.

The sun on her face, grass between her toes, a fish on her hook, and dirt under her fingernails from working in the garden or digging worms—these were the things that brought Marigold pleasure. Next to being outside, she loved her critters and her bees above all but God and family. How could someone like Eli Thalman, son of a successful tailor and clothing merchant, be sweet on someone like her, she wondered.

"I have noticed," Marigold whispered.

Pansy Joy allowed her sister time to gather her thoughts as they continued on their way to Pansy Joy's cabin. The sisters stopped in the road at the path that led to the Eldridge farm.

Goldenrod stood at attention, listening, waiting for Marigold to speak.

"Did you notice he doesn't come to church?"

Pansy Joy nodded.

"Not only are we an unlikely pair—him with his city ways, and me with my country ways—he is Jewish," said Marigold. "Even if there was some interest or sparks of affection, you know the 'unequally yoked' thing."

"That is true," said Pansy Joy, "and I am not saying it is not true, but you know, I think it is possible to be unequally yoked with someone who sits under the same preaching in the same church house."

"What do you mean?"

"Two people can belong to the same congregation, but have very different outlooks on life, ministry, and how to treat others," said Pansy Joy. "I am afraid there are members of our own local assembly who are not 'yoked up' in agreement on some really important things."

Marigold considered her sister's words. Some frightful activities had been happening around Briar Hollow in the dark of the night. "Do you really think those yellow-bellied lynchers could be from our church?"

"I wish I could say no," said Pansy Joy, "but I have to say, I can't get away from this uneasy feeling I have been having about it."

"You don't think Eli's family is involved then?"

"Honestly, Marigold, I don't." Pansy Joy contorted her lips, deep in thought. "I think it is easy to blame new folks for new problems, but the Thalmans have suffered their fair share of prejudice since they came last year."

"They seem to be doing well at their business. Their store is always buzzing with folks coming and going."

"They make the best suits in the county. That is for sure. But just because people use their services or buy their products, well, that is not the same thing as accepting them as friends."

Marigold thought on the times church folks gathered for picnics and socials, and how Eli and his family did not participate. Even Lark, who had eloped with Eli's older brother, Reuben, kept to herself and her family these days. The Thalmans were active in the business community, but Marigold rarely saw them in social settings.

Pansy Joy gave her sister a hug. "I have to go now, Mar. I am sure Garth is ready for me to be home. Maggie and Blythe are surely up from their naps by now."

"Tell him I said thanks for sharing you today," said Marigold.

"I will," said Pansy Joy, "and you give Pa and Lucas my love."

Pansy Joy quickly covered the short path leading to the small cabin she shared with her husband and two children on the Eldridge Farm. Her in-law's house, a quarter of a mile away, sat on the same property. Father and son worked together farming the land that had been in their family for three generations.

Once inside the cabin, it took a moment for Pansy Joy's eyes to adjust to the dim light and make out the figures of her husband and son both asleep in the rocking chair. Emotion flooded in her at the sight of her loved ones, mingled with thoughts of her earlier conversation with her sister. She knew Marigold was a tomboy and a playful girl at that, but she also knew that behind the freckles and grins and pranks was a heart of gold. Marigold loved deeply, and was deeply loyal, as well. "Surely, Lord, you have something special for her," she whispered in prayer.

Pansy Joy placed her basket on the table and lifted her little one from her husband's arms. Garth opened his eyes, but kept silent.

Blythe stirred as Pansy Joy carried him to her bedroom, but then settled back down when she placed him in his flannel-lined cradle.

"Hello, sleepyhead," said Pansy Joy when she returned from the bedroom.

"Hello, beautiful."

A sweet smile swept across Pansy Joy's face. "Was Blythe fussy?"

"No. He slept well, but after about an hour, I heard him chattering like a magpie. I picked him up, and he was so warm and sweet, I just wanted to hold him for a minute. Well, you saw what happened from there."

"Yes, I did, and I am sure that was a nicer way to spend the afternoon than tinkering with one of your contraptions out in the barn." Pansy Joy retrieved an envelope from her basket and handed it to her husband. "Mr. Perkins had a letter for you."

"I wasn't expecting anything," said Garth.

"It is from a Mr. Kelley in Minnesota."

Garth flipped the envelope to confirm the return address. "I don't know a Mr. Kelley in Minnesota." He placed the envelope on his lap and looked up at his wife. "I will open it after you tell me how things went in town."

"Fine," said Pansy Joy, "just fine."

Garth studied his wife's features. She usually bubbled with vitality and the joy that was part of her name, but the tone of her voice was a bit flatter than normal.

"Your lips are saying 'fine', but my eyes and ears are telling me there is more to the story."

Pansy Joy looked into her husband's face and offered a soft smile. His attentiveness and concern made him all the more dear. "Well, my love, all the business was handled without any problems at all. Marigold and I took some of Pa's old clothes into the Thalmans, and they are going to use them to make a custom suit for his birthday."

"That is one way to get a perfect fit without a fitting," said Garth. "And . . . ."

"And," said Pansy Joy, "there is no way I could miss the looks flying between Eli and Marigold."

Garth nodded. "Is that what has you looking so woebegone?"

"I just want Marigold to be as happy as we are. She is almost 20 years old and never shown any interest in anyone before. It does make me sad that there is no real chance of a match with the only fellow who has ever caught her eye."

"I see." Garth stood and folded Pansy Joy into his arms. How he loved her, his precious girl. He had known she was the one for him since grammar school days. It had been hard to wait until she turned 16 to marry her, but he did not regret it, and he never tired of the way he felt when she was in his arms.

"You know," said Garth, "I am all for settling down with a good woman, but we have to trust God with the matchmaking, darlin'."

Pansy Joy pulled back enough to look into her husband's face. "Are you saying God doesn't use people to accomplish His will?"

Garth lowered his gaze and probed his wife's brown eyes filled with mischief and a challenge. "I don't think I said that."

"That is good, because Reverend Dryfus was just preaching about that on Sunday morning."

"I know, wife, I was there," said Garth. "All right, Mrs. Pansy Joy Johnson Eldridge, what is going on in that pretty little head of yours? One minute you are about teared up because there is no chance for a match; and the next you are acting like the handmaiden of the Lord on official business."

Pansy Joy twirled from her husband's embrace and giggled as she reached for her apron and tied it around her burgeoning waistline. "Oh, I don't know, Garth. Maybe it is just being with child that makes my emotions swing so."

"You are not getting off that easy."

"Getting off? I am getting on," said Pansy Joy with a grin. She pulled the pot of beans forward to the front burner of the cast iron stove. "I am getting on with the supper fixings."

"And that is all the fixings you are fixing to do?"

"You are fixing to see, I guess."

CHAPTER 2

M arigold's steps slowed while her thoughts raced. Oblivious to the purples, golds, and oranges that marked the coming of fall and her twentieth birthday, she meandered in a mental fog, wondering at the changes in her over the last two months.

What was it about Eli Thalman that kept pulling at her heart? Marigold uttered a half-suppressed laugh at her own foolish question. *He is gorgeous, that is what!* Marigold flipped a braid over her shoulder and shook her head, continuing her musings as she finished her walk home.

Am I knocked into a cocked hat over a curly-headed, dark-eyed fellow? What would I think about a man who was only drawn to a woman because she was easy on the eyes?

There was more to the attraction, she knew, but she could not precisely put her finger on it. Perhaps it was his gentleness, but that thought spun her like the wind in a whirligig. Marigold was well aware she was nigh on the outside edge of gentle. Her Pa called her rambunctious, and she had a reputation for being a prankster.

Perhaps it was the way he treated her like a lady. When other young men were willing to take her on in a spitting contest or arm wrestling match, Eli's countenance and conduct told her that he considered her in a different light. Eli made Marigold feel like a lady, and that was a new sensation—one she was coming to appreciate even if she wasn't quite ready to put her hair up for good.

The Thalmans had been in Washington for over a year, but Marigold had met Eli only two months previous. Logan Mayfield, a relative of sorts, had ordered several suits from Thalman and Sons Clothiers. Eli had delivered them when Marigold was at Briar Hollow helping Logan's wife, Penny, prepare a new garden plot.

Marigold spent much of her time at the clearing between the copse of woodland and the orchards her pa, Matthias Johnson, husbanded. Her sister, Rosalie, and brother-in-law, Zion Coldwell, lived in the little cabin in the hollow where she and her siblings had been born and raised. Zion now used the clearing for the horse farm he worked in partnership with Logan Mayfield, his sister Penny's husband.

Prior to proposing to Penny, Logan had purchased five acres of the land across the creek that marked the perimeter of the Coldwell property. The first order of business had been building a bridge sturdy enough to support a wagon and team. To protect the bridge and provide some privacy, Logan commissioned a timber-truss structure with a roof and siding. The covering created an almost complete enclosure and a grand entrance to the Mayfield property.

While the bridge was under construction, Logan and Garth drew up plans for a modest home for his family, his wife and widowed mother. A wealthy man, Logan had the financial resources to build a grand house, but decided to first build a three-bedroom cabin on the south side of the property. In the future, if he decided to build a manse, the little dwelling would make a lovely guesthouse. In the meantime, the smaller building provided a place to live, and Penny, Logan, and Millicent were very pleased.

The clip-clop of a horse's hooves on wood marked Eli's arrival before his fringed surrey cleared the opening of the covered bridge. Penny and Marigold had been clearing stones from a plot of ground in preparation for next year's garden. The sun in their eyes kept the girls from making out the figure in the vehicle.

Both girls stood as the horse came to a stop and a handsome gentleman disembarked from the surrey.

"Good afternoon, ladies," said the dark-eyed, dark-haired stranger.

"Good afternoon," said Penny.

"Afternoon," said Marigold.

"My name is Eli Thalman. I was told I would find Mr. Mayfield across the bridge past Briar Hollow. Is this the correct location?"

"Yes, it is," said Penny. "I am Mrs. Mayfield, and this is Miss Marigold Johnson."

"It is a pleasure to meet you." Eli doffed his wide, straw-brimmed hat, giving the girls a peek at his glistening curls as he tipped his head in greeting. The combination of his exotic good looks and the mystery of his unexpected appearance muted Marigold's normal chatter.

She looked at her soil-caked hands, clasped them behind her back, and then nodded her head in return greeting. The corners of her mouth turned upward in a pleasant smile.

"What can I do for you, Mr. Thalman?" Penny wiped what dirt she could get off her hands onto her apron.

"Your husband ordered three suits from my father. He has already had them fitted, and the hemming and pressing were finished this morning. We wanted to offer a courtesy delivery in appreciation of his business."

Eli smiled. His lips were full beneath a distinctive nose. A trim beard and moustache covered the lower portion of his elongated face, and he wore wire spectacles.

Marigold could hardly believe the way his smile affected her. So this is what other girls meant when they said they had butterflies in their stomachs.

"So, here I am," said Eli. "Is Mr. Mayfield in?"

"He has gone to Maysville for the day," said Penny. "He will be so sorry to have missed you."

"I am sorry, too," said Eli. "Would you like me to return tomorrow?"

"Oh, no," said Penny. "It was so kind of you to come today. Please, just bring them in, if you don't mind."

Eli surveyed the home site in search of male presence, and then turned his attention back to Penny. "Are you ladies alone?"

Marigold sensed Eli's hesitancy. He was obviously uncomfortable about entering the home alone with the girls. "Mr. Mayfield's mother is inside."

Eli nodded and smiled his appreciation to Marigold. "In that case, I will be happy to bring them in."

"That would be fine as cream gravy," said Marigold, her hands still clasped behind her calico dress, a sweet smile playing across her freckled face.

Eli grinned. "Is cream gravy fine, then?"

Marigold's eyes grew large. "You have never had cream gravy?"

"Not to my knowledge," said Eli.

"We have some most every day," said Marigold. "There is nothing better to do with bacon drippings than whip up some cream gravy."

"Ema has never cooked with bacon drippings."

"Ema?"

"That is the Hebrew word for mother."

"Oh," said Marigold. "And what do you call your pa?"

"I call him Abba."

Marigold's thoughts swirled. "Ema and Abba."

"Marigold, we are keeping Mr. Thalman from his business," said Penny. "Let's wash up while he retrieves the suits."

"All right," said Marigold, although she was reluctant to end the conversation. She loved learning. Not so much book-learning, but through experiences and conversation. Without question, she was certainly interested in studying Eli Thalman.

The girls disappeared inside the cabin. Penny had a tub of soapy water on hand left from washing the morning dishes. She scrubbed up first, followed by Marigold, who was just wiping her hands when Eli knocked on the door.

Marigold hurried to open it while Penny knocked on her mother-in-law's bedroom door to let her know they had company. Logan had built his mother's room with a generous window, and Millicent had a practice of reading in her cushioned rocking chair in the peaceful haven.

Penny ducked her head inside the doorway after Millicent answered her knock.

"We have company," said Penny. "Logan's new suits are being delivered."

"How nice," said Millicent. "I will be right there."

Penny returned to the living area where Marigold had admitted Eli, his arms filled with three fine suits made of high quality fabric and with intricate attention to detail. "Just lay them across the table, and I will hang them in my room."

"Shouldn't we offer Mr. Thalman some refreshment?" asked Marigold.

"Yes, of course," Penny said, following her thinking, "but I would like to see the suits for a moment, and then we can clear the table for refreshments."

"Thank you for the invitation, but I need to get back to town before sunset. Ema would be disappointed if I missed the candle lighting." Eli smiled. He placed the suits on the table and then stepped back. "I would not want to miss it, either."

Millicent heard the conversation as she moved from her bedroom to the living area. "Sabbath candles are lit 18 minutes before sunset," said Millicent.

Eli nodded. "That is right."

"Eli Thalman, this is my mother-in-law, Millicent Mayfield."

"It is a pleasure to meet you," said Eli.

"And you," said Millicent. Her eyes turned to the suits on the table. "Oh, these are lovely, Mr. Thalman. I can't wait to see Logan wear them."

"My father always says, 'clothes make the man,'" said Eli.

"I am sure Logan will wear one to church this weekend," said Marigold. Thoughts of Sunday service sent Marigold into mental inventory. She had never seen the Thalmans at church, and with the talk of Sabbath candles, it dawned on her that he must be Jewish.

Eli watched the ciphering behind Marigold's big brown eyes. He saw the "click" when the pieces came together, and when she turned to look into his face, he admired her thoughtful countenance. There was a spark in those brown eyes that drew him.

"Ladies, if you will pardon me, I will take my leave."

By the time Marigold passed Briar Hollow, her thoughts had been all over the map. She resisted the urge to visit Rosalie or Penny, and continued past the orchard to the lane that led to the cabin she shared with her father, Matthias Johnson, and her nine-year-old brother, Lucas.

The apple trees were abloom with fruit, some puddled beneath the canopies of laden branches. Although she was thankful for the abundant yield, the surplus meant extra hours in the kitchen when she much preferred being outdoors.

Rosalie knew every apple recipe on the continent, and not one slice would go to waste. What apples were not sold would be put to good use. Marigold could almost smell the applesauce, apple cakes, apple pies, apple fritters, and apple chutney. They would bake apples and stew apples. And then they would make apple butter, apple relish, and apple jelly.

Besides all the cooking and canning, they would also be drying apples and pressing apples into cider and juice. If that was not enough, Rosalie made potpourri, candle holders, stamps, and even bird feeders out of apples. Apple season was just reaching full swing, and Marigold was already sick, sick, sick at the thought of apples, apples, and more apples.

Lucas looked up from his yoyo to see his sister walking his way. He had perfected Sleeping and Walk the Dog, and was working diligently at mastering the Man on the Flying Trapeze. It was one of the most difficult maneuvers, and when he looked up to see Marigold, he missed catching the yoyo. Instead of accepting the obvious miss, he made a quick adjustment to end in an easier trick.

"Looking good, Lukey," said Marigold. "You are better on that than I ever was. Nice Pinwheel."

"Thanks, but I was working on The Man on the Flying Trapeze. Ben Dryfus says he is going to get it down before I do, and, well, we will just see about that."

Marigold ruffled her brother's saddle-brown hair.

"Would you stop treating me like a dog?" Lucas pulled back from his sister. "Go pet Daisy."

"Whoa," said Marigold. "Don't be such an old croaker."

Lucas dropped the yoyo and let it hang from its string. He focused on the wooden spool, watching it spin and come to a stop.

"Looks like you need to get rid of some tension, there," said Marigold.

"Yeah."

"You know, every time you throw it, the string gets tighter," said Marigold. "That is why you need to stop and let the tension out."

Lucas lifted his green eyes to his sister's face. He knew Marigold well enough to know she was talking about more than just the wooden spool in his hand. When his older sisters had been bitten by the love bug and married off years ago, Marigold had been his companion. She was the one who could read his emotions before he said one word.

Lucas hefted his shoulders and let out a long breath.

"That is better. I can see the tension dropping off now." Marigold sat on one of the stumps around the fire ring. She patted the stump next to her. "Why don't you tell me what has got you lower than a snail's foot."

Lucas sat down on the stump. Daisy, their brownish-colored mutt of no known heritage, sauntered between the siblings and rubbed against Lucas' shin. Her skinny tail stuck up like a cattail waving in the breeze.

"You are not all balled up over a yoyo trick now, are you, little brother?"

"Nah. Not really."

"What has got your back up? You know you can tell me."

Lucas wound the string around the shaft of his yoyo, searching for the right words. "I am worried about Abram and Abby."

"Oh." Marigold nodded.

Since Balim and Minnie had moved to Briar Hollow with their children, Abram and Abby, Lucas had watched over them. He had been the little one for so long, he took to the role of protector in a heartwarming way. Watching Lucas with the children, ages one-and-a-half and four, reminded Marigold of the momma swan who nested along their creek. She spotted her several times gliding across the water with her little ones on her back, tucked beneath her wings so they would not fall off on the way back to their nest.

"Don't you think Balim and Minnie take good care of them?" asked Marigold.

"I know Balim is strong," said Lucas, "but what about those men with the white hoods?"

"They are a bunch of cowards," said Marigold.

"I heard Sheriff Nash talking to Pa about them. He said so far this year there have been lynchings in Frankfurt, Louisville, and Owensboro, and there were two in Paris—one just last week."

"Did Pa know you were listening to his conversation with the sheriff?"

"I wasn't eavesdropping, Marigold." Lucas's bottom lip projected out, and he folded his arms across his chest.

"I didn't say you were," said Marigold. "I just wondered if Pa was aware you had all this information."

"They were sitting on the porch," said Lucas. "You know how Pa likes to whittle in the evening."

"Yes, I do. I am constantly sweeping away the shavings."

"You were over at the hollow for some reason or another, and they were sitting on the porch talking. I was practicing with my yoyo in the yard. I couldn't help overhearing."

"You know, Lucas, a lot of that Klan activity is political, especially farther south, where Democrats are trying to make sure Republicans and blacks don't get elected. They try to bulldoze folks with fear and intimidation, but there is not so much of that going on around here."

"Are you sure?"

"Do you know what I am sure of?" asked Marigold.

"What is that?"

"I am sure there is a God in heaven Who is watching over you, and me, and Abram and Abby."

Marigold slapped her palms on her thighs. "And I am also feeling quite sure it is high time for an apple toss."

A smile broke across Lucas' heart-shaped face. "Isn't it a little early in the season?"

"We'll just pick some of the really bruised ones," said Marigold. "I am already plumb sick thinking about being cooped up canning and cooking for days. Let's show a few of 'em who's boss. What do you say?"

"Apple toss," said Lucas. He held his yoyo in front of him with his left hand, and then pulled the string with his right hand back behind his ear. "And then maybe some archery."

"Skewered apples," said Marigold. "But don't tell Rosalie, or she will have us roast them on an open fire or something."

CHAPTER 3

"Be careful," Rosalie watched as Penny pulled a jar of apple jelly from a big pot of boiling water.

"Oh, I am," said Penny. She lifted a second jar and placed it on a towel about an inch from the first. "I can hardly believe how nice these old jars look after you soaked them in vinegar water."

Rosalie nodded as she scraped pulp from the sieve into a pan. "It is the best way to get the film off. Who wants to put new jelly in old jars?"

"That reminds me of a Scripture," said Penny.

"The new wine in old wineskins?"

"Yes." Penny removed the last jar from the pot and began filling it again with the rest of the batch. "I have always puzzled over that passage."

"I know what you mean," said Rosalie. "Reverend Dryfus said it relates to Jesus' teaching and traditional Judaism—that what Jesus brought was something new that could not be contained in rituals and laws."

"I get that," said Penny, "but what puzzles me is the part after putting the new wine in new bottles. The verse right after that one says that if a person drank the old wine, they would not want the new. I can't imagine not wanting grace . . . not wanting a savior. Were not the Jews hoping for and looking for a Messiah?"

"Have you ever noticed," said Rosalie, "that the verse says *straightway*?"

"I guess I never gave that much thought."

"Think about it. It says those who drank the old wine did not straightway desire the new, but it does not mean they never would."

A knock sounded on the door. Rosalie answered, and a bright shaft of light struck the floor of the Coldwell cabin.

"Hi," Rosalie greeted her youngest sister. Marigold entered carrying a bushel of a mixed variety of apples.

"Hey." Marigold placed the basket on the floor and moved to the stove. "I'm sorry I am late. Any samples?"

Penny lifted a spoon that had been inverted on the thick wooden counter. A bit of jelly clung to it. "Here's my test spoon. There is enough for a taste on it."

Marigold lifted the spoon to her mouth and savored the sweet, fruity jelly. "Mm. The only thing better would be to have some on a cracker. Sweet and salty together are the perfect mix."

"I like sweet and sweet," said Penny.

"I like both," said Rosalie, "but a bit of apple jelly is the perfect complement to a crisp, salty cracker."

"Speaking of salty crackers," said Marigold, "Pa sent over another bushel of windfall apples."

"Aw," said Rosalie, "Pa isn't a salty cracker."

"He can be, when his leg is hurting and the trees are producing more than we can handle."

"Momma always knew how to sweeten him up when he got persnickety," said Rosalie. "Theirs was a combination of sweet and salty that worked."

"They say opposites attract," said Penny, "although Logan and I are pretty similar in our temperaments."

"You are now," said Marigold. "You two used to fight like Kilkenny cats."

Penny blushed and smiled at the same time. "We did have a rough start, but that is all in the past."

"The first time you met, you were like a she-bear protecting her cubs," said Marigold.

Penny crossed her arms in front of her chest and shook her head at her sister-in-law.

"Yeah, just like that." Marigold pointed at Penny's arms.

Penny pursed her lips, a look of indignation on her delicate features.

Marigold pointed at her face. "And just like that."

"Marigold Johnson, you stop that," said Penny. "You know it was not decent or proper for him to stand there at the swimming hole having conversation when we were not properly dressed."

"Oh, never mind, you two," said Rosalie. "We have work to do. Let the past be the past. I am sure Penny and Logan have all kinds of talks in all sorts of states of dress now that they are husband and wife." Rosalie winked at her sister-in-law.

Penny uncrossed her arms and leaned over the canning pot, a tight-lipped smile on her delicate face. "My, it is getting hot in here, isn't it?"

Marigold feigned a cough into her fisted hand. "Did you forget there is a single lady here?"

"Single, yes," said Rosalie. "The lady part, now that is something I would like to see more of." Rosalie noted Marigold's bare feet, messy braids, and lack of head covering. "One of these days you are going to come in with a hat on, and I don't know if I will recognize you."

"I most always wear a hat when I am tending the bees," said Marigold. She brushed off her sister's teasing words. "That reminds, me, I need to transfer larvae from my brood comb into cups."

"Not before we take care of these apples, I hope," said Rosalie.

"It can wait until later. I just need to get them in an established colony sometime today."

"I did not know beekeeping required such precision timing," said Penny.

"Most often it doesn't, but rearing new queens is a different story. Once I get the larvae in the hives, I don't have to do anything for ten days."

"That is good, because we have plenty to keep us busy right now." With deft hands, Rosalie poured sugar into the pan and mixed it with the pulp left over from making jelly.

"Would you put that on the stove and stay with it until the mixture turns clear?" Rosalie handed the pan to Marigold.

"Sure. What are you making with this?"

"Fruit paste. Katie found the recipe in the *Louisville Daily Courier* and sent it to me. I thought I would give it a try."

"Fruit paste? What do you do with that?" asked Marigold.

"Once what you are fixing to cook up is ready, we will spread it out on a greased dish and let it air dry. Then we flip it onto a cloth for more drying." Rosalie closed the sugar container and slipped it on a shelf.

"When it is not sticky anymore, we can cut it into strips or squares. It can be used for flavorings in cakes, cookies and puddings, like citron."

Marigold crinkled her nose at her sister and continued to stir the mixture on the cast iron stove. "So domesticated."

Rosalie shook her head and laughed. "Oh, Marigold, I am sure you will get domesticated yourself, one of these days. And then you will be coming to me for recipes."

"I have the basics down," Marigold defended her culinary skills. "Flap jacks, bacon, beans, and johnny cake."

"What if your fella's name isn't Johnny?" asked Penny. "What kind of cake would you fix him then?"

"Huh?" Marigold stopped stirring and stared.

"Just suppose his name was something else. Maybe someday you will be serving up some George cakes . . . or maybe some Eli cakes."

"Oh, hobble your lip, Penny Mayfield."

"Or maybe you will be making unleavened cakes, like it says in the Bible."

"Oh, Penny, stop teasing." Rosalie chuckled. "That is talking about bread anyway."

"I think it is high time Marigold got her share of the teasing around here. She has been dishing it out for years."

"That is true enough," said Rosalie, "but if we are going to be cooped up in here for the next couple of hours, we better be kind."

Penny picked up a white towel and waved it. "Ok, ok. I surrender. It is just so fun being the teaser rather than the teased for a change."

Marigold leaned over the pan and resumed stirring. "Eli cakes," she muttered.

Rosalie and Penny exchanged glances. Marigold's bright disposition had obviously been tamped down by their banter.

With nimble fingers, Penny wiped down the first batch of jars and moved them over to make room for the second. Rosalie lifted the basket Marigold had brought from the orchard onto the tabletop, reached for an apple, and pared away the bruised portion.

"All this talk has me in the mood for an apple cake," said Rosalie.

"You have enough apples there to make cake for the county," said Penny.

"I know." Rosalie grinned. "I did not mean to use all this for cake—just a few." Rosalie swiped a strand of hair off her forehead with the back of her hand. "I am tired of kitchen work already. Let's make applesauce out of this batch. It is so much quicker than jelly."

"Sounds good to me," said Penny. "You can even leave the skins on, as far as I am concerned. I like the flavor they add."

"Jonathan, Pippin, King David, and Maiden Blush," said Rosalie. "With four different apples, we are sure to have a tasty sauce."

"It will be colorful, too, if you don't peel them," said Penny. "You have two shades of red, orange, and a yellow blush."

"And they are all apples," said Marigold, still stirring and studying the contents of her pan.

"Of course they are," said Penny. "What did you expect? Plums?"

"Nope."

"Marigold," said Rosalie, "It is not like you to be so curt. Why don't you tell us what's got you troubled?"

"Troubled?" Marigold shrugged. "I am not troubled. I just have a lot on my mind."

"Would it help to talk?" asked Penny, remorse for her ribbing written on her face.

Marigold lifted the pan from the stovetop. "Let's take care of this first."

Rosalie set down her knife and the apple she was working on. "Let me help you." Marigold held the pan while Rosalie scraped the contents onto a shallow, greased dish. "There you go."

With lumbering steps, Marigold plodded to the washbasin and dropped the pan in the sudsy water.

"OK, sister-sister," said Penny. "What's on your mind?"

Marigold offered a slight smile at Penny's use of the nickname she had given her, her sister's sister-in-law. "I don't mean to be glum," she said, as she reached for a knife. She carved the bruise off a King David apple, and then sliced it in half to remove the core and seeds.

"It is just that an apple is an apple, regardless of its skin color, just like a person is a person. They are all the same species."

"That is true," said Rosalie. "They are actually in the rose family."

"Oh," Penny smiled. "I never put that together before. No wonder they flower so beautifully in the spring."

"I am just about full up to the gizzard with all the spouting off about people because of the color of their skin." Marigold cut the apple in her hand into slices, dropped it into a large pot, and picked up another to repeat the process.

"Did you see that?" Marigold lifted her eyes from her work and looked from one woman to the next.

"That was a King David. The first one was a Jonathan. They had the same insides, cores, seeds and meat, and they both had skin and stems."

"You would think a King David and a Jonathan would be friends," Rosalie grinned. "They were in the Bible."

Marigold huffed a quasi-laugh. "That is true."

"I understand what you are saying," said Penny, "that people are basically the same, regardless of the color of their skin. But, Marigold, you are preaching to the converted. Everyone here agrees with you."

"I know. But the sad truth is," said Marigold, "that folks are set in their ways. Right or wrong, they just don't want to change."

Penny looked at Rosalie and nodded. "It is like the wineskins we were talking about earlier."

"What is that?" Marigold asked.

"We were talking about the passage of Scripture that says people don't put new wine into old wineskins. How people who have their old wineskins, or ways of thinking and doing things, aren't at first willing to take on new ones."

"And Rosalie had a great thought," said Penny. "That although it sounded like the Jewish leaders were turning away from grace and salvation, there was hope for them."

"How is that?"

"I never noticed the word *straightway* in that passage before," said Penny. "The Bible does say the ones who had the old wineskins did not straightway desire the new wine, but that does not mean that they never would. There is always hope, Marigold. We can't give up on people."

"I know," said Marigold. "I just don't know what it is going to take for people to let go of old, wrong thinking."

"I will say this," said Rosalie. "Not every old thought or way is wrong. Things aren't wrong or right because they are old or new. Some folks call themselves progressives, but if you are standing at the edge of a cliff, moving forward isn't progress. It is suicide."

"Well, you can't deny that," said Marigold, "but you know what I am talking about."

The girls worked in silence for a bit. The fragrance of apples filled the room, and the only sounds were made by knives cutting into the fruit and chunks being plunked into the pan. Penny broke the silence.

"What is it going to take?" Penny reiterated Marigold's question. "It is going to take regeneration."

Marigold turned to look into Penny's face, her blue eyes filled with compassion and resolve. "Old wineskins can't hold new wine, or they will burst. The answer is this: old wineskins must be made new. And only Jesus can do that."

CHAPTER 4

A cheerful tune whistled out Marigold's puckered lips, her steps light on the macadamized road that would take her to town. After the applesauce canning, she convinced Rosalie that their father should have new socks for his new suit. It was true, she told herself, and it also just happened to be a great excuse to get out of the house on this beautiful fall day.

"I will go to the Matheny's and get some nice yarn, and you can knit them," Marigold had suggested.

"Get enough for two pair, would you? A nice wool-cotton blend." Rosalie lifted an index finger to the side of her cheek. "Do you think you should get a fabric sample from the tailor to make sure they are a good match?"

Marigold spun on her heel to hide the pleasure Rosalie's suggestion ignited. Of course, she had hoped to have a chance to see Eli, but to go on a direct assignment to the Thalman's shop was more than she had imagined.

"Good afternoon," Father Peter McMahon's greeting stopped Marigold in her steps on the street outside the St. Patrick church.

"Good afternoon," said Marigold. "Getting things ready for the new school year?"

"Yes, indeed," said the priest. "I believe the boys of the parish will be pleased with their classroom, even though it is in the basement."

"They will appreciate recess, all the more." Marigold lifted her freckled face to the sun and smiled.

Sister Marguerite Marie hurried down the street, her black habit rustling. Beneath her veil, she wore a white wimple that covered her head and neck and a worried expression on her face. "Father," she breathed out in an airy tone. "I am so glad you are here."

"What is it, Sister? You seem a bit rattled."

"I just came from the post office. There were two young men there. One of them was Bob Danhauer, but I don't know the other."

"Is everyone well?" the priest asked.

"There was a big black man who was there first. I was just getting ready to leave, and he was chatting with Mr. Jenkins. When the boys came in, things got ugly."

"Was Bob involved?"

"He wasn't the one who started things, but his friend said Mr. Jenkins better give him his mail first; that he was white, and he should be served before a black man—although he did not say it in such nice language."

"What happened?" asked Marigold, her eyes bright with concern.

"Mr. Jenkins tried to diffuse the situation, and the black man kept cool, but that first young man would not stop talking. He was stalking around like a cat after a mouse. He even poked him in the chest."

"Did anyone get hurt?" asked Reverend McMahon.

"No, but I have a sick feeling that someone may." The nun shook her head and tucked in her bottom lip. "By the time they left, both boys were throwing out threats."

"Do you think you should talk to Sheriff Nash?" asked Marigold.

"I wish it were not the case, but I think prudence dictates," the priest turned to his coworker. "Let's go speak to him, Sister, while the details are fresh in your memory."

"Yes, Father."

Marigold watched as the two walked towards the sheriff's office. A cyclonic twist of thoughts spun through her head, and uneasiness moved into her spirit. *Lord, watch over my hometown,* she prayed.

During the war, Kentucky's border-state status made it one of the primary places brother truly fought against brother. Its citizenry was split on the central issues of the war—a division symbolized by the fact that Abraham Lincoln and Jefferson Davis, both Civil War presidents, were born in Kentucky.

Governor Magoffin had sympathized with the south, but worked to keep Kentucky from seceding. When President Lincoln asked for troops, however, Magoffin said, "I will send not a man nor a dollar for the wicked purpose of subduing my sister Southern states."

Kentucky's declaration of neutrality, which angered Southern sympathizers, was violated first by the Confederates, and, in response, by the Union Army. Although Kentucky did not take sides in the war, the commonwealth endured harsh conflicts—from military skirmishes to bushwacking bands of unruly soldiers who looted and robbed.

In the year following the war, Kentucky was the scene of much turmoil. By remaining in the union, its citizens were spared harsh Reconstruction measures, but as a former slave state, they faced severe economic challenges, including a sharp drop in food production.

The end of the war brought with it lingering bitterness between those who had supported opposing sides, and violence erupted into disheartening feuds. With the newly formed Ku Klux Klan, former slaves continued to be harassed and intimidated.

Marigold's previously bright countenance darkened by concern over the altercation, but she resumed her walk to Thalman and Sons Clothiers. She passed the post office, and forcibly kept herself from walking in and talking to Mr. Jenkins.

When she reached her destination, Asher Thalman opened the door of the shop for her before she could reach for the knob.

"Good afternoon, Miss Johnson," he said, a broad smile stretched across his face.

"Good afternoon to you." Marigold offered a reserved smile in return.

"How can I help you today?"

Marigold heard sounds coming from the back room, the clicking rhythm of a sewing machine needle accompanied by the slower thump of a treadle. Masculine voices in friendly conversation rose above the sounds of their trade.

"I know we just ordered Pa's suit, and it is not ready yet," said Marigold. "My sister would like to knit some matching socks. I was wondering if I might have a snip of fabric to match some yarn."

"Certainly, certainly," said Asher. "Excuse me just a moment."

The young man disappeared in the back room. Marigold waited, taking in the sights of the cozy shop. At the back, a large counter stood in front of a wall lined with shelves. Hats perched along the top two rows, while bolts of fabric filled the lower ones. To her left, a small dressing room tucked in the corner near the entrance to the back workroom, and a sitting area with a carved table and four upholstered Belter chairs stood in the adjacent corner.

Two wirework mannequins graced the front of the display window. One wore an outfit of black-and-grey-checked trousers, a fawn-colored vest over a white shirt, a black bow tie, and a black frock coat. The second donned a black suit with a more formal long coat, pewter vest, white shirt and bright blue cravat. On the window, in Copperplate script, the words "Thalman and Sons" were painted in an arch over a horizontal and larger "Clothiers."

Asher emerged from the workroom, followed by a grinning Eli.

"My brother will help you, Miss Johnson." Asher stepped behind the counter and set to work replacing bolts of fabric from the counter to the shelf in color order, from dark to light.

"Hello." Eli blinked. Warmth filled his dark eyes, and the corners of his lips swept upward in a pleasing curve.

Marigold's natural boldness dissipated under his scrutiny. For a moment, she turned her gaze to her fingers clasped together at her waist, and then lifted her head to address the subject at hand.

If only he was not so distracting, she thought as she composed herself, amused at her response to this curly-haired man with the wire spectacles perched on his prominent nose.

"Hello," said Marigold. "Did your brother tell you what I came for?"

"Yes, he did." Eli opened his hand, revealing a piece of the fabric Marigold and Pansy Joy had selected for their father's suit. "At your service, miss."

"How very efficient," said Marigold. "Thank you, sir."

Marigold lifted her hand to receive the sample. Eli placed his left hand beneath hers, and with his right, carefully transferred the fabric into Marigold's open palm. Her fingers curled around the bit of navy cloth, and for one tender moment, Eli cupped her hand in both of his in a warm handshake.

A tingle ran up Marigold's arm and into her heart. The exchange was brief, and not inappropriate, but Marigold sensed affection in his touch.

Eli dropped his hands to his sides, his dark eyes probing Marigold's. "You are planning to knit socks?"

Marigold wrapped her right hand around her clasped fist and drew both hands to her chest. A shy smile played across her freckled face. "Actually, my sister is a dreadful good knitter," she confessed. "I just came to fetch the supplies."

"I see."

Marigold took a deep breath. She wanted to stay, but had no viable reason to do so.

"May I offer a suggestion?" Eli asked.

"Of course."

"You and your sister chose a very conservative suit," said Eli. He motioned to the mannequin wearing the checkered pants. "Patterns are very popular right now. If your sister is a skilled knitter, your father might enjoy some striped or checked socks."

Marigold considered the suggestion. Matthias Johnson was not a flashy dresser, to say the least, but he did have personality. She and Pansy Joy had chosen the navy because it would be fitting for any occasion "from marrying to burying" her father would say. Still, the thought of fun stockings made her smile.

"That would be fine as cream gravy." Marigold's face lit up in a full smile. "What color would you suggest?"

She opened her hand to study the navy fabric.

Eli smiled. "Things are slow here right now. Would you like me to accompany you to the mercantile to assist you in your selection?"

Marigold's lips formed a silent "oh," her surprise and pleasure evident in her expression. "That would be grand," she said, "just grand."

"I will just let Abba know." Eli disappeared in the back room and then reappeared. "I will be back in a few minutes," he said to Asher, as he opened the door for Marigold.

"Thank you," said Marigold, feeling like a lady under the influence of Eli's gentlemanly conduct. She walked through the door, skirts swishing, and out into the sunshine. "And thank you for your help."

"My pleasure." Eli dropped into rhythm beside Marigold.

"My color-matching skills don't hold a candle to Rosalie's. She is all the time working on quilts and putting colors and patterns together. I think it is a gift."

"We all have our gifts," said Eli. "I am sure you have your own unique talents. What do you like to do?"

"Well," said Marigold, "my favorite activities are all outdoors. I help out a lot at the orchard and the horse farm."

"All that sunshine must brighten your freckles."

Marigold knew how Rosalie had always been embarrassed by her freckles and assumed a lady should be, since Rosalie was the personification of ladylikeness. But there was something in her that embraced her sprinkling of sun kisses.

"It may at that."

Marigold's lighthearted answer delighted Eli. He found too many girls were so caught up in looking just so and acting just so, they hardly seemed real.

"What else do you do?" he asked.

"I do have my own business," she said. "I am a beekeeper."

"Really? Do you ever get stung?"

"It is only natural that if you spend a lot of time with bees, you will get stung now and again. I wear protective gear, though, and I know when to work, and when not to work."

"How can you know that?" asked Eli.

"Bees are fussier when the weather is cold, cloudy or windy. To keep them from getting into a shindy, I just wait until the weather is good, as much as I can. Right now I am raising some queens, and those have to be timed just right."

"Raising queens," said Eli. "What a thought."

"Having a productive queen is vital," said Marigold. "If I need to work with the bees, I sometimes put a little smoke around the hive. That makes them calm. Peaceful bees are less likely to sting."

The couple neared the post office. Marigold quieted, and her countenance darkened. Eli, who had been listening and watching attentively, noted the change.

"Are you well, Miss Johnson?"

"Hm?" Marigold half-heard his question.

"Oh, yes, I am sorry." She slowed her steps and looked inside the post office window. Mr. Jenkins appeared to be alone at his station.

Marigold debated sharing her heart with Eli. Wonder got the best of her.

"Mr. Thalman?"

"Yes?" Eli gave his full attention to the golden-haired girl on the walk beside him.

"Have you ever wondered what it is like to be hated by folks for no other reason than the color of your skin?"

Eli drew back at her pointed question, surprised at the turn the conversation had taken. He studied the tightness of her lips and furrow of her brow. She was serious, of that he was certain.

"Actually, Miss Johnson, I am sorry to say that I do not have to wonder about prejudice. My family has experienced it firsthand."

Marigold's fog-filled head cleared as Eli's words drew her to keen attention. Once again, she found herself speechless in his presence.

Eli watched her puzzling in silence. "You know my family and I only came to Washington last year."

"Yes," said Marigold. "You came from the western part of the state, did not you?"

"Yes. Paducah."

"That's right. I remember now."

"We were forced to leave the town because we are Jewish."

Marigold's eyes widened, and she sucked in a breath. "Forced? What kind of hard case would bulldoze a nice family like yours?"

"General Ulysses S. Grant."

"Are you bluffing me?" Marigold blinked and crossed her arms over her chest.

"Not at all," said Eli. "It was General Order No. 11."

"What does that mean?"

"It seems General Grant had a perception that Jewish merchants were profiteering in Paducah, and he wanted them out. In December of 1862, he issued an order that said the Jews as a class, violated trade regulations and had to leave within 24 hours from receipt of his order."

"But why would he think that? And why would he act so harshly?"

"Only General Grant knows what is truly in his heart, but it seems he associated my family with the illicit business activities of some."

"What exactly is profiteering?" asked Marigold.

"Profiteering means someone is making excessively high profits through the sale of scarce or rationed goods."

"Your pa seems like an honest man to me."

Eli smiled. "I am glad you think so—and I agree. But regardless of our opinions, one week after Grant's order, on January 4, 1863, all the Jews in Paducah were expelled from the city."

"That is why you came to Washington?"

"That is why. We stopped in Owensboro for awhile where we stayed with some family friends, the Suntheimers, before Abba decided to set up the shop here in Washington."

"I had no idea," said Marigold. "I am so sorry."

"You are sorry I came to Washington?"

A curious look played in Eli's expressive features.

"Oh, no." Marigold shook her head. A spark returned to her big brown eyes, and a slow smile made its way across her face. "I did not mean that at all."

CHAPTER 5

"Thank you all for coming tonight," said Reverend Dryfus. He looked over his congregation as they began to file out of the pews and out the front door of the church. He had been reluctant to use the pulpit for topics such as he had covered at the evening prayer meeting, but with the recent lynching in Paris, and the altercation at the post office, he had felt compelled to do so.

Tensions were high in the community.

"Thank you, Reverend." Matthias Johnson stood in front of the pulpit and waited for the minister to step down. "We need to come together for prayer at times like these."

"Yes, we do."

Matthias leaned on his gnarly old cane. "I know the Good Book says we aren't to live troubled or afraid, but I have an inkling we haven't heard the last of these mudsills and their promiscuous ways."

"I wish I could disagree with you, Elder Johnson, but the same inkling is inkling at me." The minister pulled his lips into a taught line and nodded his farewell to Matthias as Logan and Penny made their way to his side.

"Thanks for the good word." Logan extended his hand. Reverend Dryfus shook it and tipped his head at Penny.

"And thank you for leading us in prayer," said Penny. She stood at her husband's side with her small hand threaded through his bent elbow.

"My pleasure," said Reverend Dryfus. "That is a fine looking suit you are wearing, brother."

Logan smiled and ran the palm of his hand over the quality wool of his new frock coat. "Hiram Thalman does good work."

Penny beamed at her husband. "He looks like a politician, don't you think, Reverend Dryfus?"

"Hold that thought, Buttercup," said Logan. "Garth is the one getting letters from politicians, not me."

"What is that?" asked Reverend Dryfus.

"Garth has received correspondence from a Mr. Kelley about developing a national organization to unify farmers."

"Is that right?"

"Yes, it seems he has a vision of helping rebuild America, bringing grangers together from the north and the south to unite in an organization to help serve the needs of farm families."

"It is really an honor for Garth to be sought out like this," said Penny.

"It sounds like Mr. Kelley's ideas for uniting farming families would be beneficial to the community at large," said Reverend Dryfus. "It is good to see a group of men coming together to build up instead of tear down."

"Amen to that," said Logan. "No white hoods needed."

The road was filled with family as the participants of the evening prayer meeting made their way home. The sun had already set, and the men used lanterns to light their way. The night was warm and pleasant, complemented by the scent of sweet autumn clematis wafting in the light breeze.

"So, Mr. Kelley is calling people together to discuss his ideas of providing educational opportunities for farmers, as well as just social events to get together and have a good time—encourage one another," said Garth.

"I could see this developing into a major political force," said Logan. "If you get enough people together in one place, with the same goals in mind . . . ."

"Unity," said Rosalie, "it is a powerful force."

The sound of hooves pounding on the macadamized road interrupted the conversation.

"Hang on, Mattie." Rosalie wheeled the wagon bearing her little one to the side of the road.

"Dahlia, Maggie," Zion shooed the older children to safety, "get back."

The sound grew louder. Two horses rushed past. The white hoods of the riders flapped as they drove their horses hard down the road.

"Just what I was afearin'," said Matthias Johnson. "Those two can't be up to any good."

"Did anyone recognize them?" asked Zion.

"It is too dark," said Rosalie.

"Pa," Dahlia tugged at her father's overcoat, "were those ghosts?"

Zion scooped his mahogany-headed daughter into his arms. "Oh, no, baby girl. They were just some fellas probably playing some kind of a prank." Zion ran the back of a forefinger against Dahlia's porcelain cheek. "Nothing for you to worry about."

"That is just the problem," said Marigold. "A lot of white folks don't worry about it because they don't think it affects them."

Marigold crossed her arms in front of her chest and stomped a booted foot. "I hate prejudice."

"Nobody here likes it," said Rosalie. "I hope no one was hurt."

"Me, too," said Garth. "Let me know if you find out what is up with those hooligans. I am sure Pansy Joy needs a break from nursing Blythe, so I am going to head in."

Garth left the party on the road and turned down the lane to his farmhouse that sat on the property adjacent Coldwell Horse Farm.

"I will," said Zion.

"I hope Blythe is feeling better," said Rosalie. "If the poultice helped, I can bring another in the morning."

"Thanks, sis."

The group resumed their walk, a bit anxious to be home. The Mayfields and Coldwells turned into the lane that led to Briar Hollow, while the Johnsons continued past the orchard to their place on the other side.

They had just begun their entrance into the juniper-lined lane when gooseflesh crawled up Rosalie's neck and ran down her arms. "Zion," she whispered.

"Yes?"

"Something is not right."

"Lord, cover us," Logan breathed out a prayer, "in Jesus' name."

"You girls stay in the lane with the little ones while Logan and I check things out," said Zion. The two men entered the clearing. Nothing seemed amiss at the horse barn to the right or the gardens to the left. They crept past the hen house. The Coldwell cabin was dark and silent, but a light was on in Balim's place.

When Balim had returned to Briar Hollow the previous year, he had helped Zion build the new horse barn. When they had completed the task, they converted the existing barn into a two-family house. Balim's family lived in the bottom of the house and used the front door. The top had been turned into a bunkhouse where Carver, Zion's other ranch hand, lived. He had a private entrance by way of an outside staircase on the back of the building.

"Where is Angus?" Logan whispered.

"In town. He was meeting up with Cooper after supper, talking some blacksmithing business."

"Balim?"

"He went to Maysville to visit Revered Green."

"That is right." Logan nodded. "Minnie and the kids were here alone?"

"Yes," said Zion. "The light is on. Let's go check on them."

Zion lifted his lantern as they neared the house. A paper was attached to the front door by a nail. The script was bold, but before the men were close enough to make out the words, they heard the sounds of whimpering coming from inside the building.

"Minnie?" Zion called. "It is Zion. Is everything ok?"

Shuffling sounded inside the house. The curtain moved, and Minnie peeked out the window to verify her callers before opening the door.

"Massa Zion, thank God Almighty it's you."

"Minnie, what happened?"

"Me and the little ones was inside for the night. I was readin' them a story when they came a hollerin' and knockin' at the door."

"Who was it?" asked Logan.

"They was wearing white hoods, Massa Logan. I couldn' tell."

"What did they want?" Zion lifted the lamp to read the crude writing on the paper tacked to the door.

"They hollered, 'Open the door.' I was afraid, but I knowed they'd bust it in if'n I didn' do as they said, so I did."

"Look at this," Zion ripped the paper off the door. "Whites reign or you hang."

"Oh, Massa Zion, they's after my Balim."

"Why, Minnie? Did they say?"

"It must be about the ruckus at the post office." Minnie twisted her hands, her brows knit tightly together.

"That was Balim?" Zion was surprised he was just learning this information. Reverend Dryfus had told of the encounter, but not that his own dear friend was involved.

"Yessuh," said Minnie. "Balim didn' want to worry you none, so he said not to say nothin'."

"I can just hear him now," said Zion, "'If I hold my peace, de Lawd's gwanna fight my battles.'"

A grin broke through Minnie's worried expression. "You knows my man, Massa Zion. That you does."

Logan shook his head. Disgust at this loathsome behavior from one human being to another caused him to snarl and huff in an uncharacteristic manner. "So what happened?"

"I think they come to whoop him or warn him," said Minnie. "I'm not sure which."

"Since they came prepared with a note, I would say this was a warning," said Zion.

"'Taint no comfort to my chilluns." Minnie motioned to the little ones huddled on a blanket by the rocking chair. "They scarce blinked an eyelid since those hooded villains rode in."

Zion looked at the children. They did indeed look terrified. "Let me get Rosalie and Penny. They'll help you calm them down and get them to bed."

"I can hardly believe something like this happened right here in Briar Hollow." Rosalie stood in her bedroom brushing her thick auburn hair. "This place has always been like a sanctuary to me, and now I feel unsafe—defiled, in a way."

"Whoever those lowlifes were knew we would not be home," said Zion. "I don't think we are dealing with strangers."

"Oh, Zion." Rosalie dropped her brush to her side and turned to face her husband. "That is even more frightening."

Zion patted the bed, and Rosalie slipped under the quilt beside him. She tucked herself under his arm, and threw one of her slender arms across Zion's broad chest. Zion stroked her silken hair, enjoying the feel of its tresses loose beneath his hand instead of restrained in the braid Rosalie usually wore to bed to keep her long hair from tangling at night.

Rosalie listened to her husband's steady heartbeat. The anxiety that fought to rise in her chest quieted in his embrace. She knew he was praying for her—for their loved ones.

"I think it would be good if we did not leave Balim's family here alone for awhile." Zion felt Rosalie's nod of agreement against his chest.

"Yes," said Rosalie. "Why did Balim go to Maysville today?"

"He has been talking with a minister at the First African Church, Elisha Winfield Green. He is one of the organizers of the Convention of Colored Ministers of the State of Kentucky."

"Does Balim want to join the Convention? Become a preacher?"

Zion chortled. "Balim's been a preacher for years. He has just never done it from behind a pulpit."

"That is true."

"Actually, the Convention is working on founding a college to educate black ministers. Balim has always been a helpful sort, but ever since his time at the Dawn Settlement in Canada, he has had a new mission. He wants to help black people 'catch up' in society—help them get training and education they did not have access to as slaves."

"He has a heart of gold," said Rosalie, "but I am a bit unruffled that he did not tell you about the incident in the post office today."

"Put your worries to rest now, my sweet Rose of Sharon." Zion tipped his wife's face to his and pressed a tender kiss on the tip of her nose. "You know what the Word says about worrying for tomorrow."

Rosalie sighed. "Tomorrow will worry about itself. Each day has enough trouble of its own."

CHAPTER 6

"Lucas, you will have to stop with the yoyoing if you are going to watch me," said Marigold through her net-covered hat. "We don't want to rile up the bees."

"What are you doing, exactly?" Lucas asked as he twined the string into the groove of his toy.

"Four days ago I put an empty brood comb into my breeder hive so the queen could lay eggs in it. It is time to switch the larvae into the colony," said Marigold. "First I have to transfer them to these wax queen cell cups I attached to this frame."

Lucas watched as Marigold adeptly lifted the larvae from the brood comb and transferred them, one-by-one, into the little wax cups.

"Will each one of those be a queen?"

"We will know in fourteen days," said Marigold, "but that is the plan."

"I thought you usually worked with your bees in the morning," said Lucas.

"Well, I most often do, but the most important thing is to be here when most of the bees aren't. I did not have time until this afternoon, and it needed to be taken care of today."

Lucas unwound and rewound the string on his yoyo, debating on continuing to watch his sister or leave and practice his tricks. While he was still making deliberations, Eli Thalman walked down the lane and into the hollow.

"Lucas," Marigold spoke in a hushed tone, "would you see if Mr. Thalman would come over here?"

"Why don't you just holler for him, like you do me?"

"Because I don't want to make a lot of noise and disturb the bees."

Lucas contemplated for a moment and then walked from the hive between the wildflower garden and a row of orchard trees to meet Eli on the lane.

"Howdy, Mr. Thalman." Lucas held out a hand, and Eli shook it.

"Hello, Lucas." Eli noticed the yoyo and smiled. "Know any tricks on that?"

"Some." Lucas lifted the toy in his palm. "Ben Dryfus and I have a little competition going on to see who can get the Man on the Flying Trapeze first."

"That takes some time to master," said Eli.

"Do you yoyo?"

"I do." Eli nodded. "With a father who is a tailor, I have had a lot of access to wooden spools. I have made my own for years."

"Really?"

Marigold cleared her throat loud enough for Lucas to remember his mission. "Oh, Marigold sent me over to fetch you."

"She did?" Eli's smile widened.

"Yeah, she is making queens, so she couldn't holler for you, like usual."

Eli chuckled. "I see. Well, I will just walk over and be quiet about it."

"Ok," said Lucas. "I am gonna go practice. She did not want me making any commotion by the hive."

"That is probably a good idea." Eli patted the boy on the shoulder. "And Lucas, if you don't mind a suggestion, I found the most important part of mastering any yoyo trick is making sure to keep the tension out of the string."

"Thanks," said Lucas. "I have been a little lazy about that."

Lucas unwound the string on his yoyo, and starting at the top of the spool, pulled it all the way down, watching it untangle as he worked his fingers to the end.

Eli watched him go, and then made his way to meet Marigold. Her hat-and-net-covered head bowed over a log as she carefully placed the last larvae into a wax cup with wooden tweezers.

"Good afternoon, Dr. Johnson," said Eli.

"Doctor?" Marigold guffawed and shook her head. "Hardly."

"You do look like you are in surgery."

"It is a dreadfully delicate procedure," said Marigold with a grin, "a matter of life and death."

"Is that right?" Eli's dark eyes sparkled at Marigold as she straightened and lifted the frame for him to see.

"It is. These are my new queens."

"I see," said Eli. "So if you are not a doctor, you must be a lady to be keeping company in such a royal court."

Marigold laughed out loud. "I have never been mistaken for nobility before." Eli's words, in contrast to her tomboy reputation, raised a rosy blush on her freckled cheeks.

"What is life without some new firsts?"

"I do like adventures." Marigold smiled and turned to the hive, lifting the telescoping lid off the top of the rectangular wooden box. Inside, nine of the ten slots were filled with removable frames filled with honeycomb. Bees moved about the combs, but remained calm as Marigold slipped the frame holding the larvae into the open space.

"I guess you do like adventures," said Eli, "working with bees without any gloves."

"I wear them sometimes, but this hive isn't really aggressive, and it is much easier to work without them." Marigold slipped the lid back on top of the hive. "When you work with gloves, there is a greater chance of accidentally squishing the bees. And when one bee gets injured, it can set others off."

Eli admired Marigold's competence and confidence as she worked with the bees other girls would run from.

"Speaking of 'setting others off,'" said Eli, "that is why I came by. I heard about what happened last night. Is everyone all right? Is there anything I can do?"

Marigold's lips tightened into a thin line. Slowly, she untied the ribbon around her neck and pulled the hat off her golden braids.

"That is right kind of you." Marigold forced a slight smile, and Eli watched the emotions play behind her big eyes. Anger, worry, uncertainty—each had their turn in her sparkling brown pools. "Minnie and the little ones were plumb dragged out this morning, but I guess they are holding up all right after the fuss."

"It is a shame and disgrace how they were treated. And how about you?" Eli's dark eyes studied the girl before him. A sturdy, athletic young lady, tanned and freckled, Marigold's normally vibrant countenance was undeniably subdued.

Marigold cast a glance to the ground and twisted her lips in thought. Her shoulders hefted with a sigh. "I am trying to keep a right spirit, but to tell you the truth, every time I think of those spineless cowards threatening Minnie and those innocent children—well, I get madder than a swarm of fighting-mad bees."

"That is understandable," said Eli.

"You don't think it is wrong to be mad?"

"Anger is like a thorn in the heart," Eli offered sympathy with a smile, "but the Holy Scriptures reveal many times that wickedness provoked even the Lord to anger."

Marigold absorbed his words and felt a load of guilt lift from her shoulders. "You are right. I had forgotten." She took a deep breath and exhaled. "Pa is all the time quoting the Apostle Paul: 'Be ye angry, and sin not: let not the sun go down upon your wrath.'"

"King Solomon wrote that anger rests in the bosom of fools."

"Eli Thalman!" Marigold's lower lip dropped and her eyes widened. "First you encourage me, and then you call me a fool." She placed her hands on her hips. "I do not know what to think about you."

"You misunderstand, my friend." Eli grinned, entertained by Marigold's animation. "King Solomon did not say anger never visited wise men, but it is the fool who lets it rest in his bosom—in agreement with your Teacher Paul."

"Oh." Marigold crossed her hands over her chest, rolled her eyes, and shook her head. "I am so glad you came to offer your concern. I sure feel a heap better."

Eli laughed. "I am glad you are glad."

Marigold watched Eli's eyes, full of mystery and yet so tender. When he smiled, they softened, revealing a gentle spirit—one that had a taming effect on Briar Hollow's most rambunctious female.

The two stood in silence, the sound of barn work and horses echoed in the background. The sky was a beautiful blue adorned with puffs of billowing cumulous clouds. A vee of geese honked overhead on their journey south, and the crisp air scented by nearby apple trees made for a perfect fall day.

Marigold bent at the waist to reach for the hat she had tossed to the ground.

"Allow me." Eli narrowed the space between himself and the hat with one long step, picked up the netted headgear, and extended it to Marigold.

"Miss Johnson." Eli bowed.

Sweet sensations flooded Marigold's senses. Unaccustomed to acts of chivalry directed towards her, she stared for a moment before slowly reaching for the offering.

Eli straightened and adjusted the arms of his wire-rimmed spectacles with both hands. He searched for words—some reason, any reason—to remain in Marigold's presence. He wanted to continue talking with this girl who brought life to him in a way no one else had ever done. He loved the lilt of her laughter, the modulation of her words as the pitch and tone changed with the emotions behind them. He longed to fill his mind with her expressive features that replayed so often in his thoughts when he was alone.

As he searched for an appropriate topic, Zion rode in on his prized stallion, West.

"Hey, Marigold, Eli." Zion dismounted and patted his Thoroughbred on the neck.

"Hello, Zion." Marigold greeted her brother-in-law with unusual formality.

"Good afternoon," said Eli. "What is the good word?"

"Hm." Zion rubbed his chin between his thumb and forefinger. "A good word, you say?"

"Yes, sir." Eli nodded. "If you have one."

"As a matter of fact, I do."

"Really?" Marigold's eyes widened, and she gave Zion her full attention. "Did you find anything out about those blowhards?"

"Nothing certain," Zion shook his head and scowled, "but Sheriff Nash is looking into things. He has a pulse on what's happening around these parts. If anyone can get a lead on it, he can."

"Then what is the good word?" asked Marigold.

"The good news is Pansy Joy and Florence Erlanger decided we need some positive distraction around here, and they have worked up an idea to have a harvest party."

"That sounds fun," said Marigold, "but where is it going to be? Pansy Joy's place, or the Comfort Lodge?"

"Yes." Zion gave one definitive nod of his head and smirked.

Marigold laughed. "Which one, silly?"

"Both," said Zion. "Those two have got all kinds of things planned, starting with a pumpkin and apple cook-off at the Lodge, followed by a hay ride to the Eldridge farm for a corn maze, and then back to their big barn for a singing."

"Oh, that does sound like fun," said Marigold.

"I would like to extend an invitation to you, Eli, if you are free," said Zion. "To all your family."

"That is a good word," said Eli, a broad smile on his elongated face. "I will speak with Abba and Ema."

"We would be mighty pleased to have you come and celebrate the harvest with us," said Zion. "You do celebrate harvest, don't you?"

"In our own way, yes," said Eli. "It is called the Feast of Weeks, or Pentecost, and is always held exactly 50 days after Passover."

"Pentecost?" Marigold's curiosity was piqued. Raised in church, she had heard of Pentecost all her life, but she related it to an experience, not a holy day. She had never connected the Old and New Testament concepts. "That is the harvest celebration?"

"Every year," said Eli. "Pentecost began in Israel as the celebration of the spring wheat."

"And for New Testament believers," said Zion, "it became the celebration of the first spiritual harvest of souls on the birthday of the Church. It was on the day of Pentecost 3,000 people were filled with God's Spirit in Jerusalem."

Zion wanted to share much more with Eli—to launch into the revelation of Jesus, the Messiah, but he chose his words carefully and kept them short. "I can't imagine what it was like that day when the Spirit of God first moved into that room and filled the place like a rushing mighty wind and tongues of fire sat on the believers."

"I have just been inspired to do a Bible study," said Marigold.

"That is always a good idea." Zion smiled at Marigold, and then turned to Eli. "Do you and your family study Scripture?"

"Yes, we do," said Eli. "What you are saying brings to mind words of an old rabbi who said on the day of the giving of the Law, God's voice looked like a 'fiery substance' that split into 70 languages heard among all the nations."

"That is amazing," said Zion. "I would love to learn more."

"Perhaps we will find a time to do that," said Eli, hopeful that a trip to study Scripture at Briar Hollow would also include time with a Miss Marigold Johnson. "For now, I must check with Mr. Mayfield on the items he inquired about for Mr. Johnson's birthday gift and then get back to the shop."

"What has Logan gone and done now?" asked Zion. "Did not the girls order a full suit?"

"Yes, they did, but Mr. Mayfield wanted him to have a new cane, top hat, and pocket watch. I received a telegram from my supplier in Louisville, and I wanted to go over the details before finalizing the order."

Marigold sucked in a breath and let it out with an exaggerated *hooey*. "Pa is going to be cutting a swell, for sure," she said.

Zion ruffled his chestnut hair with his big hand and grinned. "Folks will think he turned politician."

CHAPTER 7

"An empty barrel reverberates badly," said Hiram Thalman as he shook his head. Sorrow filled his dark eyes.

"Yes, Abba," said Eli. "Loud words and shaking threats make more noise when they are echoing from the hollow chamber of a desolate soul."

"I am sorry to hear of these threats in Washington," said Asher from his spot at the ironing board. He unfolded a new handkerchief and pressed the rolled-hem flat. "I was hoping after the war things would calm down."

"Yes," said Hiram, "I, as well, but as the saying goes, 'a wolf loses his hair, not his nature.'"

"You always have a *saying*, Abba." Eli smiled. "I believe you would enjoy a conversation with Miss Johnson. She has the most entertaining word-stock."

"She was at the Mayfield's?" Asher lifted his eyes from his work to his brother's face.

"Yes," said Eli with a gleam in his eyes easily detected by his brother. "She is a beekeeper, did you know?"

"That makes sense," said Hiram. "Bees and orchards are good companions. The bees pollinate the trees, and the trees provide the nectar for honey."

"That brings to mind one of Ema's sayings," said Asher. "With honey, you can catch more flies than with vinegar." Asher folded a pressed handkerchief and reached for another. "Did Miss Johnson offer you some honey, brother?"

Eli looked intently at his brother who was busily at work ignoring him. He could not miss the underlying question masked in Asher's seemingly innocuous words.

"Actually, Mr. Coldwell invited our entire family to a harvest celebration Sunday afternoon."

"Harvest." Hiram smiled. "That is something to celebrate."

"What do they do at a harvest party?" asked Asher.

"I don't have all the details," said Eli, "but Zion said something about a pumpkin and apple baking contest, a corn maze, a hay ride and singing."

Hiram pulled the collar he was sewing from the machine, snipped the threads, turned it right side out, and began working the corners into points. "Who will be there?"

"I am not sure if there will be more, but Zion's family, which includes the Johnsons, Mayfields and Eldridges, as well as the Erlangers."

Hiram rose from his seat at the sewing machine and handed the collar to Asher. "Please press this," he said, and then turned to face Eli. "It would be nice to get to know our neighbors better."

Eli studied his dear father's face. The exodus from Paducah had taken its toll on him. The fine lines on his distinguished face seemed deeper. His dark eyes did not sparkle as brightly as Eli remembered before their move. Eli sensed his father's conundrum. He had established himself in Paducah and made friends with the other merchants and residents. While he enjoyed companionship, he had been reluctant to freely engage socially in their new community. The recent outburst of prejudice-based hostility only fed his reticence.

The interior door to the upper residence flew open at the hand of Eden, Eli's sister. "I've got it, Ema," said the 14-year-old girl. Eden held the door open for her mother to pass through and then closed it behind her.

Judith crossed the floor of the shop with a tray in hand that she placed on the corner table. Steam rose from the pot on the tray, and china cups clinked as she began to poor. "*Tatte*, boys," Judith called through the door of the workroom.

"Why don't you show them what we've brought?" Judith nodded at the cloth-covered basket on her daughter's arm.

"Yes, Ema." Eden smiled and slipped inside the workroom door. "Abba, Asher, Eli—Ema and I have made a special treat for you."

"Hm. Let me guess, my dumpling." Hiram stroked his beard in serious contemplation. Eden's eyes twinkled with excitement.

"Macaroons?"

Eden's lips turned up at the corners in a sweet smile. She shook her head. "Guess again."

"*Mandelbrot?*"

Eden shook her head again. "One more time."

"I know," said Asher. "Abba's favorite, *rugelach*."

"That is a good guess, but still not right." Eden opened the towel and lifted the basket for her father to see its contents, still warm from the oven—a spicy cake made with buckwheat honey and dried fruits.

"Ay-ya-ya." Hiram took a deep breath and closed his eyes. "Your sister brings us *lekach*, boys, and it is not even New Year's Day!"

"Come," said Judith from the main room of the shop. "I prepared *gogol mogul* for your rough throat, *Tatte*." Judith dropped a bit of honey in the mixture of egg yolk and hot milk. "It will go nicely with your *lekach*."

"Thank you, *Bubbala*."

Eli watched the exchange between his mother and father. He knew their marriage had been arranged by their parents, and it was nice to see how they had chosen to love each other, for better, for worse. Their marriage was more than a complementary arrangement. Hiram and Judith were clearly affectionate. The terms of endearment and tender expressions they shared in private and in public testified to their true love.

The men washed in the basin in the workroom and then seated themselves around the table. Judith finished pouring the *gogol mogul* for her husband and tea for the rest of the family. She sliced the honey cake and placed a piece at each place setting. Eden retrieved a stool from behind the work counter, and Eli scooted his chair to the side to make room for her at the table.

"Blessed are You, LORD, our God, King of the universe," Hiram prayed, "Who creates varieties of nourishment."

Everyone waited for the patriarch to take the first bite. Eden watched her father's face as he made a great show of sampling her baked goods. Slowly, carefully, he submerged the prongs of his fork into his piece of cake. He lifted it for visual inspection, turning the utensil from side to side, and then nodding his approval. With a deep inhale, he breathed in the sweet, spicy fragrance, and then finally brought the fork to his mouth, sliding the bite slowly off the fork.

"Ah, my daughter," said Hiram after chewing and swallowing the first bite, "you will make a fine wife some day."

"From your mouth to God's ears," said Eden with a smile. "Your turn, Asher and Eli! *Ess!*"

"You don't have to tell me twice to eat *lekach*," said Asher.

"Thank you, Eden and Ema," said Eli.

Silence filled the room, interrupted only by the sound of forks on plates and cups on saucers as the family shared their afternoon snack.

"To what do we owe this special treat," asked Hiram, "and in the middle of the day, at that?"

Judith reached for her husband's free hand and gave it a squeeze. "Eden and I were a bit sad this morning. I guess yesterday's threats brought back memories of not so long ago. We just wanted to do something different—something that we would do on a special day, to break the bit of gloominess."

"I, for one," said Asher with a bite of honey cake tucked into one cheek, "am glad you did."

"Speaking of breaking the gloominess," said Eli, "we have been invited to a harvest party on Sunday afternoon."

"A party?" Eden sat on the edge of her stool. "Where? Who invited us?"

"Calm down, daughter," said Hiram. "We have not decided yet if we will go."

"Why wouldn't we, Abba?" Eden's shoulders slumped, and confusion filled her dark eyes.

"Sunday afternoons are usually free," said Eli. "The store is closed, and we have no religious obligations."

"That is true," said Hiram. He lifted his cup from its saucer and took a long sip. His eyes met Judith's across the carved table. After all their years of marriage, he read her easily. In two words he mentally summed up what he saw on his wife's dear face: reserved hopefulness. Their family had gone through much during the last few years. The children had been sheltered from most of the sorrows prejudice had inflicted upon them.

Still, as husband and wife had discussed many times, the Thalmans recognized they were still part of the human race. Their God called them to be set apart in their worship and consecrated lifestyles, but He did not call them to be isolationists. They were part of a holy nation, to be sure, but that nation was spread abroad and dispersed among the continents of the world.

"I have no ill feelings towards anyone in the community," said Hiram. "Perhaps I am being overcautious, Eden. It is not for myself, but for you, my child. With the move from Paducah and then Owensboro, I suppose I am being careful about developing friendships."

"Oh, Abba, you are friendly with everyone," said Asher.

"Being friendly is not the same as being friends," said Hiram. "True friendship goes much deeper than that."

"It sounds like such a good time, Abba," said Eden. "I would like to go if you approve."

"Ema and I will discuss it in private," said Hiram, "and we will let you know at breakfast tomorrow."

With decisive steps, Marigold crossed the covered bridge between Briar Hollow and the Mayfield's property. Armed with a wire basket filled with eggs, she whistled *Onward Christian Soldier* in time with the pulse of her footfalls. The scene when she emerged from the bridge's cover, was beautiful, as always, enhanced by the dramatic tunneled entrance.

Following Millicent Mayfield's meticulously landscaped path, Marigold kept her pace and song until she reached the open front door of the Mayfield cabin. Logan had installed a hanging net from the doorpost that allowed the fresh fall air to flow into the house. Marigold peeked inside the parlor, but Penny was not in sight. She rapped on the doorframe. "Penny? Are you home?"

"Hi, Marigold." Penny moved from the kitchen to the front door, wiping her hands on her work apron. "Come in. I can't stop what I am doing right now, but we can visit while I finish waxing the rutabagas."

"So that is why you wanted that batch of beeswax," said Marigold. "Did you have any trouble cleaning it?"

"No," said Penny. "I did just what you said. I put it in the bag in the hot water and the wax melted and came through the fabric. It all floated on top and the junk stayed inside. When the water cooled, I just scooped off the good, clean wax."

"I am glad that worked for you," said Marigold. "Did you have enough?"

"I think so," said Penny. "Come see."

The girls moved to the stove and kitchen work space where a bushel of rutabagas had already had their foliage trimmed to about an inch off the crown. Several had been processed, on which Marigold noticed the roots had traces of dirt beneath the wax coating. "Don't you wash them before you wax them?"

"Rosalie said just to wipe them. If they get wet, they are more likely to mildew or rot." Penny picked up a root and dipped it in the hot wax. "You just do this long enough to coat them, because we don't want them to cook, just preserve them. Rosalie says this will keep the moisture in over the winter months."

"Are you going to do the turnips, too?"

"Yes, and the parsnips."

"I can almost taste vegetable stew right now," said Marigold.

"Are you hungry?"

"No. I am good." Marigold remembered the basket in her hand and placed it on the table. "I brought you some eggs."

"Oh, thank you! And I will send some of these home with you."

"You want me to leave already?" Marigold thrust her hands on her hips and punched out her bottom lip.

Penny shook her head and giggled. "Of course not, you silly goose."

Marigold watched her friend's graceful movements as she moved the rutabagas through the waxing process. Penny was not only delicately beautiful, she was so ladylike—two areas in which Marigold was recently finding herself woefully lacking. Of course she knew she was not gorgeous or graceful, it just had not bothered her before—before Eli came around and made her wish she was both.

"I saw Eli leave a while ago," said Marigold. With the tip of her index finger she traced the lip of the wire basket.

"Yes. He came to finalize some details with Logan about our contribution to your pa's birthday gift."

"He told me," said Marigold. "Pa is liable to bust his buttons when he sees the entire getup. He is getting the whole kit and caboodle, isn't he?"

"Your pa deserves everything he is getting," said Penny. "Think about it. None of us would be here if he hadn't settled in this place. He poured blood, sweat and tears into Briar Hollow, and we are all the beneficiaries of his labor of love."

"I guess I never thought of it that way," said Marigold.

"The Bible says to give honor to whom honor is due, and we just happen to think Matthias Johnson is an honorable man."

"He is second to none," said Marigold, "and he is going to look like a real Thoroughbred in his new bib and band, a gentleman of the first water."

"Speaking of gentlemen, I have to say, Eli Thalman has been more than mannerly the way he has serviced us with such special care. He helped us find just the right watch with a gold guard and chain."

"That is nice."

"He recommended burgundy gloves, especially with the navy suit."

"Mmhm."

"I am really excited about the cane," said Penny. "It is a medium-dark ash with a carved ivory pommel."

"Ivory."

"And the hat," Penny added, "well, Eli wanted to make sure we knew the beaver was not being processed with mercury. Isn't that sweet?"

"Why is that important?" asked Marigold.

"It is mostly for the safety of the hatters, so they don't get 'mad hatters disease.' I can only imagine it is safer for the customers wearing them, too."

"Really?" Marigold's lips contorted and she raised her gaze to the ceiling.

"Are you all right?"

"Sure," said Marigold. "That is just a lot of soft solder for one junior tailor."

"I am not flattering," said Penny. "I am just telling the truth."

Marigold dropped her head and let out a sigh. "I know."

CHAPTER 8

The hum of voices and bustling activity in the lower meeting room of the Paxton Inn was just loud enough to provide a safe place for the conversation at the corner table.

"I have had enough of them and their uppity ways." Trigg Simon took a drink from a pewter goblet and set it hard on the table.

"We all have," said Fred McGhee, "but it looks like your boy River done put the fear of God in that group in Briar Hollow."

Trigg's top lip curled up on one side in a smirk. "Shoot, Luke, or give up the gun. That is my philosophy. Sitting around does not accomplish anything."

"I was surprised Danhauer went with him," said Burke Calhoun. "Do you think he will shoot his mouth off about us?"

"He was with River at the post office when that beefy bull got between him and his mail," said Trigg.

"If we don't put them in their place, they will be getting all kinds of stumped notions," said Burke Calhoun. "Governor Magoffin didn't do us no favors by trying to keep the state neutral. Shoddy, self-serving politics, that is what it was."

"I am as riled up about it as you," said Trigg, "but who knows what Magoffin had to deal with being sandwiched between the Union and Confederacy? At least we aren't dealing with carpetbaggers, and there is no going back and doing things over now."

Fred pulled a quirley from of his shirt pocket, struck a match against his fingernail and lit the hand-rolled cigarette. "I blame the Methodists."

Trigg leaned back in his chair, a bemused look on his dark features. "What does religion have to do with uppity blacks?"

"You know those circuit riders got folks around these parts all fired up—converting slaveholders and slaves alike."

Trigg raised his eyebrows and gave Fred a sideways glance. "And your point?"

"The holy rollers were preaching 'Reform! Reform!'" said Fred. "They were all in a frenzy about religion and trying to get folks involved in politics on all kinds of social issues— slaveholding, alcohol—even women's rights."

"What is the world coming to?" Burke cupped his chin in his hand and shook his head. "And they think all this 'transforming the world' business is God's plan."

"God's plan." Trigg guffawed. "I have got plans of my own."

"I trust you do, Grand Cyclops." Fred sniggered and flicked ashes in the urn on the table. "That big fellow woke up the wrong passenger messing with your River."

Burke leaned into the table, his reddened eyes turned to slits. "What do you have in mind?"

"My boy told me he saw books in that house," said Trigg. "That is reason enough to burn him out."

"We can't back down," said Burke. "The last thing blacks need is education. Before you know it, they will want the vote."

"I don't care a continental what they want." Trigg slammed a fist into the table. "I am going to put a spoke in that wheel right quick."

"I am in, you know," Fred stumped out the end of his quirley in the urn, "but do you really think we could burn him out of his house right there in Briar Hollow? There are lots of folks living there, and I have a clear recollection of the sporting events at last year's Germantown Fair. Coldwell's whip handling and Mayfield's shooting skills are not to be trifled with."

"You have a point," said Trigg, "but I have got a bad feeling about this Balim bidder. With his double offense of reading materials and uppity ways at the post office, I think we need to make an example of this one."

A glint lit in Burke's hooded eyes. "A quick trip to the bone orchard?"

Trigg nodded. "A lynching."

"There is a big tree in a clearing in the woods across the road from the hollow—near the old hunting lean-to that burned down last year," said McGhee.

"Yeah," said Burke. "I know it. It is near the old Corbin place."

"Right," said Fred. "There is still a barn standing nearby, ain't there?"

"I believe so." Trigg turned to Fred and looked him in the eye. "We will have to work out a time to pull this off. Do you think you can get the lowdown on their schedule, McGhee?"

Fred gave a few quick nods. "Will do."

"All right then. We will wind this business up and put the squelch on these indulgent notions before they corrupt the whole of Mason County."

"What is that you are working on?" Balim watched his wife cut four-inch circles out of fabric from the scrap bag using a paper template.

"Cutting." Minnie kept her eyes on her task. She made the final snip on the last circle from the bit of red check, and then picked up a yellow calico print.

"I can see that, woman."

"Oh," said Minnie, slowly nodded her head, "so you can see. I was beginnin' to wonder."

"I see plenty," said Balim, "fo sho and fo certain."

"Mmhm."

Balim noted the set of his wife's chin and the way her lips were drawn in. He knew his Minnie-girl well enough to know that she did not have to give herself to such concentration to cut circles out of scraps.

"I know you is upset about what happened with those bullies."

"I is," said Minnie, the snips of her scissors coming quicker and louder.

"I am sorry I weren't here," said Balim, "but I am thankful Jehovah-Shammah was nigh. He is and ever will be 'de Lawd is There.'"

Minnie dropped her scissors and fabric on the table and placed both hands on her ample hips. She turned to face Balim, and said, "If you wasn't out beatin' the devil 'round the stump, you would've been here to see to the family the good Lawd give you."

Sweet Lawd Jesus, help me. Balim offered a silent prayer. His usually warm and wonderful wife was acting completely out of character. Those hooded horsemen had scared her plumb right out of her skin.

Balim reached a beefy hand towards his wife, but she abruptly turned a shoulder to him. "Ah, Minnie-girl, you know I'd never shirk my most precious calling. You and Abram and Abby are my first concern."

"Then why's you out running all over the county when they is villains loose lynching folks like us?"

Endearment etched itself on Balim's big face. His eyes turned to tender pools. "I hear ya, puddin', but when I left to meet with Revrun Green, they hadn't been any serious threats around these parts." Balim placed a hand on Minnie's shoulder and turned her to face him. "I wouldna left if I thought you and the little ones was in danger."

Minnie's shoulders slumped beneath the weight of her concern and the reality of Balim's words. She knew he was telling the truth—that he would do his best to protect them—but those same words also created a stark reminder that no one could be under the protection of another at all times. She was going to have to muster some faith of her own.

"Lucas told me there was goings on in lots of places 'round the state," said Minnie. "I guess hearing about folks getting lynched in as close by as Frankfurt and Louisville, well, it just seems the violence is creeping this way."

"What is a whippersnapper like Lucas doing talking about lynchings?"

"He overheard the sheriff and Massa Zion, and he was worried 'bout Abram and Abby." Minnie pulled a handkerchief from her sleeve and blew her nose. "He is almost as scared as me and the chilluns. He loves 'em so."

"They's good people here." Balim pulled his wife into an embrace. "We 'taint alone in our troubles."

Minnie sniffed against her husband's broad chest and then let out a long sigh, releasing some of the tension that had steadily built into a mountain of worry on her calico-covered shoulders.

"Promise me ya won't go out by yoself, Balim," Minnie whispered.

Balim released his grip around his wife and cupped her face in both hands. He studied her obsidian eyes, hoping she could read his heart as he read hers.

"I am sorry." He shook his head. "I can't promise ya that, Minnie."

Minnie stared at her husband, concern on her ebony face. "Why, Balim? Why won'tcha be safe?"

Balim stepped back and looked out the window of their home. The simple curtains riffling in the breeze framed the view of the hollow beyond their door. Light spilled inside the building in a great shaft that struck a pose between the window frame and the new wood floor.

"'Cuz I won't go back to slavery of no kind." Balim turned to face his wife.

"Don't ya see, Minnie? That is what these folks is trying to do. They is people in this state and all over the country that is still on slavery's side, no matter who won the war, and they is gwanna do what they can to weigh us down—keep us under control. That is why I want to help out with the Convention. Education is the key for our people."

Peals of laughter and the ringing of a bell grew louder as the children arrived back at the cabin in a make-shift goat cart. Lucas often led Abram and Abby in a big lap around the hollow in the cart he had made of a simple wooden box with a board seat. Balim had helped him with the wheels, axles and shaft; Zion with the bridle and harness; and Rosalie had made a cushion for the bench seat. With Marigold's assistance, Lucas had trained Blossom, their calmest Nubian goat, to pull the wagon.

"One mo! One mo!" Abby bounced on the cushioned seat. Abram sat beside his sister, grinning up at Lucas with adoration in his eyes.

"That is it for now," said Lucas. "I have chores to do."

Abram bounded down from the bench seat, while Lucas lifted Abby and set her safely on the ground.

"T'morrow?" Abram asked.

"I don't see why not," said Lucas.

"Yay!" Abby wrapped her arms around Lucas, her head reaching just above his belt line.

"What is all the commotion out here?" said Balim as he and Minnie walked out into the afternoon sunshine.

"Pappy!" Abram ran to his father's side and jumped up and down. "Lucas said he will teach me to drive the cart all by myself soon!"

"You must be doing a good job," said Balim.

"Oh, he is." Lucas nodded. "He will be driving Abby and Dahlia around in no time."

"Where is that little niece of yours?" asked Minnie.

"She is in the house with the girls. They are cutting circles for something."

Balim gave his wife a sideways glance and a grin. "You never did tell me what you was cuttin' all them circles fo."

"All us holler ladies is cuttin' circles out of our scraps to make a yoyo quilt."

"A yoyo quilt?" Lucas was puzzled over the idea. "Yoyos are made out of wood or stone."

"Not this kind," said Minnie. "You will see when it is all done up. It'll be something special with bits from everybody's basket."

"Thanks for taking the little ones out on your cart," said Balim. "It was a nice distraction."

"That is what Rosalie said about the harvest party," said Lucas, "that it would be a nice distraction."

"That it will," said Balim, "and it will be good to think on things that are of a good report."

A look of gratitude washed over Minnie's face as she remembered the words that had kept her from bitterness and anxiety so many times in the past. "Whatsoever things is true, and honest and just and pure and lovely," she said, "things of good report; if they's any virtue or praise, think on these things."

"That's right, Minnie-girl" said Balim. "That is just what we is gwanna do."

CHAPTER 9

"We are certainly having our share of parties around here," said Penny.

Rosalie nodded and made the final snip on a piece of blue calico. "I can't wait for Pa's birthday. He is going to be so surprised, and I think he is going to love his new suit. I really like the navy color you girls picked."

"I do, too," said Pansy Joy. "Did you start on the socks yet?"

"You should see the colors Marigold brought home from the mercantile." Rosalie grinned. "Eli helped her pick them out, and he said stripes and checks were really in fashion this year."

"Striped and checkered socks?" Pansy Joy's eyes grew wide. "For our Pa? He is going to look like a dude. What colors?"

"Eli said that with a 'ditto suit,' where the pants and jacket match, it would be nice to use burgundy and fawn accent colors. So I have those two and navy to work with."

"I can't wait to see his face when he sees the whole ensemble," said Penny. "He will be as modern as Logan with his wide neck tie. Do you think we should get him a stickpin?"

"That is a bit fussy for Pa, don't you think?" said Pansy Joy. "But I know he is going to love the new walking stick. I wish we could give it to him right now."

"It would be nice if he could wear it to the harvest party," said Penny with a laugh. "That might be a bit fancy for a hay ride, though, and I don't think we will have everything ready by then."

"I like the idea of having the harvest party at both the farm and the Comfort Lodge. It is going to be a lot of fun." Pansy Joy leaned over the table and continued drawing circles on a remnant of yellow gingham.

"Is it going to be at your house, or your in-law's?" asked Rosalie.

"I really wanted to have it at our place, but ever since Katie got married and moved away, Momma Maggie just hasn't had the same sparkle in her eyes. I think decorating for a fall party will liven her up a bit."

"It is only a few days away," said Penny from her station at the ironing board. "Do you need help? Millicent is a beautiful decorator, and it would give her something to do."

Rosalie picked up the piece of fabric on the top of the colorful pile Pansy Joy was making. She positioned the scissors to cut the first chalked circle, and a sigh passed through her thin lips.

"You sure are quiet today, Rosalie," said Penny. "Are you feeling all right? Is everything ok?"

Rosalie offered a slight smile to her sister-in-law. "I guess I am at that . . . quiet, I mean." She placed the scissors and fabric on her lap and folded her hands on top of them. "I am fine. I just have a lot on my mind."

"Like what?" asked Pansy Joy.

"Well, I miss Kate more than I ever imagined. She has been my best friend since we were born." Rosalie pushed back a stray strand of auburn hair and looked from one girl to the next. "Not that you two aren't fine company.

"And if the truth be told, I guess there is a part of me that sometimes wishes I had a mother-in-law around. Not just for me, but for Dahlia and Mattie."

"I wish that, too," said Penny. Her blue eyes cast a faraway glance into her past. "I still think about her and wonder how she would feel if she could see how our lives have played out."

"I am sorry," said Rosalie. "I did not mean to take us both into the melancholies."

"A quick trip to the melancholies I can tolerate, as long as it is a short visit and the memories are sweet," said Penny. "And I only have sweet memories of Mother . . . and Father."

Penny placed the flat iron she had been using on top of the warm stove and picked up a second iron that had been heating on the stovetop.

The front door of the Coldwell cabin flung open and Marigold swept inside. The smell of fall and apples followed her.

"What are you bunch of coffee boilers doing in here?" Marigold closed the door and surveyed the room, chewing on a piece of wax.

"Coffee boilers?" Pansy Joy shook her head. "We are the ones working. What are you doing?"

"I have been collecting honey." Marigold opened her hand and extended it palm up. "Anybody want some wax?"

"This iron could use some," said Penny. "Zion sanded it off, but some beeswax would help keep it from sticking to this starched cloth."

"If it is warm enough I can do it right now."

"Oh, it's warm. I just took it off the stove."

Marigold crossed the room and took the iron from Penny's hand. She turned it over and held it near her cheek to check the temperature and then pulled back.

Pthu.

"Marigold Johnson!" Penny threw her hands on her hips. "Did you really need to spit on it?"

"It's the best way to tell if it is hot enough."

"I appreciate your willingness to help," said Penny, "but I have been using this for awhile and it probably needs to be cleaned first anyway."

"Suit yourself, sister-sister." Marigold shrugged and handed off the iron and wax to Penny. "I came to see Rosalie anyhow."

Rosalie turned her green eyes to her sister and noted the not-so-neat condition of her braid and dress. "You are not going to spit on me, are you?"

Marigold threw her head back and guffawed. "I don't think that would be a right nice way to treat someone before I asked for a favor, now. Would it?"

"What kind of favor?" asked Rosalie.

"I was wondering if you had any extra canning jars. One of my hives finished capping off the honeycombs, so I pulled the frames and cut the wax caps off. They are hanging in the barn right now, but I need some extra glass jars to put it in after I filter it."

"That is a good problem to have," said Pansy Joy, "too much honey."

"Yep." Marigold's brown eyes sparkled. "The bee yard has just been buzzing away."

"Are you going to take some to Matheny's to sell?" asked Pansy Joy.

"I am thinking I might do some dickering."

"With who?" asked Rosalie.

"Actually, with the Mathenys," Marigold answered. "I saw a notice for a new-fangled gizmo I'd like to get for Abram and Abby."

"What kind of gizmo?" asked Pansy Joy.

"It is called a *metamorphoscope*. The last time I was in town I saw a poster at the mercantile saying they were going to start carrying them. It said they were 'Intended for the Amusement of Good Children.'"

Rosalie set aside her handwork and stood. "Abram and Abby are certainly good children, and they could use a little fun right now."

"What does this *metamor*-thing do?" asked Pansy Joy.

"It is like a book that has colored pictures, but the tops and the bottom parts move up and down on paper hinges."

"Fascinating." Rosalie moved to the corner storage cabinet and opened the bottom shelf. "What kind of pictures?"

"Mostly people and animals. They change heads and bodies when you move the tops and bottoms."

Rosalie pulled two canning jars from the cupboard. She stood and turned to Marigold, and there was no missing the concern in her green eyes.

"Let fly, Rosalie." Marigold twisted her lips and shook her head. "I can tell by that look on your face you are about to put a spoke in the wheel."

"I don't have any spokes for your wheel." Rosalie smiled at her impetuous younger sister. "I think it is sweet as can be you want to do something nice for the little ones. I am just wondering if those pictures might be scary to them, with changing heads and body parts."

"I haven't seen it yet," said Marigold, "but you could be sound on the goose. I didn't think of that."

"Changing pictures can be fun," said Penny, "but maybe something different would be better."

"Like what?" Marigold tapped her mouth with her forefinger.

"I know!" Penny's eyes grew bright. "A kaleidoscope!"

"Well, that is a horse of another color," said Marigold.

"I love it." Relief washed over Rosalie's features. "And I love that you want to do something nice for Abram and Abby."

Marigold tilted her head and a quirky smile splayed on her freckled face. "The more I think on it, the more it seems like a right fittin' choice."

"Why is that?" asked Penny.

"Because it is the different colors and shapes that make the patterns so nice." Her grin stretched into a tooth-filled smile.

Rosalie retrieved two more jars from the cabinet and set them on the table. "You seem like a woman on a mission."

"I guess I am, at that," said Marigold. "It just struck me that it takes all kinds of people to make the world go 'round. And kaleidoscope pictures would not be special at all if it were not for the different colors and shapes."

"That is true." Rosalie closed the cabinet door and turned to her sister with a smile. "You are quite the philosopher today."

"I am going to see if I can dicker with old Matheny for a kaleidoscope." Marigold gave a firm nod that sent her honey-colored braids bobbing. "And then I am going to use it to tell Abram and Abby how they make the world a better place."

"Well, that is just fine as cream gravy," said Pansy Joy, mimicking one of her sister's favorite sayings.

"Hey, now." Marigold reached for a jar and tucked it under her arm.

"You know, Marigold, since your frames aren't going to be emptied until tomorrow you could help us with this yoyo quilt."

"Aw. Quilting is too domestic for me. I do not like following patterns and all that precision cutting and sewing."

"Perfect," said Rosalie. "We aren't doing that kind of quilting."

"You aren't?"

"No," said Rosalie. "We are just snipping circles for a yoyo quilt. It is really more of a 'spread' than a quilt. It is not even going to have any batting or backing on it."

"That doesn't sound very functional," said Marigold.

"They can be more decorative than warm." Pansy Joy fanned out the stack of brilliantly hued remnants. "But wouldn't it be a shame to waste these pieces? It is going to be so colorful and fun."

"And you can lay it on top of a blanket for warmth," said Penny.

Marigold shuffled her feet and looked out the window. It was a perfect fall day and it was beckoning to her. "Well, that doesn't sound as horrible as those fancy schmancy patterns you do. Who is it for, anyway?"

Penny schooled her facial expressions. She looked to Rosalie, who looked to Pansy Joy, who began carefully stacking the fabric into a neat pile.

"Rosalie?" Marigold pointed her question to her oldest sister.

"You never know when you might need a quilt for a gift." Rosalie stammered out the words. "There could be a tragedy somewhere and um folks could need a blanket, or . . . ."

"Right. A nice, cozy, warm yoyo quilt?" Marigold rolled her eyes.

"Well, things do happen," Penny came to Rosalie's aid. "Sometimes they happen fast, and it is always good to be prepared."

"Whatever you say." Marigold reached for the door handle. "I think you are right. I need to get some things prepared myself."

"Oh, you," Pansy Joy called out to her sister as Marigold shut the door behind her and stepped into the crisp fall day. The cool air was such a relief after a hot Kentucky summer.

"Howdy, Miss Mar'gold." Minnie greeted the girl with a tip of her head and a slight smile.

"Hey, Minnie. How are you?"

"I is as well as can be expected, I reckon." Minnie lifted her arm. A basket dangled from it filled with fabric circles. "I am just deliverin' these here circles fo the quilt to Miss Rozlee."

"That quilt." Marigold shook her head. "It is haunting me."

"What you mean by dat?"

"Oh, nothing. How are the kids?"

"They is all right. Massa Lucas done took 'em on another ride in that goat cart of his. They is on your Pa's side of the orchard. Gonna help Lucas pick up the fallen apples."

"That makes a boring job more fun, for sure," said Marigold.

"I have been hankerin' for some boring 'round these here parts here lately."

CHAPTER 10

"What did you find out?" Burke Calhoun leaned against the old barn.

Leaves crunched beneath Fred McGhee's boots as he closed the space separating him from Burke Calhoun and Trigg Simon.

"Everything we need to know." McGhee nodded and paused. Beneath his floppy felt hat, his thin lips contorted into a sneer.

"Well, open your big bazoo, McGhee." Trigg Simon squared his shoulders and looked Fred in the eyes. "I don't want to hang around here all day."

"Me either." Burke Calhoun scanned the scene at the old Corbin place. The house was long gone with only crumbling foundations in sight, and the barn was in disrepair with gaps between the wood slats. The front door hung precariously by its bottom hinge. Inside was a partitioned area that included a heavy chain measured out in iron rings. The barn was filthy and dilapidated. Dark, damp, and rank with odors, the place gave him the creeps.

"Pull in your horns, Trigg" said McGhee. He was enjoying his momentary leg up on Simon. The two had been friends for years, but he tired at times of Simon's domineering ways. They were peers, but he acted much too often for McGhee's liking, as if he ruled the roost.

"I will when you stop wondering around like a fart in a pickle barrel."

Fred shook his head. "Far be it from me to keep you waiting, Grand Cyclops."

"Don't cock a snook at me, McGhee," said Trigg. "And stop shaking in your boots, Calhoun. I can see you are plumb spooked. I have business to tend to, so just let's get on with the findings so we can make our plans."

"There is a party Sunday night," said Fred.

"For who?" asked Burke.

"I am not sure who all is coming, but I know the Coldwells, Mayfields, Johnsons, Erlangers and Eldridges are all planning to go. Maybe some folks from town, too."

"What about their ranch hand?" Burke ran his fingers through his hair. "What's his name? Carver?"

"Angus Carver," said Fred. "I imagine he will be going."

"And the flannel-mouthed, colored ox?" asked Trigg, "and his family?"

"You know them folks at the holler is all give in to abolitionism. They treat the lot of them like kinfolk." Fred spit on the ground. "It is flat out sickening."

"I know that," said Trigg, "but do you think they will be going to the party?"

"Well," said McGhee, drawling out the word and stroking his chin, "I was thinking if something was to happen to one of their young-uns, they might stay behind."

A lopsided smile broke out on Trigg's face. "That is good thinking."

"What did you have in mind?" asked Burke.

Marigold whistled for the entirety of her walk from Briar Hollow into Washington. She felt like skipping, but the basket was too heavy for that. She peeked at the six, quart-sized jars of sweet, sticky goodness and adjusted one of the ribbons Rosalie had given her to make the containers look extra nice.

One of the first Kentucky settlements, and the first city named after the first president, the town of Washington's origins lay with the North American bison. The great buffalos crossed the Ohio River at Maysville, four miles away, and in their search for salt, they cut a broad path that led south into Washington. That path became the main road from Maysville all the way to Lexington, 80-plus miles away.

Established as the county seat of Mason, Kentucky, in 1848, Washington was a well established settlement with flourishing mercantile houses, taverns, mechanics shops, and churches. Rope walks created safe paths from building to building, including the limestone courthouse, a venerable structure with a modest steeple that looked like a pencil writing in the sky. A two-story white clapboard building with black shutters on its many windows, the city's renowned Paxton Inn, bustled continually with activities of all sorts. It was only a short while ago it had served as a secret station on the Underground Railroad. Runaways hid in concealed chambers in the inn's staircases during the day and were taken to their next stations after dark.

Briar Hollow, located outside the city's boundaries, had also been a refuge for escaping slaves as they traveled the Underground Railroad.

Tinkle. Tinkle.

The sound of the bells hanging from the mercantile door sang out as Marigold opened it and stepped inside. Familiar sights and scents greeted her entry into the area's largest store. The mercantile held a vast selection of goods: everything from ladies' unmentionables to garden hoes, all of which were dispersed throughout the store in categorized displays. Barrels of flour and sugar stood across from the ammunition counter. Wagon tongues and beef tongues, ribbons and rifles, bonnets and bric-a-brac were all laid out in the same building. The variety of the merchandise testified to Washington's unique location. Neighboring Maysville was considered the pioneer gateway to the west, and businesses in Washington catered to those traveling out as well as those staying on.

"How are you today, Marigold?"

Martha Matheny, a plumpish, middle-aged woman called from behind the counter. She wore her favorite work ensemble, a pagoda-sleeved gown with multiple rows of blue plaid cotton skirts trimmed in deep navy. Marigold noted that the lady's smile did not quite reach up to her eyes this fine fall morning.

"I am dandy," said Marigold. "Finer than a frog's hair, actually."

A slight smile played across Martha's face. "That is pretty fine, isn't it?"

"Yes, ma'am. It is." Marigold nodded. "It is so fine you can't even see it."

Martha nodded and then shook her head at the girl who always had a way of brightening up the room. The mercantile had darkened for her just six months ago when her daughter Lark had eloped with Reuben Thalman.

"What can I do for you today?" Martha noticed the basket Marigold held with both hands. For years she had been less than friendly with the Johnsons, but life had tempered her pride as of late.

"Did you bring me some of that good honey of yours?"

"I did." Marigold lifted the basket to the counter top. "Six jars of pure delight."

Martha pulled out a ribbon-clad jar and inspected the contents. "It does look good."

"I brought you a sample," said Marigold as she reached in the basket and drew out a napkin, "so you can check the quality without opening any of the jars."

"How thoughtful." Martha unfolded the napkin and uncovered a half of a honey sandwich on fresh white bread.

"Split that right open so you can see it and taste the honey better."

"It certainly looks pure," said Martha, "and it has a beautiful amber color."

"I filtered it right thoroughly." Marigold grinned and tipped her head. "Go ahead. Taste it."

Martha nibbled a corner of the sample.

Mmm.

Martha Matheny's pleasure was written clearly on her face.

"We have such a variety of flowers at Briar Hollow," said Marigold, "our bees make the grandest blossom honey."

"It is very good," said Martha. "Lark would love this. Honey has always been her favorite sweet."

A wistful expression filled Martha Matheny's eyes.

"How is Lark?"

"She and Rueben are out making a circuit on the wagon," Martha sighed. "She says it is a great adventure. That is how Mr. Thalman got his start before he opened his shop."

"Hiram Thalman was a peddler?"

"I like to think of it as a traveling mercantile." Martha placed the remainder of her sample back on the napkin. "I will just be glad when they get back in town."

"I think it is right noble they don't want to ride on your coattails, or Mr. Thalman's. They want to make their own way by their own efforts."

"Well, I sure miss her around here. Her father and the twins do, too."

"I imagine they will stay in town once she has the baby, don't you?"

Some of her old fire lit the older woman's eyes. "I will be making sure of that, now. Yes, I will."

Martha picked up the remainder of Marigold's sample, popped it in her mouth and savored the sweetness on her tongue. "This is so good. How much were you thinking for it?"

"I was hoping to make a trade with you," said Marigold.

"A trade? What would you like, and I will look at the pricing."

Marigold glanced across the room to a counter filled with toys. "I was hoping I could dicker some honey for a kaleidoscope."

"A kaleidoscope? I know it is not your brother's birthday. I can never forget his leap year birthday."

"No. It is not for Lukey. Do you have one?"

"We have more than one. Why don't you take a look?"

Marigold whisked down the aisle and stood before the array of toys: a porcelain doll, a bilbo catcher, checkers, nursery rhyme books, humming tops, marbles, backgammon, chess, dominoes, and two kinds of kaleidoscopes.

She looked at a silver one, but then selected a brass one with double stained glass wheels for closer examination. It felt sturdy in her hands. The brass cylinder was solid, with a central rod attached to a pair of colorful stained glass wheels. The two wheels were separate from each other, so they could turn independently or at the same time. The first color wheel was divided in eight sections, and the second in four, each section in a vibrant color.

Marigold spun the wheels and an amazing display of color combinations and shapes played before her big brown eyes. Carefully, she placed the kaleidoscope back in its stand and carried the set to the counter. "How about this one?"

Martha Matheny studied the girl she had known since birth. She had always been a bit wild—definitely a tomboy running here and there with messy braids flying behind her. Something had changed in the girl, like it had in herself. *Things* just did not seem as important as they once did.

The cost of the kaleidoscope was greater than the value of the honey, but something pricked the older woman's heart.

"That is a lovely gift? What age are you thinking of?"

Marigold hesitated. She did not feel right about blabbing her plans to give it to Abby and Abram. Mrs. Matheny probably wouldn't understand. Besides, she did not like to do her giving in public.

"It would be for a family," said Marigold.

"Oh. Anyone I know?"

"I'd rather not say." Marigold turned the wheels of the kaleidoscope from where it rested in its stand. "Nothing personal, Mrs. Matheny. It is just . . . well, it is personal."

Mrs. Matheny studied the girl, usually so bold, but reticent and somewhat aloof. "It must be a very special family."

Martha reached behind the counter and retrieved a sheet of brown packaging paper.

"I tell you what," she said as she picked up the kaleidoscope from the stand and began wrapping it, "if you throw in the basket, we will call it even. What do you say?"

"I would say you are a good apple, Mrs. Matheny." A great smile stretched across Marigold's freckled face. "And believe me, I know apples."

CHAPTER 11

Marigold stepped on the rope walk outside the mercantile with the kaleidoscope carefully wrapped and tied with a string. The sun that had played peek-a-boo on the walk into town had gone into full hiding, but Marigold's smile refused to be darkened by the changing weather.

Marigold began her trek home grinning from ear to ear. Less than a mile from town she saw the familiar sign for Comfort Lodge, which lay a mile south of Briar Hollow. She quickly closed the 100 yards to the entrance and thought about stopping in, especially with the cloud cover thickening, but she had havens the rest of the way home with Pansy Joy's place just up on the right and that only a short distance from the Coldwell/Mayfield side of Briar Hollow.

Born and raised in Kentucky, Marigold was used to the state's quick changing weather patterns, but still she grimaced when she felt the first droplets fall from the darkening sky.

"Oh, bosh. I don't want this to get wet." Marigold tucked the package as far under her arm as possible.

I should have worn a hat, she thought. *I could have used it to cover the package, at least.*

The sound of hooves drew her attention to the road ahead. Saddled figures were galloping down the road. As they neared she made out one of the men, Trigg Simon. The other two she recognized but did not know their names.

The men continued on their way into town while Marigold made plans to dart into Garth and Pansy Joy's place. Their farm was the next stop on the right. The clip-clopping of hooves on the macadamized road sounded a second time. The rain was coming down harder. Marigold raised her eyes to see a single-horse surrey heading her direction.

It looked familiar, with its fringed canopy, and when she heard the driver say, "whoa," she knew for sure.

Eli.

With precision movements, Eli set the brake and stepped gracefully down from the carriage. "Dear lady," he bowed before Marigold. "May I offer you a ride?"

"You bet your sweet life!" A large shipping container spanned the back bench, leaving only the seat next to Eli for a passenger. Before Eli could stand upright, Marigold circled in front of the surrey aiming to scramble inside.

"Allow me." Eli hurried to the passenger side of the carriage and assisted Marigold to her seat. Marigold had been lifted into wagons and carts and carriages all her life, but there was something about Eli Thalman's hands around her waist that made her cheeks flame and her insides wiggle.

He was just so different from everyone else she had ever met. To Marigold's way of thinking, his dark curly hair and trim beard were arranged just right around his elongated his face. A pair of wire-rimmed glasses perched on his prominent nose drawing her attention to his kind, black eyes. He was tallish and trim and always dressed neatly. He smelled good, too; not like the menfolk who worked on the horse farm or in the orchard.

Eli wore a white linen shirt with a high upstanding collar and one of the newer wide neckties. In his father's store, he often worked in a simple vest, but today he donned a black waistcoat that was cut straight across the front with lapels and notched collars.

Yes, there was something about Eli Thalman that intrigued Marigold Johnson.

Eli moved to the driver's side of the carriage and hoisted himself into the seat. He could not help noticing how quiet Marigold became once she settled her green calico skirts and package in the surrey.

Her hair the color of spun honey was caught in two braids on either side of her freckled, round face, and her brown eyes seemed wider than usual as she sat next to him with her hands clasped firmly around the package in her lap. Beyond her wholesome attractiveness, Eli saw much more: a resilient, real, and delightful young woman.

Reins in hand, Eli glanced over his shoulder to make sure the road was clear and then cued the horse to pull out hard to the right. Once the surrey was facing north to take Marigold home, Eli tossed a warm smile her way.

"What brings you out in the rain today?"

"I did not go out in the rain," Marigold laughed. "The rain came out on me."

Eli chuckled. "I see."

"I am glad you came along when you did, though," said Marigold. "I was going to high tail it to Pansy Joy's, but I am sure Pa will be glad I will be home in time to fix supper."

"Were you buying groceries in town, then?" Eli nodded to the package in her lap.

"Oh, no. This is not food."

Hooves clip-clopped.

Rain dripped on the canopy.

An awkward smile unfolded on Marigold's face and she squeezed her lips tightly together.

"A secret then, you have, is it?" Eli asked.

"If I told you, it would not be a secret."

Eli nodded his curl- and yarmulke-laden head. "Every heart has secrets."

"Does yours?" Marigold's breathy tone sounded foreign to her ears, and she worked to keep her focus on the road in front of her.

"Of course," said Eli, "but I am willing to tell you my secret— if you like."

Marigold squirmed on the bench seat. Just a few elephant-sized inches separated her from this intriguing man. Her emotions played like a lightning storm. She cast a quick glance at his smiling face, sucked in her bottom lip, and then looked away.

"What . . . what secret would that be?" she asked.

Adorable, Eli captured the look on Marigold's face and tucked it away to think on later. Her response to him both frightened and beguiled him. How could he, a devout Jew, be so magnetized to this one who was forbidden to him? She was not like the strange or foolish woman he read so often about in *Mishlei.* She was more like the wise woman King Solomon wrote so favorably about in his book of proverbs.

Eli knew that more than a few inches of black tufted leather stuffed with horse hair separated him from Marigold. There was a "person" sitting in that space. His name was Jesus.

Eli was familiar enough with Christian teachings to know those who called themselves Christians believed that Jesus was

God. This belief was incompatible with his theology. Jews were monotheists, they only believed in and worshiped one God.

The *Shema.* It was the core of the Hebrew faith. Every morning and night Eli recited those most sacred words recorded by Moses: "Hear, O Israel: The LORD our God is one LORD: And thou shalt love the LORD thy God with all thine heart, and with all thy soul, and with all thy might."

How could Jesus be God, and his God, the Lord of the *Shema*, both be God? There could only be one "Holy One," after all. It just was not logical. Besides that, all of his life Eli had been told that Jesus did not fulfill the messianic prophecies. He did not build the Third Temple or bring a universal knowledge of the God of Israel, as Ezekiel wrote. Jesus did not gather all the Jews back to Israel and there was certainly no world peace, as Isaiah prophesied.

If Jesus did not meet the criteria for the messiah, how could He be the anointed one?

Eli had never been so close to a girl before without a chaperone. His mind searched to reconcile his religious beliefs with his feelings. All the while her hand seemed to call to him, "Hold me! Hold me!"

His thoughts and emotions spun in a *mitsve tants,* each clinging to the sash of Eli's soul as they spun in the traditional Jewish dance. Eli shooed the chaos away and chose instead to enjoy the moment. It was just an innocent favor, he reasoned to himself. He was only giving a girl a ride home in the rain. A nice girl.

"The secret of what is in my package," said Eli.

Relief flooded Marigold as the conversation turned to safer ground and a sigh escaped with her words. "That would be fine."

"Fine as cream gravy?" Eli winked.

That wink did not feel safe. No—not at all. Marigold knew she was not feeling a threatening kind of unsafe, but something else altogether.

"I have been to Maysville today," said Eli.

"You have?" Marigold raised her eyebrows in hopes her expression seemed more relaxed than she was feeling.

"Yes. That is where I picked up the crate in the back seat." Eli held the reins with one hand and motioned to the back of the surrey. "A steamboat came in with supplies Abba had ordered. I drove out to pick them up."

"I guess you have to keep your shelves stocked if you want to keep your customers happy," said Marigold.

"Happy." Eli nodded. "Yes, happy."

Marigold turned her head and studied Eli's profile. "You aren't making that word sound any too appealing."

"I am sorry," said Eli. "Ema often says 'One always *thinks* that others are happy.'"

"I suppose that is true enough."

"I do like to think we contribute to that in a small way with our work."

"Don't you think so?" Marigold asked. "I mean, for the most part, folks around here are generally sunny-side up." She glanced at the package in her hands. "Well, most folks, anyway."

CHAPTER 12

"You can let me off at Briar Hollow," said Marigold. "I want to drop this package off at my sister's place."

"Certainly." Eli signaled the horse to slow and then to turn right into the juniper-lined lane. A quarter mile of scenic beauty created a grand entrance into Briar Hollow. Treetops seemed to bow to one another, their limbs intertwined in an embrace that formed a blue-green canopy. Ferns covered the ground, and the earthiness of their smell mingled with the fragrance of the evergreens and saturated the air.

"I have never seen trees like these before," said Eli. The junipers flanking the entrance to the hollow were 30 feet tall with reddish-brown bark, round-topped and well proportioned with broad, interlaced fibrous strips of small branchlets.

"Pa brought those from Texas," said Marigold. "He planted them here, and it is a good thing, too. Junipers and apple trees are not a good mix."

"Junipers?"

"Yes," said Marigold. "They are the weeping kind. They aren't native to around here."

"You certainly know a lot about plants."

"I love nature." Marigold scanned the scene, including one of her favorite spots, a three-foot mushroom circle surrounded by a ring of foamflowers in fall bloom. "See that?"

Eli looked in the direction she pointed. "That round spot on the ground?"

"That round spot on the ground?" Marigold mimicked with a note of sarcasm. "That is our fairy ring!"

Eli relished the life he saw in Marigold's face, but was surprised she actually believe in mini, magical flying beings. "Do you believe in fairies?" he asked.

"Can you prove they don't exist?" Marigold's brows arched over her expressive brown eyes.

"So do you believe in dragons and unicorns, too?"

"I did not say I believed in fairies," said Marigold, "but I do believe in dragons and unicorns. They are in the Bible, after all."

"You must mean Leviathan. That could be a dragon," said Eli, "but a unicorn?"

"That is in there, too."

"A flying horse?" Eli shook his head, his lips curved up in a smirk.

"I didn't say that," said Marigold, "but unicorns are. I did an essay on animals in the Bible my last year of school. Why, even Noah Webster put in his dictionary that a unicorn was an animal with a horn called a *monoceros*."

"Is that right?" Eli's tender dark eyes filled with a merry mix of warmth and amusement.

"It is," said Marigold, with set jaw and arms folded across her chest.

"Oh, I am not doubting you, Miss Johnson." Eli tipped his head in cheerful deference. "It is just the *Talmud* and your Bible don't always use the same words."

Marigold willed her arms to unfold from her defensive stance but only succeeded in dropping her left arm to her side while her right hand clutched the opposite elbow. "Well, I remember very clearly it was in Psalms."

Eli nodded. "Ah—the *Tehillim*. See, your Bible uses the word Psalms, and the *Talmud* uses *Tehillim*, which means 'songs of praise.'"

"Different words that mean pretty much the same thing. I bet there is a heap more alike than there are differences," said Marigold.

Eli reached beneath his vest and pulled out an embossed leather-bound book. "Do you remember the chapter that mentioned the unicorn?"

Marigold peered at the book with the unfamiliar markings on the cover and then looked at Eli's face so intently focused on hers. A wave of pink rose from her neck and washed over her freckled face. She mentally scrambled for the answer to Eli's question.

With a hard squint, she worked to bring her thoughts into focus and recall the passage.

"Hmm. Let me think."

She drew her lips into a tight line and shook her head.

"Oh, I remember!" Marigold's eyelids flew open, and a big smile broke across her face. "It is 92. I remember because it is after one of my favorites, Psalm 91."

Eli nodded and flipped through the pages of his book. He scanned the lines and then pointed to Verse 10. "But You have raised my horn like that of a wild ox; to soak me with fresh oil."

"Well, isn't that Simon pure?" Marigold offered Eli a toothy grin. "Just look at that. Pa told me the original language said 'wild bull,' and yours says wild ox."

"And Noah Webster's dictionary said rhinocerous."

"And a male rhinocerous is a bull," said Marigold, "and that is certainly wild."

Eli chuckled. "It seems the renditions reconcile, after all."

"Seems rightly so." Marigold tilted her head and looked into the sky beyond Eli's dark curls. "I wonder why the King James translators used the word 'unicorn.'"

"I am not sure, but as long as there is no conflict with the original writings, it does not seem that important."

Eli closed his book and replaced it in his shirt pocket. "As a matter of fact, Abba often says, 'To learn the whole Talmud is a great accomplishment; to learn one good virtue is even greater.'"

"That is a thought you can tie to," said Marigold. The surrey had been stopped for several minutes. Drops of rain hit the canopy and slid off onto the lane with plinks and splashes. "Well, we have talked about the whole kit and caboodle from fairies, to unicorns to . . . ."

Eli waited as Marigold searched for words. She had picked up the package from her lap and was obviously preparing to make her exit inside the Coldwell cabin.

Plink. Splash. Plink. Splash. A Black Java chicken sang her egg laying song from her spot in the nesting box. A whinny floated out from the horse barn. Marigold gave up looking for words to finish her sentence. She did not want to talk. She just wanted to sit next to Eli under the fringe-lined canopy and listen to the peaceful sounds in Briar Hollow.

Eli sensed her reticence to leave, and it pleased him. There was a hush in the hollow that seemed almost sacred from the blending of their talk about God's creation and God's Word. He found himself refreshed by the time he spent with this girl.

"Briar Hollow is a beautiful place," said Eli.

"Some of the Good Lord's best handiwork, Pa says."

"Yes," Eli nodded. "Such artistry from God's hand. It almost demands a reverence of its own."

"I imagine you enjoy getting out of the shop," said Marigold. "I mean, not like it is not a nice shop and all."

"Of course," said Eli. "I know what you mean." The young man sighed and straightened his hat. "But speaking of the shop, I better be getting back. I am sure Abba has been expecting me for quite some time. And Ema will be worrying until I am home safe, especially in the rain."

"I reckon so," said Marigold.

Eli slipped down from his seat and circled around the surrey. Marigold sat her package on the seat and placed her hands on Eli's shoulders. Eli took her by the elbows and assisted her safely to the ground, making sure to avoid the muddy wheels.

"Don't forget this," Eli lifted the paper-wrapped package and handed it to Marigold, surprised by the weight of its contents. "If those are candies, maybe I am in the wrong business." Eli grinned.

"What is that?" Marigold scrunched her eyebrows and wondered what Eli meant.

"Washington might need a dentist more than a tailor."

"Eli Thalman, you do take the rag off the bush," Marigold laughed, and then dashed to the door with her package tucked under her arm. She threw open the door, bound inside and then turned to wave goodbye.

"Thanks for the ride!"

Eli circled around the surrey to the driver's side and lifted himself into the seat.

What a girl.

What a conversation.

He chuckled. Delight sparkled in his dark eyes.

Rosalie watched from her rocking chair as Marigold shut the door, package in hand. The smile splayed across her freckled face was evident even from behind. "It looks like you had a successful trip."

"Hm?" Marigold spun and caught sight of Rosalie nursing Mattie in the fireside rocking chair. The scene was a striking picture of maternal love, innocent baby sweetness and Rosalie's fine features. Marigold's countenance fell.

The change in her sister's expression was palpable. "Is something wrong?" Rosalie asked.

Marigold scrambled to rein in her runaway emotions. The sight of Rosalie looking so serenely perfect and lovely and maternal had sent her spiraling into thoughts of doubts and inadequacies. It was obvious to anyone with working eyeballs Marigold would never be the delicate beauty her sister was. Rosalie always said the right thing, wore the right thing, did the right thing. Marigold esteemed herself to be woefully lacking.

"Oh," Marigold attempted to shake off the looming melancholy, "actually I had a successful trip into town. Mrs. Matheny made me an even trade for the kaleidoscope, but I had to throw in the basket. I hope you don't mind."

"Not at all," Rosalie smiled. "There is plenty of straw around here to make another one, and I like having winter projects."

"That reminds me, I wanted you to use your basket making skills to show me how to make a straw bee skep."

"I will be happy to," said Rosalie, "but I thought you really liked the wooden hives with the removable frames?"

"Oh, I do," said Marigold. "It is just I can use a skep to capture swarms."

"Don't you have enough bees to fill your hives? You need to get more?"

"I do, but the swarms I am interested in capturing are my own bees—the ones that, come spring, might up and leave the hives. They sometimes split off like that when colonies get too big."

Rosalie lifted her sleeping infant to her shoulder and patted his back. A soft burp signaled the end of the feeding, and she rose to place the baby in his cradle. "I will be right back," she said, and then slipped into her bedroom with her bundle.

Marigold crossed the room and placed her package on the table. With nimble fingers she untied the string and unwrapped the paper from around the kaleidoscope. Her thoughts swirled like the pieces of glass in the gadget. So much of her life had been shaken up and shuffled that she felt unsure of herself—an unwelcome feeling she was unaccustomed to entertaining.

Rosalie walked to the table smoothing her skirts. "That is a nice one," she said.

"I thought so, too," said Marigold. "It is really sturdy, and I like that it has its own stand."

"Can I give it a try?"

"Sure," Marigold handed the brass cylinder to her oldest sister. Rosalie looked in the viewer and turned the stained glass wheels.

"They are going to love this," said Rosalie, "such brilliant colors—and it is a new picture with every twist!"

"When I was leaving the mercantile, before it started to rain, I was thinking about how life is like a kaleidoscope in so many ways. Things are constantly changing into new combinations and pictures."

"I wonder if you ever get the same exact picture," said Rosalie as she continued turning the wheels that changed the colorful geometric designs.

"If it is like life, I don't know," said Marigold. "Is any day like yesterday? It might look the same, but it is not. Nothing ever happens twice exactly the same."

Rosalie carefully placed the kaleidoscope on its stand. "I suppose that is good, don't you?"

"How is that?" Marigold lifted her eyes to meet her sister's reflective gaze.

"I think it is good because it teaches us to appreciate each day we live as a unique gift from God. Some days are brighter than the next. One may look similar to others, but think about how every morning's sunrise is an incomparable creation of God.

"Can't you close your eyes and picture God's hand turning the earth on its rotation around the sun in the same way I just turned the wheels on the kaleidoscope? Think about it. The sunrise you saw yesterday is not the same as today's, and it won't be the same as tomorrow's. But every single one is a unique and beautiful declaration of the arrival of a brand new day."

Marigold closed her eyes and pictured the sunrise she had seen that very morning. It had been worth waking up for as she had watched the sun peek over the trees and spread an incredibly magical glow of gold and orange across the hollow. Several horses had stood by the corral fence, only their silhouettes discernable in the brilliant morning light that reflected off the smooth surface of the creek in radiant glimmers.

"Life has so many colors, Marigold," Rosalie reached across the table and patted her sister's forearm. "The world is like my wildflower garden, filled with pinks and purples, greens and blues."

"I get what you are saying," said Marigold. "It just seems here lately there has been an unusual amount of shoddy, hard case greys in our little berg."

"You have a beautiful heart, Marigold," Rosalie smiled in a way that reminded her sister of the picture of their Ma hanging in their father's bedroom. "You see every person as the individual God made them to be, and you want everyone to live in harmony. I believe that can happen—that the colors of life can come together like the pieces of glass in the kaleidoscope and make a beautiful picture. But it won't happen if people don't let go of old hurts and wrong mindsets. We just survived a great Civil War, and we need to pray and be good examples. Hopefully that can make some difference—at least here in our 'little berg,' as you say."

Marigold placed her hand over Rosalie's small fingers still resting on her arm. "You have a good heart too, Rosalie. I guess I have just been thinking more than usual with the recent lynchings and what happened in the post office when I was in town the other day. I don't want to live in the past, but I am sometimes afraid for the future."

"I understand that. I can't say I never get a fearful thought for myself or others, but then I remind myself that Jesus said not to live troubled or afraid. You know we are not supposed to worry about tomorrow, because tomorrow will worry about itself, and each day has enough trouble of its own."

"I know," said Marigold. "I guess if each new day is a turn of God's kaleidoscope, we can't really live in the fullness of today until we stop worrying about tomorrow and leave yesterday in the past where it belongs."

CHAPTER 13

"This meeting of the Ladies Auxiliary of the Anti-Horse Thief Society is called to order," Ophelia Simon scanned the group of ladies taking tea in the spacious parlor of the Comfort Lodge. "The first order of business is to thank Mrs. Florence Erlanger for hosting us."

With teacups balanced carefully on their knees, the ladies smiled and applauded their appreciation. Afternoon sunlight streamed in the windows of Comfort Lodge and washed over the meeting room that covered the entire base beneath the rental rooms on the second floor above. The smell of earl gray and cinnamon filled the air.

Ophelia Simon sat upright in her parlor chair, her feet tucked carefully beneath her seat. She wore a lavender and purple plaid tea dress that overlaid a white chemisette with a high, laced neckline. The gown's puffy pagoda sleeves were trimmed in the same ribbon that piped the waistline of the dress before it flared out to the floor in full skirts.

"As you know, lawless men have banded themselves together to plunder the honest citizens of our fair commonwealth. Law abiding people have found it necessary to take action for the defense of our property. The men have recently formed the local chapter of the Anti-Horse Thief Society, and today the Ladies Auxiliary will be voting on our board members and to accept the same constitution and bylaws as our sister chapter in Missouri."

"And on the amount of dues," chimed in Martha Matheny.

"What are the dues for?" asked Maggie Eldridge.

"That is a good question, Mrs. Eldridge," said Martha.

"The money goes for rewards for the recovery of stolen horses and prosecution of the thieves," said Ophelia.

Rosalie raised her hand. Mrs. Simon acknowledged her with a nod, "Yes, Mrs. Coldwell. You have a question?"

"I do. Thank you," said Rosalie. "I think it is a wonderful idea to do whatever we can to make things safer in the community, but would you please explain exactly how the society works?"

"Of course," Ophelia offered a cordial smile. She was more than happy to be the person "in the know" and enlighten the ladies she had called to her meeting.

"The society's motto is 'Protect the Innocent; Bring the Guilty to Justice,'" said Ophelia. "If a man steals a horse, selected men band together to ride after him. If they capture the thief, they deliver him to the authorities, unless there is no doubt of guilt, and in that case, they just go ahead and hang the thief. The Anti-Horse Thief Society provides a $10 reward to be split among the men who catch the thieves."

"That sounds like legalizing vigilantes to me," said Marigold.

Ophelia turned her head and looked squarely at Marigold. "I assure you, Miss Johnson, the goal is to work hand in hand with law enforcement as much as possible. The Society has been established as a means for law-abiding citizens to keep from becoming helpless victims."

"Then why the 'secret' organization?" asked Marigold.

"It is not really a 'secret,' since almost anyone can join. But to be clear, our role in the Ladies Auxiliary is to aid in social functions, not riding after malefactors."

"So I can't ride after the horse thieves and collect on the reward?"

Marigold knew she was pushing the line on good manners, but she could not resist. Mrs. Simon was just far too proper for her to take seriously, and something did not seem right. The words and intentions of the Society organizers seemed in apple pie order, but did not hold a candle to what she was feeling inside.

Ophelia looked from Marigold to Rosalie, and then back to Marigold again, her lips in a thin line across her expressionless face. "I believe, Miss Johnson, you are jesting, but the subject of stolen horses is far from humorous."

"That is true enough, Mrs. Simon." Marigold clasped her hands in her lap and conjured up her most angelic countenance. She could feel Rosalie's eyes resting heavy on her.

"As you know, my husband, Trigg, is the president of our new group," said Mrs. Simon. "You ladies are here because your men have signed on as members. If any society members have a horse stolen, the proper course of action is to contact my husband. He will assign several members to hunt for the trail of the thief and work it until they apprehend the criminal and turn him over to the Vigilance Committee when necessary."

"If you had been a couple of inches closer, I would have kicked you in the shin." Rosalie looked sideways at her sister as the two stepped out on the road that would take them the short distance from Comfort Lodge to Briar Hollow.

"Now that would not have been proper," said Marigold, "and I am certain Mrs. Simon would not have approved."

"I am certain Mrs. Simon did not approve of your comments at the meeting."

"Oh, bosh. She may think she is a big bug—her husband, too, but I am not impressed," said Marigold. "It just seems like things could get out of hand quick as a whip with a secret society, especially if tempers get to flaring or folks have grudges. I know she said it was not a vigilante group, but it makes me think of the Klan, and I have my concerns—especially with recent goings on and Trigg Simon heading things up."

The girls walked a few moments in silence, each lost in their own reflections. Rosalie was concerned by her sister's stewings and doings. She had been out of sorts lately, and her outburst at the meeting and seemingly unwarranted apprehension about a pillar in the community did not add up in Rosalie's calculations.

"Why does Mr. Simon's involvement have you concerned?" asked Rosalie.

Marigold pondered her sister's question. She did not have a good answer. There was something that was not feeling right down in her knower.

"I can't say exactly. There is just something stuck in my gizzard."

Rosalie shook her head and smiled. She understood the understandable—Marigold's discernment at work. Her tomboy sister had a sensitive, perceptive heart that not everyone recognized or appreciated.

"Why don't you tell me what you do know, and I will be praying with you."

"Well," said Marigold, clasping her hands behind her back as she continued her saunter towards home, "first things first."

"That is a good place to start," said Rosalie.

"You know the old saying, 'the apple doesn't fall far from the tree,' right?"

"I think I know every old saying about apples." Rosalie smiled and a playful spark lit her green eyes.

"That is for sure and for certain." Marigold flashed a quick grin at her sister. "But I am talking about folks, not fruit. It was Trigg Simon's son River who had the incident at the post office with Balim the other day."

"I see," Rosalie adjusted her crocheted shawl more tightly around her slight shoulders. "I understand how you might put two-and-two together there, but we do need to be careful with that line of thinking. God gives everyone a free will to make their own individual choices."

"I know that, but I also know if two cucumbers sit in the same pickle jar, they will likely come out tasting the same."

"I can't argue with that bit of wisdom."

The girls arrived at the entrance of the familiar tree-lined lane marked by a hand-painted sign made of several wooden boards joined together. The words "Briar Hollow" were painted in red scrolled letters, not too fancy, but not too plain. From the large sign a board was hung painted with bold block letters: "Coldwell Horse Farm."

"And then," said Marigold, "just yesterday when I was walking home from the mercantile with the kaleidoscope, Trigg Simon came blowing past me on that silver pied horse of his. He was with a couple of other fellows from town. I did not get a good look at them because it was starting to rain, and they had lit a shuck for town. He did not say hey or nay, just galloped on by."

"You don't have to get a look at Mr. Simon to know when he is riding your way. Zion has admired his horse since it arrived from England last year."

"It is a beauty," said Marigold, "a show-stopper for sure. I have never seen a horse with silver star-shaped dapples. And that white mane and tail that reaches clear to the ground are a sight to behold."

"I have always liked feathers on a horse," said Rosalie, "and Pied Piper's completely cover his hooves. They are just striking. Zion would like to breed him with the Quarter Horse. Of course, he would love to buy a Gypsy Vanner mare and breed her, too, but they aren't easy to find. Such a beautiful horse."

The girls exited the juniper-lined lane, the fragrance of pine lingered in the air as Rosalie drank in the splendor of her beloved Briar Hollow. Balim called it a "li'l patch a heav'n," and Rosalie agreed with him.

The hollow was an inviting circular clearing between the woods on the west and the creek on the east. To the north, left of the lane, a wildflower garden greeted the approach to the cabin. The blooms were close to finished for the year with only some turtlehead and cardinal flowers holding out in the crisp fall air.

The orchards lay in neat rows beyond the cabin, and between the cabin and creek, an enclosed rose garden and a grape arbor flanked the worn path to the orchard. The roses were still colorful, especially the Damascus ones Rosalie favored to make lotions and fragrant rosewaters she used to rinse her hair. Sharon Johnson, Rosalie's mother, had taught her that the fragrance of roses was more than just a pleasure to the senses. It had therapeutic properties that soothed the mind and nerves.

As she scanned the grounds, she let her eyes rest on one of her favorite places, the bench beneath the grape arbor. The leaves on the vines that climbed the sides and tops of the wooden structure had changed from green to yellow for the season, but this was a timeless place for her. There were so many memories of talks with her mother and father. She would never forget the time Zion had come to call on her there. She had dropped the scissors on her foot and ended up on the ground in his arms.

Across from the cabin was the kitchen garden neighbored by a hen house; and where once a small serviceable barn had been, now stood the two-family house shared by Balim's family and the Coldwell's farm hand Angus Carver. On the southern perimeter, on the site of the old apple barn now stood the beautiful round barn and corral Zion had built for the fine stock of Coldwell Horse Farm.

Since her marriage to Zion, Rosalie had come to appreciate the expensive nature and risks of raising Thoroughbreds and fine horses.

"Maybe Pied Piper inspired Mr. Simon to start the local chapter of the Anti-Horse Thief Society," said Rosalie. "I can't imagine what he paid for him, and to have him shipped across the ocean."

"Maybe." Marigold plodded up the steps to the narrow covered porch that spanned the face of cabin with its steep-pitched roof and fieldstone chimney. She plopped in the nearest of the two rocking chairs separated by the tree stump table. "I just can't escape that niggling feeling that haunts me betimes. Sometimes I wish I did not get it, but the truth is, I have learned to trust it."

"That is because what you call a 'niggling feeling' could well be a spiritual gift at work," said Rosalie. "Discernment is a spiritual gift, and the Lord has given different people different gifts for His purposes."

"Do you think that is it?"

Rosalie seated herself in the rocking chair next to her sister. "It could be. Discernment means you are able to distinguish or judge a person, a situation, or even a statement because the Spirit in you knows good from evil, even when there is no hard evidence. It is a gift God gave to the church so His people would not be led astray by false teachers and would have a warning in times of danger."

The cabin door flew open and a cacophony of hoots, cackles and wails proceeded the children's launch from the cabin into the sunshine. Dahlia was the first out and ran to her mother. She lifted her arms and Rosalie scooped her firstborn into her lap. Abram came next, giggling and holding Abby's pudgy hand, followed by Lucas with a bare-bottomed Mattie tucked under one arm and a diaper in his free hand.

"Wait, you rascals," said Lucas. "I wasn't finished!"

"Well, if that don't take the rag off!" Marigold threw her head back and burst out in a howl of laughter. "I think this shindy is a sign of a potential danger, for sure and for certain."

CHAPTER 14

"Eli," Asher called into the workroom of Thalman and Sons Clothiers, a broad smile spread across his face. "Miss Johnson is in need of some assistance. Could you come here, please?"

"I will be right there." Eli grinned as he finished pressing the edge of a shirtfront over in a double fold to create a placket for the buttonholes. With a quick motion, he set the iron down on the table beside him and hurried into the customer area of the shop where Marigold waited. Her cheeks were flushed a rosy pink, and her brown eyes sparkled. Honey wisps escaped the confines of their matching braids and wreathed her freckled face in a most becoming way.

She wore a button-front green calico work dress with box pleats starting at the waistline and falling to the floor. The bodice was simple with full, cuffed sleeves that Marigold had just noticed she had forgotten to unroll. She grinned at Eli, unrolled her left sleeve with her right hand and buttoned the cuff.

"Miss Johnson." Eli watched as the golden girl fixed her second sleeve looking sheepishly from the sleeve to his face and back again.

Marigold finished buttoning the second cuff and smoothed her skirt with both hands. "Mr. Thalman, how are you?"

"I am well, thank you. What can I do for you today?"

"Well," said Marigold, shifting her weight from one foot to the other, "we have a bit of an emergency at Briar Hollow."

"Is everything ok?" Eli asked. Marigold's bright demeanor did not seem to reconcile with her use of the word emergency. "How can I help?"

A hand flew over her mouth as Marigold tipped her head down and then looked up with mirth in her big brown eyes. "It is nothing life threatening, or anything."

"That is good. I was worried for a moment."

"It's just . . . Baby Mattie."

"Your sister's little one? Is he well?"

"Oh, he is well," Marigold giggled. "He is so well we can't keep him in his diapers."

Relief and amusement washed over Eli's face. He adjusted his spectacles and gave Marigold his full attention. "Please, go on," he said with a smile.

"It's like this," said Marigold, "Mattie is such an active baby Rosalie has been having a hard time with straight pins for his diaper. This afternoon Lucas was watching him while Rosalie and I were at the Ladies Auxiliary meeting for the Anti-Horse Thief Society, and Lucas drew blood on himself and nearly poked the baby when he had to change him."

"That sounds like a real emergency," said Eli. "How can a simple tailor like me help you in your distress?"

"Rosalie sent me to town for some safety pins, but Mrs. Matheny is all out at the mercantile. Do you have any you could spare? I am willing to pay, and it is for a worthy cause."

A full smile broke out on Eli's bearded face and he shook his head in amusement. "Wait right here," he said. "I will ask Abba if I may share some with you."

Eli started through the workroom door, and then turned to throw a look at Marigold followed by a cheesy grin.

The dual combination of Eli's dark good looks and charming ways sent waves rippling inside Marigold Johnson. She tried not to stare after him, especially with Asher looking on from his spot behind the counter. With peculiar interest, she studied the hats perched on the top shelves of the cozy shop, and then the two mannequins in the front of the display window.

Asher worked silently removing bolts of ecru fabric from the shipping container Marigold recognized as the one Eli had brought in from Maysville when he rescued her from the rain. She noted the coarseness of the twilled cotton fabric and wondered why he was stocking the shelves with fabric so inferior to the adjacent bolts of fine wools.

"Abba, Miss Johnson was hoping we might spare some safety pins for her nephew," said Eli.

"Her nephew?" asked Hiram. "What would a little one need safety pins for?"

"Nappies."

Understanding lit in Hiram Thalman's eyes. "I see," he nodded.

"It seems the little one is so energetic the straight pins are threatening injury to himself and all who attend him."

"I may be a worn out old shoe," Hiram chortled and stroked his beard, "but well I remember the days of you and your brother and sister in nappies."

"I suppose it wasn't *that* long ago."

"Not so, not so," said Hiram, "You may share what we have, of course, my son."

"Thank you." Eli walked to the shelf lined with tins and retrieved the container that kept their store of safety pins. With each step he longed more and more to ask his father if he and Ema had made a decision about the upcoming harvest party. He decided to wait. If the answer was no, he did not want to spoil his brief opportunity to spend time with Marigold.

With quick strides and a pleasant expression on his face, Eli crossed from the workroom to the counter in the shop and wrapped a handful of pins in paper that he folded into an envelope. "Here you go." He extended the package to Marigold.

"Thank you so much. Tell your pa he is Ace high." Marigold closed her fingers around the pins and reached in her pocket for her coin purse. "How much do I owe you?"

Eli pursed his lips and studied Marigold with penetrating eyes that dove straight into her soul. She knew she could hear a pin if it dropped in the seconds that seemed like minutes she waited for Eli's answer.

"Let's just consider this an act of neighborly kindness," said Eli. "Neighbors and friends help each other out in emergencies. Right?"

"That they do," said Marigold fidgeting internally beneath his gaze.

"That they do," Eli echoed.

"But they also say 'one good turn deserves another,'" said Marigold, "I can't stay in your debt now, can I?"

"Perhaps we can think of a way you can ease your conscience of any burden of debt," said Eli.

"Yea," said Asher, "how about a little honey?"

Marigold blinked and whipped her head to look the young man in the eye. Color raced up her cheeks.

"Honey?" Eli asked his brother with a quizzical look on his face.

"Yea—honey," said Asher. "I was in the mercantile yesterday and Mrs. Matheny was selling the last jar of Miss Johnson's famous honey. She said it was the best she had tasted in years."

Marigold exhaled the breath she had been holding. Eli waggled his head at his mischievous, instigating brother. There were some things brothers did not have to verbalize, and Eli's interest in Marigold Johnson had surely not gone unnoticed by his sibling.

The flash of color that had dashed up Marigold's cheeks eased its way down. "I can bring you some directly," she said. "I just need to get some more jars. I wiped out mine and Rosalie's supply."

"I will run upstairs and ask Ema if she has one you can use," said Asher with a wink.

Marigold slipped her coin purse back in her pocket and took a deep breath. Eli watched his brother charge up the steps to their living quarters and then turned his attention to the young lady before him.

"So you were at a Ladies Auxiliary meeting?"

"Yes," said Marigold. "Rosalie said I should go since all our menfolk have joined up in the Anti-Horse Thief Society. Horses are Zion's business, after all."

"That is understandable," said Eli. "A man must look after his livelihood."

"That is for sure and for certain," said Marigold. "By the way, speaking of livelihood, I could not help noticing the fabric your brother was unpacking. Are you got to make suits out of that?"

"You must mean the *serge de Nimes* we had shipped in from Europe," said Eli.

"*Serge-de-what?*" asked Marigold.

"Serge de Nimes," said Eli as he walked to the display and unrolled a span of the rugged cotton twill. "It is sometimes called denim for short."

"That seems a might rough for suit fabric."

Eli chortled.

"No offense meant," said Marigold.

"Oh, no offense taken, Miss Johnson," said Eli. "Abba always says, 'If one asks, one does not err.'"

Marigold rubbed her fingers over the rough textile. "I didn't mean to shoot my mouth off, it is just the fabric is so different from everything else in your shop."

"Exactly," said Eli. "Remember when we were speaking of secrets the other day?"

Images of sharing the bench seat with Eli in the Thalman's surrey replayed in Marigold's mind. No. She had not forgotten that time, or the conversation about secrets that had intoxicated her thoughts so many times since.

"I remember."

"I was picking up the *serge de Nimes* for my family's secret plan to help Reuben and Lark get established in a business that will keep them in town once the baby comes."

A pleasant smile swept over Marigold's face and she tilted her head with piqued interest. "Really? Can you tell me about it? Or is it too secret?"

Eli stroked his bearded chin between his thumb and forefinger with feigned concentration. "Hm. You withheld your secrets from me. Should I do the same?"

Marigold's smile sank into pursed lips. "Well, that is rich." She folded her arms across her chest. "I did not tease you, now, did I?"

"Perhaps you did not," said Eli, "at least on purpose."

A bemused expression filled Marigold's brown eyes. Before she could speak, the door to the living quarters opened and Asher clomped down the stairs, jar in hand.

"Here you go, Miss Johnson," said Asher with a grin.

"Thank you," said Marigold, "I will be happy to fill this for you."

"And I will be pleased to sample your famous honey."

"I was just showing Miss Johnson the *serge de Nimes*," Eli patted the bolt of ecru fabric.

"What do you think of our plan?" Asher reached for a bolt from the shipping container, gave it a quick inspection, and then placed it on the shelf beside its traveling companions.

"I have not heard all the details yet," said Marigold. "Would you like to tell me?"

Asher gave his brother a sideways glance, and Eli nodded his approval with a smile, "Go ahead, brother."

Asher flipped the fabric on the bolt Eli had opened on the counter to reveal the backside of the material. "See this diagonal ribbing here? It is created when the weft passes under two or more warp fibers. This is a twill weave, and it means the fabric is very strong."

"I see."

"This new denim fabric has been used to make dungarees for miners out west. It is far more durable than other materials, and Eli thought we could use it to help Rueben get established in his own business. We are going to making dungarees for the working people of Mason County that hold up to wear and hard use. Reuben can introduce them by selling them on his travels."

"We are confident that once people see what a good value these denim dungarees are, they will tell others about them and demand will increase," said Eli. "The goal is to develop a name for Rueben that will help him set up a shop with a ready market of customers."

Marigold's recent contact with Mrs. Matheny had stirred a compassion for the woman. She obviously missed her daughter very much. Sure, there had been times in the past Marigold had tired of Martha Matheny's uppity ways and hearing about her stupid angel food cake. The woman obviously thought it was a legend in Washington, when everyone knew it was only because her husband was on the judging committee that her pasty old cake won any ribbons at all at the Germantown Fair. As long as Marigold could remember, Martha Matheny had bustled and preened around Washington like a rooster in the henhouse. But when it came right down to it, if she was honest with herself, Marigold rather missed the spunky Mrs. Matheny.

"I think that is grand idea," Marigold clasped her hand together, the package of pins sandwiched between them. "Oh, I better get back. Rosalie is expecting me home straightaway. That is why I rode Absalom in, so I could hightail it into town and get right back."

"Give her our regards," said Asher.

"I will walk you out." Eli led the way to the door and held it open for Marigold to pass through and then followed her out onto the rope walk.

"You will keep my secret now, won't you?" Eli asked as Marigold mounted Absalom with beautiful form.

"Of course," said Marigold. She flashed him a tooth-filled smile. "I am very good at keeping secrets."

CHAPTER 15

"Oh, they are wonderful," said Rosalie. "Not only did I manage to get the diaper on without stabbing either one of us, but it was so much easier to pull his soaker over the top with the safety pins."

"I am proud to hear it," said Marigold. "And now I am off to check my hives. The newer ones were not ready yet when I harvested last time. I am hoping to find at least one filled with cured and capped honey for Mrs. Thalman."

Of course, for Mrs. Thalman, thought Rosalie as she watched her golden-haired sister practically skip out the cabin door.

Sunlight streaked through the door jambs. Through squinted eyes, Rosalie caught the quick exchange of howdies between Marigold and her husband before Zion's broad silhouette filled the opening.

Greeted by the tantalizing aroma of bacon and coffee, Zion lifted his straw hat and riffled a shock of thick chestnut hair with his free hand. A grin spread across his tanned face accentuating the dimple in his right cheek.

"And howdy to you, too, Mrs. Coldwell." Zion hung his hat on a hook by the door and sucked in a deep breath. "It smells like all kinds of wonderful in here."

Rosalie finished tying the bib around her daughter's neck and handed her a spoon. "There you go, baby girl. You can have your oatmeal after we pray."

"I washed up in the lean-to, so let's get on with the getting on." Zion's cornflower blue eyes twinkled at his girls as he seated himself between them and extended a hand to each.

"Lord, I thank You for Your bounty. I thank You for my family and home. I thank You for this day that You have made and this meal You have provided. I ask Your blessing upon this food and the hands that made it, in the precious name of Jesus."

"A-men!" Dahlia reached for the bowl her father pushed in front of her while Rosalie went for the coffeepot. With quilted potholders in both hands, she grabbed the speckled pot off the stove and filled Zion's cup with steaming brew.

"Nothing like a hot cup of Arbuckles." Zion took a swig of black coffee.

After she had filled her cup, Rosalie returned the pot to the stove and then joined her family at the table.

"Marigold was here bright and early this morning," said Zion. He took the bowl of scrambled eggs and spooned some on his plate next to several pieces of crispy thick-cut bacon.

"Yes," said Rosalie. "She was here to check her hives. She is hoping to harvest some honey."

"Didn't she just do that?" Zion took a fluffy biscuit from the napkin-lined basket and then passed the basket to Rosalie.

"She did, but the newer colonies don't fill their frames as quickly as the established ones. They were not ready yet."

"I see," said Zion. "Speaking of honey, do we have any for these bang up biscuits?"

"For now we do."

Rosalie retrieved the honey jar from the cabinet and gave it to Zion. "We may have to use molasses or preserves if Marigold keeps trading her honey away."

"Who is she trading with?" Zion crunched a bite of bacon while he lifted the honey dripper from the jar and held it over his buttered biscuit. He spun the handle, and the grooves of the dripper released the amber fluid in a sweet drizzle. "And what is she trading for?"

"The first batch was with Martha Matheny," said Rosalie. "I thought I told you about the kaleidoscope she got for Abby and Abram."

"You did," said Zion. "I just did not realize she traded her honey for it." Zion took a bite of his biscuit.

Mmm. Zion savored the tastes mingling in his mouth. "If you keep making biscuits like these, I may have to go in to the mercantile and buy some of that honey back."

"I am glad you like them," said Rosalie, "but Marigold told me Mrs. Matheny already sold out. That is why she is hoping to get some more today to give to the Thalmans who were kind enough to share some safety pins with us yesterday. That son of yours is one wiggly piggly."

Zion chuckled. "I can still see a picture in my mind of Lucas running out the door with a bare-bottomed baby in one hand and a diaper in the other."

"Sweet Lucas." Rosalie smiled. "He is so good to help out with the little ones."

"Yes, he is."

"He said he was coming over this afternoon to take the kids out on the goat cart," said Rosalie.

"Yay!" Dahlia clapped, and oatmeal from her spoon went flying. "Goat wide!"

"Oh, baby, I am glad you are happy, but let's not clap with a spoon in your hand." Rosalie wiped the oatmeal from the table with a grin.

"We should have thought of a goat cart years ago," said Zion. "Every one of them loves it, including Lucas pulling them around like a ringmaster at the circus."

Rosalie offered Dahlia a drink of milk while Zion opened a steamy biscuit and quickly prepared it with a slab of butter and drizzle of honey.

"Zion?" said Rosalie in that voice her husband knew so well.

"Yes, *my green-eyed girl from Kentucky named Rosalie*?" Zion studied his wife's delicate, heart-shaped face. How he loved that face that could say so much without a word. He took in every feature: curved eyebrows arched beautifully over celadon green eyes; porcelain skin with a freckled, upturned nose; delicate lips. He watched as with slight fingers she twirled a loose strand of thick auburn hair.

"What is on your mind, Mrs. Coldwell?" Zion loved his wife's thoughtful, nurturing nature, and he could tell something had captured her concern.

"I have been thinking."

"About?"

"Well, about Marigold."

"I see." Zion nodded his head. "And what exactly is it you have been thinking about Marigold?"

Rosalie's shoulders lifted with the release of a quiet sigh. "You know I have been more like a mother than a sister to her these last few years."

"That I do know," said Zion.

"I have learned to read her pretty well."

"Rosalie, you can read most folks pretty well."

"I don't know about most folks, but I do know my sister," said Rosalie. "I have always wanted her to find a godly man who would love and appreciate her for the treasure she is."

"And?"

"And I am afraid she is developing feelings for someone."

"That is something to celebrate, isn't it?" Zion studied his wife and waited for her reply.

Rosalie curved her fingers around her coffee cup and then looked into her husband's blue eyes. "It should be."

Zion thought back on the likely candidates. The only fellows he had seen with Marigold lately were family, and Balim, and Angus. Then he recalled Marigold and Eli Thalman talking together in the hollow the other day.

His eyes met Rosalie's.

"Eli?"

Rosalie nodded.

"Well, I'll be," said Zion. "I did come across them together the other day when Marigold was out tending her hives."

"He came over to check on her after the incident with Balim."

"That was right neighborly, wasn't it?" Zion grinned. "He is a nice young man. And he is a godly fellow. We even got to talking about Pentecost and studying Scripture."

"Really? You were talking about Pentecost?"

"Well, it is in the Old Testament, you know."

Rosalie nodded her head. "Oh, of course."

Zion assessed his distracted wife. She was usually put together and as placid as a looking glass.

"And Marigold keeps finding reasons to run into town," said Rosalie. "I used to could hardly get her to run an errand for me, and now she is back and forth every day."

"I see," said Zion. "So you think she is sweet on Eli. Do you think he is feeling the same way?"

"He has never said or done anything inappropriate," said Rosalie. "He is the utmost gentleman. The truth is, he treats her like a lady."

Zion nodded. "Do you think that is why she might be responding to him? Most folks around here just think of Marigold as one of the gang."

"It could be," said Rosalie. "I just don't want her to get hurt. You know Reverend Dryfus could not agree to marry them—and look at what happened to Lark."

Zion stood, went to the stove to refill his coffee, and then offered some to his wife.

"No, thank you," said Rosalie.

"Well, my Rose of Sharon, this could all be as simple as Marigold appreciating being treated like a lady and have nothing at all to do with romance."

Rosalie nodded slowly. "It could."

"But you don't think so, do you?"

Rosalie shook her head as slowly as she had nodded it moments before.

"How about this," said Zion. "When we were talking the other day he seemed open to comparing notes on Scripture. How about I ask him to teach me the deeper meanings of some Old Testament passages coming from a person who understands the original language? I would really like the opportunity to do that, and it could give me the chance to get to know him better."

Rosalie smiled. "That sounds like a wonderful idea."

"Perhaps I could get a feel for where he is at with his intentions towards Marigold. And you never know, the Lord might be using this to reveal Himself to Eli. It must hurt His heart to see His people not recognizing Him as their Savior."

Rosalie's green eyes brightened with unshed tears. "Oh, Zion," she said. "Of course. That may just be what God is doing, at that."

"That's my girl," said Zion.

He circled the table and gave his wife a kiss on her creamy cheek. "You know I invited them to the party. Maybe the whole family will come."

"That would be so nice," said Rosalie. "They seem to be such kind people, but since they don't go to church or other social functions, they have not really integrated in the community. I would like to get to know them better myself."

CHAPTER 16

"What happened?" asked Rosalie, breathless from her rush from the cabin.

"Sweet Lawd Jesus!" Minnie leaned over her unconscious daughter crying and praying. Abram and Dahlia were huddled on the grass near the goat cart that lay askew on the ground a few yards away. Besides a scrape here and there, the two older children looked to be uninjured.

"I am so sorry," Lucas moaned and worked diligently to unbridle the bleating goat. "I am so sorry."

"Let me see her." Rosalie fell to her knees beside the toddler and pressed the dish towel she had carried out of the cabin on the open head wound. With all the chaos, she knew she would not be able to hear if Abby was breathing, so she placed her cheek next to the little one's nostrils and prayed.

"Minnie," she whispered, "she is alive. Keep praying."

"Oh, dear God," Penny gasped as she arrived on the scene. She had heard the accident through her open window and ran across the bridge to see if she could help.

"Penny," said Rosalie in a calm and confident tone, "I need you to go in the cabin and bring my large cutting board."

"You ain't gonna do no surgery on my baby, is you?" Minnie wailed.

"No, Minnie," Rosalie placed her free hand on her friend's arm. "I am just going to move her inside where I can take better care of her. I am not sure if she has hurt her neck or back, so I want to keep her straight until I can assess her condition better."

"Oh, Lawd. Oh, Lawd."

"Lucas, are you hurt?" asked Rosalie.

A groan slipped through Lucas' clenched lips, "No, Rosalie. I am not hurt. I am just so sorry—so sorry."

"I know you are, Lukey. We will talk about that later, but right now, as soon as you get Blossom untangled, I need you to run for the men. They have been clearing trees to expand the far corral. They were probably making so much noise they haven't heard any of this commotion. Can you do that for me?"

"I will," said Lucas. "I almost have her free. I think she is ok."

"That is good, sweetheart. You are doing a good job."

The cabin door flung open and Penny rushed down the porch steps with a large, smooth cutting board.

"Minnie, can you help me?" said Rosalie.

"Oh, Lawd. I will try, Miss Rozlee. I will try."

"All I want you to do is slide the board under Abby. Penny, I need you to very carefully lift her, and we will ease her on as gently as we can."

Penny knelt next to Rosalie and placed her hands under the pudgy toddler's diaper. Rosalie used both hands to keep Abby's head, neck and spine as immobile as possible.

"I am going to count to three. When I say three, Penny, you and I are going to lift her off the ground only enough to slide the board underneath. Minnie, that is your job. Just slide that right under her."

"I will. Yes, I can do that for my baby girl. Oh, Lawd, help me."

The transfer went smoothly, but Abby lay motionless and soundless on the board.

"Penny, we're going to carry her into my cabin. I have things in there we may need," said Rosalie.

The girls lifted the corners of the board followed by Minnie sniffling and whispering prayers for her daughter.

"Auntie Penny will be right back for you," Rosalie called to Dahlia and Abram. "Lucas, don't go until Penny gets back for the little ones, ok?"

"Ok," said Lucas. He had successfully freed Blossom from her bridle and the Nubian goat was just getting her footing. An abrasion ran down her right front leg from the knee down the cannon bone almost to the toe, but she was able to stand.

Once inside the cabin Rosalie shooed Penny back outside to the children and prayed Zion would be there soon. She knew Abby's injury could be life threatening, but with the toddler's inability to communicate, she would have to make some difficult determinations. She hoped Doctor Byerly had not left Washington for his Maysville office today.

Thankfully she was not vomiting, sweating, or having seizures, but she was very pale. The fluid draining from her ear on the same side her skull had been lacerated concerned Rosalie. She lifted the towel to do a closer inspection and make sure there were no foreign objects in the wound.

"What you think, Miss Rozlee?" Minnie watched as Rosalie checked her daughter for injury.

"It is my prayer she will be just fine," said Rosalie. "The wound is bleeding heavily, but that is common with a head injury, and is not necessarily a sign that something terrible has happened.

But we do have to be aware that she could have hurt herself more inside than we can see."

With one hand still applying pressure to the wound, Rosalie lifted one of Abby's eyelids and then the other. "Both of her pupils are the same size," she said, "and that is good."

"What can I do?" Minnie asked. "Surely I can do somethin'."

"You are doing a good job keeping calm and praying," said Rosalie. "As soon as Zion gets here . . . ."

The women heard the pounding steps before the door flew open. "Oh, thank God," said Rosalie.

Zion reached the house first followed by Logan and Balim. Angus waited outside.

"What happened?" Logan looked at the makeshift examining table, disturbed by Abby's still form layed out on the cutting board.

"We don't know all the details yet," said Rosalie. "There was an accident, but Abby's breathing."

"Glory be," Balim raised his right hand to heaven and placed his left on his wife's shoulder. "Thank ya, Jesus!"

"Zion, can you ride into town for Doctor Byerly?"

"You know I can," he said.

"I will saddle West," Angus shouted over his shoulder on his way to the barn.

"The thing is, I don't know if he is in Washington or Maysville today."

"I can ride to Maysville, just in case," said Logan.

"Oh, that is a great idea." Rosalie smiled. "That way wherever he is, he will get here as soon as possible."

"Yes," said Zion. "Good thinking, Logan."

"Zion, if he is not there, would you please bring back some ice from the Matheny boys?"

"I sure will," said Zion. "Do you need anything else from town?"

"Just the doctor, if he is there."

"You've got it," said Zion. He patted Logan on the back. "We better get your horse saddled up, too. Let's go."

Fred McGhee took a drag off his quirley, held it for a moment, and then let off a plume of smoke. He was as anxious as his companion to hear from Trigg Simon what had happened since their last meeting, but he was playing it cool.

"So exactly what did your boy do?" Burke Calhoun asked.

Simon glanced around the lower meeting room of the Paxton Inn. His top lip curled up on one side in his signature smirk as he leaned on the table to give his report. "My boy River overheard how the Johnson boy was all the time giving goat cart rides to that bull's young'uns."

"Deadbeat," Calhoun scowled.

"He is between hay and grass," said McGhee, "too young to know any better if he ain't been taught right by his folks."

"Well, he needs to get educated," said Trigg, "along with a lot of folks around Washington, I would say. That is what this meeting is about, isn't it? Educating folks on the way things ought to be in our fair society?"

McGhee took another drag on his hand-rolled cigarette and nodded his agreement.

"Anyhow, River snuck over to Briar Hollow in the night and sabotaged that cart." Trigg looked from one man to the next.

"Bully!" A wide smile crept across Burke Calhoun's face. "How did you think of that?"

"I got to thinking about what Fred said the other day. The best way to hurt someone is to hurt their children," said Simon. "Even an animal won't leave their wounded. If we isolate them, we will have a chance to do a surprise attack and beef that mudsill. We'll make an example out of him that will benefit the entire community."

Simon took a swig from his cup. "With everyone gone to the party Sunday, we'll scoop him up and take him to the Corbin place."

McGhee flicked ashes in the urn on the table. "If everyone is going to be gone, why don't we just do it in Briar Hollow?"

"I don't want to take a chance on getting interrupted. There are people coming and going to and from Briar Hollow all the time," said Simon. "And there is something in me that would take some personal satisfaction in utilizing the Corbin place. Not everyone knew that old barn of his was where runaways were held up before they got returned or sent to auction."

"Not just runaways, I heard," said McGhee. "I heard Corbin 'gleaned' slaves from operations all over the tri-state area and then resold them right here at the Washington courthouse auction as runaways."

"Sounds like Corbin," said Burke. "He was a promiscuous ol' rip."

"Some might say a shrewd businessman." Trigg pushed his chair back from the table. "So we will meet at the Corbin place at dusk Sunday night."

"Right," said McGhee.

"Don't forget to bring your . . . *hat*," Calhoun snickered.

CHAPTER 17

"Whoa," Zion signaled West to halt in front of Doctor Byerly's office and dismounted before the horse stopped moving. With long strides he bounded up the steps two at a time and swung open the door to the doctor's Washington office.

"Mr. Coldwell," the nurse greeted Zion from her desk, a startled look in her eyes, "is everything all right?"

Zion scanned the receiving room. "Is Doc in?"

Lou stood up and circled around the desk. "I am sorry, Mr. Coldwell. He is in the Maysville office today. Is there something I can do for you?"

"It is Abby. She has been in an accident and Rosalie sent me to fetch Doc Byerly."

"Would you like me to come?"

Zion shook his head. "I think not. Logan rode to Maysville, and I rode here. He will fetch the doctor, and Rosalie told me to bring her some ice if he wasn't here."

"Are you sure?" asked Lou.

"I think so," said Zion. "I will just ride over to the ice house and head back. If Rosalie wants you to come I will send someone back with a wagon for you."

"What is wrong with the little one? Maybe I can send something that could help."

"She fell out of the goat cart. Cut her head pretty bad. She is unconscious at the moment, which is scary, but might be a blessing. Poor thing."

"Hopefully she won't be out for long," said Lou. "The longer she is unconscious, the more chance the injury is serious."

"I am going for that ice now," said Zion.

"I would give you laudanum for pain, but you don't want her to sleep once she wakes up." Lou unlocked the pharmacy cabinet and pulled out a small brown bottle. "I know Rosalie well enough to know she has white willow bark on hand, but this tincture would be the best method to get some in her system."

"Thanks, Lou." Zion tucked the bottle in his shirt pocket, made a quick exit and swung himself onto West in a seamless motion. He shifted his weight forward and pressed his heels together. "Giddup!"

"Is that Mr. Coldwell?" Eden pointed out the window where she stood drying the last of the breakfast dishes.

Judith Thalman turned from her kneading to peer outside. "He is moving so fast," she said, "but that certainly looks like him and his horse."

"I saw him enter the doctor's office and then run back out." Eden gave the cup in her hand one more wipe and placed it on the shelf adjacent the washbasin. "Should I let Eli know?"

"Eli?" Judith looked at her daughter and contemplated her words. "Why Eli?"

Eden felt the weight of her mother's interrogating gaze. "Because he has recently become more friendly with Mr.

Coldwell and his family. You know, Ema, since Mr. Mayfield ordered his suits and the family has been working with Abba on Mr. Johnson's birthday surprise."

"Eli has been out to their place several times the last few weeks," said Judith. She wiped a wisp of hair off her face with the back of her hand and returned to kneading. Flipping the challah dough on the floured surface, she pressed and stretched it with the heel of her hand, folded it over and rotated it several times until it had the smooth and elastic texture she was looking for. Satisfied with her efforts, she rolled the dough into a ball, placed it in a greased bowl and covered it with a cloth.

"We have some time," said Judith as she moved the bowl near the stove still slightly warm from the morning's breakfast preparations. "This needs to rise. Shall we visit Abba and your brothers in the shop?"

Eden untied her apron. "Yes, Ema. That would be nice."

Judith removed her flour-coated apron and washed her hands. "Shall we take coffee?"

"If I can have some, too," Eden smiled at her mother.

Judith allowed fourteen year-old Eden only a limited amount of coffee.

"Ay yay yay." Judith shook her head at her daughter. "Such *chutzpah* you have. You had coffee with breakfast today and you want more before noon?"

Eden shrugged and tilted her head. A twinkle lit her dark eyes. "What can I say, Ema? I think some day I will open a coffee shop and serve coffee all day long."

A chuckle slipped through Judith's lips. "I think we must make a fresh pot then."

"Thank you, Abba." Eli shoved a flat-topped straw hat with a dark band over his black curls and closed the door to the shop behind him.

Once Eden told him about Zion's rush to the doctor's office, he knew he could not be at peace until he checked on the family. He would have taken the surrey, but by the time he got to the livery and got the horse hitched up, he could make it to Briar Hollow on foot.

He walked.

He prayed.

He tried not to worry.

May the one who blessed Abraham, Isaac and Jacob, bless the sick with health. May any injured or ill at Briar Hollow merit from the Holy One of Israel protection, rescue from trouble or distress, and full recovery from any illness, whether it be minor or serious. God send Your blessings to all. Amen.

The sound of pounding hooves alerted Eli to Zion's approach before he thundered by on West, holding the saddle horn in one hand and gripping a silver bucket in the other. Eli dared not stop Zion on his obviously important mission, although he certainly wanted to ask him what had happened.

By the time Eli reached Briar Hollow he had mentally buried half the family with the plague.

"Perfect," said Rosalie. She took the ice from Zion, wrapped some in a cloth and placed it on Abby's head. "This will work to keep down any swelling."

"It is a shame Doctor Byerly was not in Washington," Zion hung his hat on the peg by the door.

"I know," said Rosalie, "but at least Logan should have him here soon."

"Lou sent this." Zion reached in his pocket and retrieved the small brown bottle. "She said the best way to get willow bark into her system was with a tincture."

"That was thoughtful," said Rosalie, "but I still need her to wake up to swallow."

"How is she?" asked Zion.

"It is hard to say for sure until she wakes up, but the good news is she is breathing well, and her heart is beating strong and regular."

"My girl has always been a healthy one," said Minnie as she dabbed the corner of her eye with a blue paisley bandana.

"I am not a doctor," said Rosalie, "but I checked her neck and back the best I know how without risking further injury. They seem fine to me. She just took a hard fall and it knocked her right out."

"Could you use smelling salts?" asked Zion.

"I could." Rosalie lifted the ice and then placed it back on Abby's injury. "Doc Byerly might, but I just think he should check her first. If she did hurt her neck or back and we roused her with smelling salts she could possibly injure herself moving around."

"So basically we are waiting for the doctor, or for Abby to wake up?" Zion watched his wife carefully tending the small child stretched out on the table where he had eaten breakfast not so long ago.

"And we is praying," said Balim.

Lucas stood at the entrance to Briar Hollow waiting to see the doctor appear on the macadamized road. He was so intent on his focus northward, he did not hear Eli's approach from the south.

"Lucas." Eli touched the boy on the shoulder, and he jumped. "I am sorry. I did not mean to startle you."

"Oh, it's ok." Lucas looked back down the road towards Maysville.

It was obvious to Eli that Lucas was not ok. Worry was etched on his heart-shaped face. His thin pink lips were taught and his eyes downcast.

"Has someone been hurt?"

Lucas turned to face Eli with a quizzical look. "Does the whole town know?"

"Know what?" Eli studied the boy's face trying to read whatever information he could gather.

Lucas' chin trembled, and he bowed his head to the ground. "About Abby."

"Balim's little girl?" Eli dropped to one knee next to Lucas. He cupped his chin in his hand and tipped his face to look into his green eyes. "No one knows that I know of. I just heard your brother-in-law ran into town for the doctor, and I wanted to make sure everyone was all right."

A sob shook Lucas' shoulders, and the tears he had worked hard to contain spilled out his sorrowful eyes. "It's all my fault. I am so sorry."

Eli patted the boy's shoulder and whispered a prayer. "Why don't you tell me what happened."

Lucas sniffled and wiped his eyes with the back of his hand. "I was giving Dahlia and Abram and Abby a ride. It was a tight fit on the bench with all three of them on the goat cart, but I thought it was safe." The scene replayed in Lucas' mind and he squeezed his eyes together wishing he could send the vision away.

"I am sure no one would ever think you would intentionally hurt them," said Eli. "Did Abby fall out?"

"The cart. I don't know what happened. The wheel broke off and all three of them fell out. Dahlia and Abram got a few scrapes and scratches, but they are ok."

"That is good," said Eli.

"But Abby—she hit her head on a rock. She hasn't woke up, and I am so worried about her."

"Oh, Lucas. I am so sorry."

"Zion rode to town for Doc Byerly, but he is in his Maysville office today."

"That is a shame," said Eli. "Is that why you are waiting here by the road?"

"When Zion rode to Washington, Logan rode to Maysville just in case. Penny is watching Dahlia and Abram, and I can't really do anything, so I was just standing here waiting and watching and trying to pray."

"Is Marigold here?"

"Oh, no," Lucas groaned. "Nobody told them yet. Do you think I should go there?"

"I tell you what," said Eli. He smiled at Lucas and ruffled his saddle-brown hair. "I am sure it is no fun telling this story over and again. Would you like me to go for you and you can be here when the doctor comes?"

"Oh, that would be grand." Lucas cracked a trepid smile. "Thank you."

CHAPTER 18

Matthias Johnson stood in an interior corridor of neat rows of fruit-laden apple trees. The wire basket, with its open end at the top of a sturdy pole, was close to filled.

"Just one more," he said as he raised the clawed basket. With the basket full, hand under hand, he lowered the pole and placed the apples one by one into a bushel basket.

"I will be glad when Lucas gets back," said Marigold. "I think you are getting soft on him, Pa—letting him take the little ones for a ride before chores."

Marigold moved from the lower branches of the same tree her father worked on to the makeshift table used for sorting apples by condition and size. Smaller apples stored better than large ones, so these were separated from the larger apples that would be used first. Those with any bruises or imperfections would be taken to Rosalie to be made into applesauce, fruit leathers or preserved by canning or drying.

The fresh, fruity aroma of apples and fall followed Eli from the Coldwell side of the orchard to the Johnson side. Rows of trees stood like soldiers in a rectangular formation so different from the eclectic composition of the rest of the grounds. On the

Coldwell side, Rosalie's wildflower and rose gardens, asparagus and pumpkin patches mingled with dottings of a shed, henhouse, and other outbuildings in an eclectic mix that harmonized with the contour of the hollow.

The Johnson side was sparse in ornamentation, although the same creek that flowed through Briar Hollow bubbled along its border. Edged with velvety grasses, the clear water flowed over a succession of rocks and ledges that formed pools along the edges and held a few lingering tadpoles. Whippoorwills nested in the shade of mixed woodland on the far side of the creek, and a chorus of meadowlarks interplayed with the song of the brook.

The property the Johnsons called home had been settled previously by Grant and Awinita Taylor. When Matthias and Sharon Johnson had moved from Texas to Kentucky, they had not had enough money to purchase both parcels of land, so the young couple settled on Briar Hollow and planted what they could on the land they had. The location was lovely, and it was important for the orchard to be near water. It was the ideal place to build their home and enterprise.

Matthias had always hoped to purchase the adjacent property, but had not been able to raise the finances before Grant Taylor bought the place to build a home for himself and his new bride. Providence intervened, however, and everything worked out for good and in perfect timing. Just as Rosalie and Zion were needing a place to set up housekeeping and launch Zion's horse farm, the Taylors decided to relocate and offered to sell their home and land to Matthias. He was more than happy to "work the orchard from the other side" and see the cabin he had built for his beloved bride Sharon filled with the love of their firstborn and her growing family.

His needs were simple. When Rosalie had married, it was just the three Johnsons left: Matthias, Marigold and Lucas. He had figured Marigold would have married and moved on by now, leaving the cabin to him and his son. He planned to give the title to the cabin and orchard to Lucas when he was no longer able to work it. With his physical limitations, that could be sooner than he wanted to consider.

A brownish colored mutt raised off her haunches and sniffed her way to Eli. Her skinny tail stuck straight up behind her waving as she walked his way.

"Hello, *kelev*." Eli watched the dog approach and look him over. She seemed calm and friendly enough. Her unexpected deep *woof* startled him.

"Somebody is here," said Marigold as she placed an apple in the fruit-picking bag Rosalie had created. Made of sturdy cotton duck, the bag's straps crossed her back and the receptacle in front was able to hold up to a half a bushel. A flap in the bottom was closed with grommets and ties but conveniently opened for Marigold to unload the apples on the sorting table.

"You better go see who it is before Daisy lights into them," said Matthias. He leaned his 6 foot 5 inch frame onto his cane with one hand and positioned himself to unload the apple picker into the bushel basket Marigold had set up on a box next to him.

"Right Pa," Marigold chuckled. "I will go. Why don't you sit down for a few minutes?"

"I will do some sorting for a bit." Matthias eased himself into a folding chair next to the table. Relief coursed through his weary, aching body.

"Good idea," she said.

Although Matthias uttered no words of complaint, Marigold

had observed more than anyone the way her father had slowed in recent months. It was clear from his movements that he was in pain most of the time, and he tired quickly. But as long as there was work to do and he was able to do it, Matthias Johnson would never settle for his rocking chair, no matter how his body begged him to.

Marigold crossed through two rows of trees and stepped into the clearing to see Eli and Daisy in a face-off. Unsure of the dog's temperament, Eli stood on the path deliberating his options.

"Don't worry about ol' Daisy," said Marigold as she crossed the clearing to the path. "She is more blow than bite."

She snapped her fingers. "Down, girl."

The dog made a lazy turn and meandered back to her watch near the cabin.

Eli removed his hat and tipped his head in greeting, "Hello, Miss Johnson."

"Hello, Mr. Thalman," she said, delight obvious on her freckled face. "What brings you out this way?"

"I wish it was a good report," said Eli, concern etched across his dark features.

Marigold's thoughts scrambled in a quick search for possible scenarios.

Eli watched as her imagination moved her brown eyes from unseen vision to unseen vision.

"Don't be offish and leave me worrying and guessing," she said. "What is it?"

"I am sorry," said Eli, "I just wanted you to have a moment to prepare yourself."

"Now I am really worried." Marigold closed the gap between them and clasped her fingers around his upper arm. She probed his obsidian eyes. "Please don't prepare me any more, Eli. Just let loose with the news before I plumb burst."

Eli offered a slight smile to reassure the girl with the beseeching brown eyes. "It is no one in your immediate family," said Eli, "but I am afraid little Abby has been injured in a goat cart accident."

Marigold's eyes widened. "Is she ok? What happened?"

"She is alive, but she is unconscious," said Eli. "Your sister is looking after her and the doctor should be arriving soon from Maysville."

"Oh no." Marigold turned her head and looked at the ground. "I can't believe this happened. Lucas is so careful with those little ones. Was anyone else hurt?"

"Dahlia and Abram were involved, but not seriously injured. Lucas said they had some scrapes and scratches."

"Dear Jesus," Marigold whispered a prayer and then sprang to attention.

"I have got to get over there." She grabbed Eli's hand. "Come with me to tell Pa, ok?"

Eli allowed himself to be led through the trees to the portable work stand set up in the fragrant orchard.

"Pa!" Marigold called as she hustled herself and Eli through the trees. "Pa!"

Matthias turned from the worktable to see his daughter's lively approach. He recognized the young man she was with as one of the new tailor's sons, but the two had never been formally introduced.

"What's the hullabaloo, daughter?" Matthias asked. "And do you want to introduce me to your caller?"

Marigold looked down her arm startled at what she saw. She simultaneously drew her head up and dropped Eli's hand quick as a wink. "Oh, I am sorry, Mr. Thalman."

Marigold collected herself and remembered her manners.

"Pa, this is Eli Thalman. Eli Thalman, this is Matthias Johnson."

"Pleased to meet you," said Matthias.

"And I you, sir."

"What's got you running, girl?"

"It is Abby, Pa. She's been hurt."

"That is not good news," said Matthias. "How serious?"

"She is unconscious. I am heading over there now to see how she is doing and if I can help."

"The doctor should be coming from Maysville any time," said Eli. "Mr. Mayfield rode in to get him."

"Well, go on, girl," said Matthias. "I think I would be more in the way than I would be help, so I will just stay here, and I will be praying. You send Lucas over with any news."

"I will."

Matthias watched as his honey-haired daughter took off like a barn cat after a mouse. Eli stood his ground, although his heart bounded after the girl who disappeared in the trees to take the path through the orchard to her sister's cabin.

"Mr. Thalman," said Matthias. With one hand on the table and the other on his cane, he pushed himself up from the chair. "I am sorry to meet you under such circumstances, but I am always right pleased to meet my good neighbors. Would you care to keep an old man company while we wait for the news?"

"In my haste to make sure all was well with your family, I deserted Abba and my brother at the shop," said Eli, "but I am sure they will permit me a few more minutes away."

"I see you are riding shank's mare," said Matthias. "Did you run all the way from town?"

"We keep our horse and surrey at the livery," said Eli. "By the time I walk there, and the horse and surrey are readied, I can cover the distance from the shop to Briar Hollow on foot."

"You've come out this way before then, have you?"

"Yes," Eli nodded. He matched his gate to Matthias' afflicted pace. "The first time was to deliver Mr. Mayfield's suits."

"Those getups are just like downtown," said Matthias. "Your pa does grand work with a needle and thread."

Eli grinned. "I see where your daughter gets her interesting euphemisms."

Matthias nodded and cut a sideways glance at the young man beside him. "You must mean Marigold. My older girls are right proper in their speaking most of the time, but Marigold—well, with that girl one word can become a herd. And herds ain't always neat and orderly."

"No, sir," said Eli, a broad smile across his elongated face.

"But they are profitable, that I have to say."

The two walked in silence a few steps. "And sometimes there are tender calves in the herds," said Eli.

Matthias Johnson could not miss the affection in young Thalman's eyes. He had seen this "elephant" before. He had married off two daughters, and recognized the courting symptoms when he saw them. As a father, he wanted nothing more than to see his youngest daughter settled in a good marriage, but as a Christian man, he had some concerns. The Good Book said Christians ought not be yoked up with unbelievers, and as fine a gentleman as Eli Thalman seemed to be, and as deep as His faith might be, he did not believe in Jesus.

"That reminds me of one of my favorite passages," said Matthias. "It is in Habakkuk: 'Although the fig tree shall not blossom, neither shall fruit be in the vines; the labour of the olive shall fail, and the fields shall yield no meat; the flock shall be cut off from the fold, and there shall be no herd in the stalls: Yet I will rejoice in the LORD, I will joy in the God of my salvation.'"

Eli nodded at the words. They were not exactly as those he had learned in the *Torah*, but he knew the passage. "God the Lord is my strength. He made my feet as swift as the hind's, and he guides me on my high places."

"Yes." Matthias nodded. "The Lord is good. He said He would guide you on your high places and me on mine."

"To be sure."

"Everybody has high places," said Matthias.

Eli looked into the older man's wizened features and sensed a depth to this man that went beyond human understanding.

"You know, I know you and your family are Jewish, but there is something Jesus taught that has helped me out many a time."

"Please feel free to share," said Eli.

"He was teaching on faith, and He said that if we had faith the size of a grain of mustard seed, we could say to a mountain, 'remove hence to yonder place,' and it would go."

"A faith that could move a mountain would be a powerful faith, indeed," said Eli.

"Well, I have pondered this many times, and you know in Isaiah where he said to 'prepare the way of the Lord' to make the high places low and the crooked places straight?"

"Yes," said Eli, nodding, "'and the glory of the Lord shall be revealed, and all flesh shall see it together; for the mouth of the Lord hath spoken it.'"

A pleasant smile lifted the corners of Matthias' mouth. "Yes," he said. "I love the writings of Isaiah."

"I, as well," said Eli.

"What I was getting at, son, is that I don't necessarily think Isaiah was talking about the hillsides and roadways of Jerusalem when he was talking about those mountains and crooked places." Matthias stopped in front of the cabin and adjusted his hat on his head. "It seems to me the mountains and valleys and crooked places God is most concerned about are those in the hearts of men like you and me."

The weight of Matthias' words thudded in Eli's soul.

The chant of a brindled bird floated from a pine across the creek and filled the silence as Eli pondered what Matthias had said.

Whippoorwill.

Whipporwill.

Matthias leaned against his cane in thought. "Ol' Habbakuk, and ol' Isaiah," he said, "they might have been talking about the same mountains as Jesus was talking about."

Eli nodded his understanding, "The mountains in a man's heart."

"That's it, son. That's it."

CHAPTER 19

"She looks to be stable," said Doctor Byerly as he continued through the necessary checks on young Abby Coldwell. "Her breathing is steady and strong. Her pupils are the same size, and that is very good."

"Why is that, Doc?" asked Zion.

"Because if one were bigger than the other, it could indicate problems with her optical nerves or even her brain."

"Mmhmm." Balim nodded. "Then that is good, it sho 'nough is."

"And her eyes aren't roving about, which is also good, because that could indicate a lesion above the brainstem."

"Oh, my, my, my, Doc Byerly," said Minnie shaking her head, "you knows words I ain't never heard of."

"The most important word to know is Jesus," said Balim, "because they is power for healing in that word, bless the Lawd."

"That is the truth," said Doctor Byerly. "No doctor ever healed anyone. We just try to line things up as much as possible for the gift of healing God put in every body to go to work. I can set a broken bone, but I can't cause it to grow back together again."

The doctor lifted the cloth over Abby's forehead and examined the wound. "This is what gives me the most concern, but I have to say, with the ice packs, the swelling has been minimal. Good job, Rosalie."

"Thank you, Doctor Byerly," said Rosalie.

"There is really not more that I can tell until she wakes up," said the doctor.

"When will that be?" asked Minnie.

"I wish I could tell you, Minnie." Doctor Byerly turned to look directly at Balim and Minnie. "The sooner the better."

"Can we take her back to our place?" asked Balim.

"I don't see why not," said the doctor. "You just need to make sure someone stays with her at all times."

He lifted the tincture of white willow bark off the table and handed it to Minnie. "If she wakes up when I am not here, give her 20 drops of this. You can mix it with water if you need to help her get it in her system. Continue with the ice packs every 20 minutes for the next couple of hours and let me know right away if there are any changes."

"Thank you Doctor." Zion walked the physician to the door.

"You are welcome, Zion. I will come back in a few hours if you don't come for me first."

Judith used a serrated knife to slice the braided challah on the cutting board. "I was beginning to wonder if you would make it back for *Shabbat,*" she said.

Eden placed a spoon in a bowl of rice pilaf and placed it next to the roast brisket on the cloth-covered supper table already set with candles and china. In a pewter tureen, matzah balls floated in a broth of aromatic chicken soup, and a salad of purple cabbage and apple rounded out the menu. "I hope little Abby will wake up soon."

"Let us not talk of sad things now," said Hiram. "It is time to light the candles and offer the blessing."

With praises and prayers, the family began their Sabbath rest with the celebratory meal and then prepared to cap it off with hot coffee and Eden's apple crumble dessert.

"Rosh Hashanah begins one week from today," said Hiram. "I wish we had a synagogue to attend."

"I know, *Tatte*," said Judith as she scooped a heaping spoon full of apple crumble in a bowl and gave it to her husband. "So do I."

"At least we are welcome here," said Asher. "The community at large has been kind to us."

"Which means so much given the circumstances that brought us here from Paducah," said Hiram.

"Abba," said Eli as he took the bowl his mother passed him and set it down in front of him on the table, "I hesitate to ask, but Sunday will soon be here. I was wondering if you and Ema have reached a decision about the harvest gathering."

Judith looked across the table at her husband, smiled and nodded.

"Your mother and I have decided that we will accept the invitation," said Hiram.

Smiles broke out around the table.

"Yay!" Eden clapped.

"But," said Hiram, holding up one finger, "we will come home before the singing."

Eli and Asher did a better job at hiding their disappointment than their sister whose countenance fell notably.

"Daughter." Judith placed her index finger under Eden's chin and turned her head to look her in the eye. "Have you thought that we will not even know their songs?"

"I suppose that is true," she said.

"Besides," Hiram interjected, "their selections would likely be frivolous songs or Christian hymns. With clear conscience, I cannot join in singing either one."

"But that said," Judith chimed in a lilting tone, "it will be wonderful to get to know our neighbors better. I for one am looking forward to the picnic and hay ride."

"Perhaps we can get some apples and honey for Rosh Hashanah," said Eden.

"I am certain Miss Johnson will remember the honey once things settle down at Briar Hollow," said Eli.

A lopsided grin played across Asher's face. "And if she doesn't, you can reminder her." Asher winked at his brother.

"Zion, I think you need to see this." Angus rested his weight on one bent knee next to the fallen goat cart, a broken axel in his hand.

"What is it?"

"Looks like sabotage to me," said Angus.

"Are you mad as a hatter, Carver?"

"No, boss," said Angus. He held up the wood cylinder for Zion's closer inspection. "Look at that."

Zion examined the axel and saw for himself what had captured Angus' concern. There was a smooth cut about two thirds in on the wood spindle and the rest of the break was splintered off.

"Somebody cut this, but not all the way through," said Zion.

"They obviously wanted this cart to be in use when it broke down." Carver shook his head in disgust.

Zion let out a huff. "When I find out who did this, I am going to clean their clock."

"I feel the same," said Angus. "That is a pathetic wicked soul for sure. Do you have any idea who would be so low as to plan and engineer an accident to injure innocent children?"

Zion took his hat off and riffled his fingers through his hair. "I don't have a name, but I have an idea."

"What do you mean?" Angus unfolded his leg and stood next to his employer.

"The same kind of lowlifes that ride in the night with white hoods."

"We will need to lay low afterwards." Trigg Simon spoke in low tones to Fred McGhee and Burke Calhoun. "I am thinking I might need to make an 'out of town business trip' this weekend."

"Don't you think it would look suspicious if all of us were to up and disappear on the same night?" said Fred McGhee. He pulled a quirley from his shirt pocket and lit it with a match.

"It is up to you fellows to work up your own alibis," said Simon. "I am just telling you mine. Nobody will suspect a thing if I say I have to be in Goose Creek. I have regular dealings with the Salt Works. T.T. Garrard will cover for me if I need him to. I have covered his carcass more than once when he got into some shenanigans with the Whites over in Clay County."

"You have any ideas?" Burke asked Fred.

"I will be your alibi, and you'll be mine," said Fred.

"That would work," Burke snickered.

"How about I meet up with you at Drake's Tavern tonight, and we will have a conversation with the bartender about our plans for Sunday night."

"You want to tell the bartender about the lynching?" Burke looked baffled.

"Are you at sea, or full as a tick?" Fred shook his head at Burke.

"I ain't lost, nor had a drink," said Burke with indignation.

"What he is saying," said Trigg, "is that you make up a story about what you two are going to be doing Sunday night and make sure the bartender hears it. That way if you need an alibi, you have each other to cover for yourselves and the back-up testimony of the bartender who will just *happen* to overhear your plans."

Fred took a drag from his hand-rolled cigarette, "Say, Calhoun, don't you need some help getting a stump out of your yard?"

"I haven't cut any trees down yet," said Burke, "but I could arrange to have a stump that needed pulling by Sunday night."

"Then we have a plan," said Fred.

"At least for the alibi," said Trigg. "We need to set a time and meeting place for Sunday night."

"Is your boy, River, going to be there?"

"Not this time," said Trigg. "He is having plenty of fun harassing and threatening folks. The other day he and his friend Danhauer put on their hoods and rode up to the house where a black family lives. He kept asking them over and over again for water that he poured in a hidden canteen. They brought him buckets of water, and then he told them, 'I ain't drank nothing since I died on the battlefield.' He rode away leaving them thinking he was a ghost."

"Oh, that is rich." Burke threw a hand on his stomach and laughed out loud.

"Leave it up to your boy to come up with that." Fred shook his head and smirked.

"Anyway, I don't see any need to risk getting him involved in any lynchings just yet. I don't normally take him up to Goose Creek on business, and his Ma might get suspicious. I don't want to do anything that would look out of the ordinary, and besides, I wouldn't have an alibi for him."

CHAPTER 20

Eli pulled the blanket over his feet and then reached up to remove his black yarmulke. He held the circle of soft fabric in both hands, lightly rubbing it between his thumbs and fingers, and recalled his father's words:

"We place the yarmulke at the very highest point of our beings to remind ourselves and signify to the world that there is something higher than mankind, and that is God's infinite wisdom. It is a symbol of recognition that there is One above who watches every deed and hears every word."

While Eli understood what his father was saying and the good intentions behind wearing this symbol to the world of his faith, he wondered why, if it was so important, the *Torah* never instructed men to cover their heads.

"God, you are with me at all times," Eli boldly prayed without his covering. "I honor my father and the teachings of the rabbis and elders, but in my heart I am drawn to reverence You and Your Word always and above all else."

His mind wondered back to his conversation with Matthias Johnson, and he felt compelled to lay aside his usual evening reading from his pocket book of *Tehillim*. Instead, he padded over to his writing desk and retrieved his *Tanakh*. Passing over the writings of Moses, he turned to the prophets, and then flipped to Isaiah.

He was familiar with this collection of oracles, prophecies, and reports, and its most dominant theme: the message of salvation. According to Isaiah, there was no hope for mankind outside of a savior.

"I am worried, Balim." Minnie slipped her hand under Abby's dark curls and massaged her daughter's scalp. "Why ain't she woke up yet?"

"You know what the doctor said when he came by last night."

"I know," said Minnie. "She is not awake, but she ain't no worse as far as he can tell."

Balim's eyes glowed with faith and hope from his recent prayer time. "If Doc Byerly thought he could do somethin' fo her, he would've done took her on over to his office, don'ya think?"

"I suppose so," said Minnie. "It's just that waitin' is so hard."

"I know, my dumplin'. I knows it right well."

"Did I hear Miss Rozlee out here a few minutes ago?" asked Balim.

"Yeah." Minnie's full lips lifted in a slight grin. "And she heard you, too."

A toothy smile spread across Balim's dark face. "Sometimes when a man is talking to Jesus, he can get a might lively."

"Lively, you say?" Minnie chuckled. "The rafters was shaking. I am surprised you did not wake Abby up yo'self."

"Now, woman, I know you is thankful you have a praying man."

"That I am." Minnie nodded and looked down at her daughter's still form. "I hate to bother her," she said, "but I's gwanna have to change her diaper or her poor bottom will be lookin' like a strawberry."

"Doc Byerly said it shouldn' bother her none," said Balim. "Go ahead and do what you have to do."

"Will ya hand me a clean diaper while I get a wet rag to wash her up?"

"Sure thing," said Balim.

Minnie unfastened Abby's diaper and began to wash her tender skin with a damp cloth.

"Dear Lawd God Almighty!" Minnie exclaimed. "She is moving, Balim. She is moving!"

"Glory be to God!" Balim boomed in a rich bass voice.

"Wake up, baby girl," Minnie called to her daughter. "Come on back to yo mammy now. You done slept long enough."

Abby balled her little hands into fists, winced, and let out a quiet moan. "Get those drops the doctor give us, Balim," said Minnie. "She is a hurtin'."

With a lightness of foot unexpected of a man of his thick build, Balim retrieved the bottle of white willow bark tincture and handed it to his wife.

"I will go get Miss Rozlee," he said with a wide grin on his face. "She is waking up, Minnie. Thank Ya, sweet Jesus. You is answering my prayers right quick. Yes, You is!"

Marigold practically skipped all the way from the orchard to town with a single jar of honey in her hands. Although it was not for sale, she had taken the time to tie a cheerful ribbon around the circle of calico she had placed over the top. She wondered if Eli would notice it was calico from the dress she had worn the last time they were together.

Silly girl, she chided herself. *Why would Eli notice such a thing?* Even as she upbraided herself for her schoolgirl thoughts, Marigold could not shake the lingering excitement that Eli might notice and want to keep the swatch of fabric as a little memento.

How did I get so, so. . . twitterpated? Is that what I am? Marigold was altogether unfamiliar with the feelings racing through her heart. *Dear God,* she prayed and wondered, *is this what love feels like? Am I in love with Eli Thalman?*

Oh, guard my heart, Jesus. Don't let me make any foolish mistakes. Your Word says if I acknowledge You, that You will direct my paths, so I am asking You to do that. Direct my path according to Your plans. And regardless of whatever may or may not happen with Eli, I pray that You will reveal Yourself to Him. You are the God of Abraham, Isaac and Jacob. Eli just doesn't know you yet as his Messiah. Show Him, Jesus, that You are God. You are the Creator and the Savior.

Reach Eli through Your Word that foretold Your coming.

The bells on the door jingled out the announcement of Marigold's arrival in the tailor's shop where Hiram Thalman sat quietly in an upholstered chair at the carved table in the corner.

"Good morning, Mr. Thalman," Marigold greeted the older man with a cheerful smile.

Hiram noted the glow and zest for life in this unusual but nevertheless comely young lady. He rose from his chair to greet her. "Good morning to you, Miss Johnson. To what do I owe the pleasure of your call?"

With a toothy smile Marigold held out the jar of honey. "I have come to pay my debt."

"Ah, the famous Briar Hollow honey." Hiram took the jar and examined the color.

"That it is," said Marigold. "I should have brought some of Clover's sweet milk to go with it."

"Milk?"

"Yes," said Marigold, "then you would be in a land of milk and honey."

Hiram smiled. "The Promised Land right here in Washington, Kentucky?"

"I am sure it is not like the Holy Land," said Marigold, "but I'd say it is a land flush with fruitfulness, all right. You should come out to Briar Hollow sometime and see the orchards. The apples are in, and I'd love to show you around."

Hiram nodded. "We could use some fresh apples to go with the honey for Rosh Hashanah next week. It is our tradition to dip apples in honey on the holy day."

"I am surprised to own up to it, because I have had apples just about every way you can fix them, but I have never had apples with honey," said Marigold. "I will have to give that a try."

Hiram watched as Marigold glanced around the shop hoping for a glimpse of a certain tailor's apprentice. "Are you working by yourself today?"

"At the moment, it seems," said Hiram. "Eli and Asher were enjoying their breakfast so much I left them to it and came down for a few minutes of quiet."

"I like breakfast and quiet," said Marigold with a grin.

The door to the living quarters opened, and Eli and Asher slipped out and traversed the steps with a quick staccato. Both of the young men wore simple outfits of wool trousers, crisp shirts and vests. A tape measure dangled around Eli's neck.

"It looks like both are over, however," said Marigold.

"Well, hello, Miss Johnson," said Asher. "What is over?"

"Quiet time for your Pa and breakfast for you."

"Yes, indeed," said Asher. "I hope your quiet time was as pleasurable as Ema's challah French toast, Abba."

"Each is sweet in its own way," said Hiram. "Miss Johnson has come with a gift of honey. Perhaps we can get some apples from the orchard for Rosh Hashanah."

"Did Abba tell you we were coming to the picnic Sunday?" Eli's dark eyes twinkled from behind his wire-rimmed glasses.

"No," said Marigold, "but I am glad to hear it. We will have a hog killing time for sure."

"Will there be butchering at a picnic?" asked Hiram.

Marigold burst out in a hearty laugh. "Oh, no, Mr. Thalman. We won't be butchering. That is just a saying."

"I look forward to learning more of your sayings, Miss Johnson," said Hiram. "Our people have many of them, as well."

"Oh, I would be right pleased to hear some of them," said Marigold.

Hiram brightened at the girl's interest. Her charm warmed the entire shop.

"There are many," he said, "but I will share the one I was thinking of earlier today. 'If you can't do as you wish, do as you can."

Marigold contemplated the weight of Hiram's words before responding. "There is a heap of wisdom on those words, for sure and for certain."

"There are plenty more where that came from," said Asher with a grin. "Abba has a saying for just about every situation."

"That reminds me of another saying," said Hiram. He cleared his throat and paused for effect. "'A wise man knows what he says; a fool says what he knows.'"

Eli grinned at the banter between his father and brother. Both sons highly respected their father, but Asher and Hiram especially enjoyed a little good-natured tit-for-tat from time to time.

For a moment, Marigold wondered if Asher had gone too far and his father was reprimanding him, but the atmosphere in the room remained light and pleasant.

"I can tell right now you and my Pa are going to enjoy one another's company at the picnic."

"We are all looking forward to it," said Hiram, "but I am afraid we need to get to work now. I am finishing your father's suit, and my boys are working on a special project for their brother Rueben. We are expecting him back in town any day."

"I need to get back too," Marigold's face lit with the remembrance of her good news. "I forgot to tell you that it looks like Abby is starting to wake up."

"Oh, that is so good to hear," said Eli. "We have been praying for her."

"Thank you," said Marigold. "She is not out of the woods yet, but she is responding to touch and moving some. We're just waiting for her to open her big beautiful eyes any minute now."

Marigold beamed a tooth-filled smile that filled her animated face. "Well, I guess I better light a shuck for home."

"Let me walk you out," said Eli. He opened the door and Marigold preceded him out into the sunshine.

"I was wondering how Lucas is doing," said Eli. "He was most troubled when I spoke with him yesterday."

Marigold clasped her hands together and toed the ground. "It is been a bit of a carousel ride, I have to say."

"A ride? What do you mean?"

"I mean that he was feeling all kinds of awful, thinking he had hurt the little ones, but now he is all balled up and madder than a wet hen."

"Mad?"

"With good reason." Marigold crossed her arms in front of her chest and her lips tightened into a thin line. She paused for a moment to collect her emotions and then spoke in a hushed tone. "They think it was sabotage."

"Sabotage?" Eli could not believe what he heard. "But who would do such a thing? Who would knowingly hurt innocent children?"

"I don't know names," said Marigold, "but Zion seems to think it might be the same lowlifes riding around in white hoods threatening folks."

Eli shook his dark head. Sorrow etched across his features. While he sympathized with Balim and his family, he also recalled some of the harshness and challenges prejudice had wrought on his own family. "I am so sorry."

"Me, too," said Marigold, "me, too."

Silence hung between them for several moments.

"I better get back to work," said Eli. He spoke the words that were in such contrast to the desires of his heart. He longed to stay out in the sunshine with this morning glory of a girl, but Abba and Asher awaited his return.

"And I better get back to Briar Hollow—and apple picking," said Marigold. "I will be sure to pick some nice ones for your holy day. I can bring them to you at the picnic."

Eli reached for the doorknob. A twinkle played in his black eyes, and a smile made its way across his bearded face. "That would be fine as cream gravy, for sure and for certain."

Marigold felt the flush begin to rise. Was Eli Thalman flirting with her? Or was he just funning? She did not know for sure, but regardless of his motives, her freckled face turned a rosy pink.

Eli winked and disappeared inside the shop.

CHAPTER 21

"Are you thinking about going to the Granger meeting?" Pansy Joy asked Garth.

"It is an honor to be asked," said Garth. He wiped his oil-covered hands with a cloth and leaned against the wooden threshing machine. It was housed in a two-story addition to the backside of the Eldrige barn, and Garth had been greasing the movable parts.

"Since the war's end, Mr. Kelley has been touring the southern states, and he believes there is a great need to gather farmers and their families to rebuild the country. He thinks an organization, like a brotherhood, would best serve the needs of the farm families."

"And what do you think?" Pansy Joy studied her husband's face. He was a hard working man of integrity, and she trusted his judgment.

"I think it is a good plan," he said, "but I confess I have some local issues that are pressing more than the national ones Mr. Kelley is concerned about. These men with hoods running around, and their threats—and what happened to poor Abby. I am trying to weigh everything out, but it is hard to think about going to a meeting when I have got uneasiness about the safety of my family and friends. Do you think that is selfish?"

Pansy Joy crossed the barn floor and placed a small hand on Garth's plaid-covered forearm. "Garth Eldridge," she said, "No. No, I think it is only natural to worry about things that directly affect our family and community. I don't think that is selfish at all. It is what a good husband and father does."

"Yes, but I don't want to lose sight of the big picture, too. Our country has suffered terribly from the war and now its raging after effects. If people would come together and work as a team to rebuild the states, that would benefit all of our children in the long run."

"I see the dilemma," said Pansy Joy. "We will just pray that God gives you direction before you would need to leave for the meeting."

Garth smiled at his petite bride. He never tired of looking into her big brown eyes so full of life and kindness. "That is just what we will do."

"I bet the folks at Comfort Lodge are buzzing around more than my bees this afternoon," said Marigold.

"A party takes a lot of work," said Matthias.

"Not as much work as apple picking," said Lucas from beneath the tree where he worked raking up fallen fruit.

Marigold stood at the portable worktable sorting through the apples Matthias and Lucas had picked from the trees. With quick motions she sorted the large apples, small apples, and bruised apples into three separate wheeled bins. "We sure have a heap of windfall apples this year," she said.

"Because we had so many hot and sunny spells followed by heavy rains," said Matthias. "We have got a bumper crop, for sure. Rosalie will make some fine cider out of the windfall apples."

"At least you don't have to sort them by size or worry about bruises," said Marigold. "Just dump them in the bruised bin."

"I don't have to sort them," said Lucas, "but it sure does take a heap of apples to get just one cup of cider." He smacked his lips together thinking of it.

"I wish I had one right now."

"It does take a lot," Marigold wiped a strand of hair off her face with the back of her hand, "but think how good the cider will be with the mix of the four different kinds of apples from the orchard. It is far better than drinking cider or juice made with just one kind."

"The Good Lord likes variety," Matthias chuckled. "I just read something like that in the book of poems Logan loaned me. That British poet William Cowper wrote 'variety's the very spice of life, that gives it all its flavour.'"

"That is true," said Marigold. "It is funny how a certain line will stick out when you are reading. I was reading one of his poems, too. I can't remember it all, but it was called, *The Negro's Complaint*."

"Well come on out with what you remember," said Matthias. "It makes the work go by a bit faster."

"I can't remember exactly. It said something about fleecy locks and black complexions. The line I remember most said, "'Skins may differ, but affection dwells in white and black the same.'"

Matthias nodded and raised the wire clawed basket on the pole to capture another apple near the top of the tree. "I haven't got that far along in the collection," he said, "but that is Simon pure. Yes, it is."

Lucas propped up the rake with both hands and wore a stern look not customary to his boyish, heart-shaped face. "I think some folks are just dimwitted," he said.

"What do you mean, Lukey?" Marigold asked.

"I mean how come folks can figure out an apple is an apple is an apple and they have different colored skins, but then can't do the same with living, breathing, talking people?"

"It is perplexing, son," said Matthias. "That it is."

Lucas filled the bin to the top with the apples he had raked from beneath the tree. "Do you want me to take these to Rosalie right now, Pa?"

"No," said Matthias. "She has got her hands full already. Let's put them in some cold salt water for a few minutes. The salt will get any bugs or worms that moved in to move out, and then all Rosalie will have to do is rinse them with some vinegar water before she gets them ready to make the cider."

"Ok." Lucas placed his hands on the wheeled bin and gave it a push. "This is heavy."

"Let me help you get it going." Marigold dropped the apple she was holding into a bin and turned to help her brother.

"Once those soak make sure you lift the apples out, not dump them," said Matthias. "No need to give Rosalie the dirt and worms."

"Yes, Pa." Lucas grunted and pushed the cart that resisted but then gave way to the force he and his sister exerted upon it. Side by side they mushed the cart down the corridor between the trees and on the path to the apple barn.

"How is your yoyo trick coming?" asked Marigold.

"I think Ben Dryfus is going to master the Man on the Flying Trapeze before I do," said Lucas. "I have been too distracted to give it my best effort."

"I know what you mean."

"I just can't hardly believe someone would purposely rig the goat cart to break down," said Lucas with consternation in his green eyes. "It is obvious from the size of the bench in it that the cart is just for little ones. Who would want to hurt a kid?"

"I don't know," said Marigold, "but when we find out, someone is going to clean his plow good, I can tell you that for sure and for certain."

"I wish I was big enough," said Lucas.

"You will be some day." Marigold smiled. "For now, you can be Abby and Abram's friend, and let the older ones do the protecting. I don't want you to get hurt. That would not do at all."

The two worked in silence for a few minutes, each lost in their own thoughts. Marigold brought salt from the cabin and added some to the bucket Lucas filled with water. Together they covered the apples for a quick soak.

"Thanks for your help," said Lucas. "I think we should just leave these here for now. I will get a bin out of the barn to transfer them to."

"All right," said Marigold. "Wipe it out first."

"I will."

Before returning to the orchard to work with her father, Marigold took a minute to dash into the cabin and retrieve a small basket and a tin mug. She stopped at the well and pumped out some cold water. After taking a long drink, she refilled the cup and returned to her father's side.

"Hey, Pa," said Marigold, lifting the tin mug to her father, "are you thirsty?"

"I could do with some refreshment," Matthias took the cup and drained it of its contents. "Thank you, girl. What have you got there?"

Marigold followed her father's gaze to the basket she had placed on the worktable. "I am going to pick some apples for the

Thalmans," she said. "Mr. Thalman said they have honey and apples on their upcoming holy day, so I thought I would pick some special ones for them."

"Ah," said Matthias. "I forgot."

"Forgot what?"

"That the Jewish new year is in the fall. That must be what they are celebrating."

"I am not sure," said Marigold with a shrug, "but I told them I'd have some apples for them tomorrow. Did I tell you they were coming to the picnic?"

Matthias gave a quick huff and shook his head. Yes, she had told him. She had told him several times.

"I reckon you did tell me that before."

Matthias studied his daughter. There was no denying she was acting peculiar lately. Of course some of it could be attributed to the recent turmoil in the community, but a pa knows his girl. It might not be the same ways a ma might know her, but Matthias was certain something was stirring in his daughter's heart.

"Marigold," Matthias spoke her name and waited for her to respond.

With her head buried in the branches of a neighboring tree, Marigold let out a muffled, "Hm?"

"Marigold."

Matthias waited.

Holding a perfectly formed apple in one hand and her basket hanging off the other, Marigold turned her freckled face to her father.

"Yeah, Pa?"

"Be careful, will you?"

"Careful?" Marigold asked, her brown eyes filled with puzzlement. "Careful of what?"

"Careful with your affections."

Matthias searched for the words. He scanned the trees and prayed. "You know that saying, 'you are the apple of my eye?'"

"Of course, Pa."

"You know that is in the Bible right?"

"I sure do." Marigold nodded, her eyes were wide and searched her father's face for clues to what he was trying to get across to her.

"I might have told you this before, but the apple that saying is talking about isn't fruit like we are picking out here in the orchard. It is talking about the round part of your eye."

Marigold had heard Matthias tell the meaning of the Jewish idiom before, but she waited for him to make his point.

"That saying is talking about the reflection you see in your eye. It comes from a Jewish saying that is talking about seeing the reflection of another person in your eyes."

"Yes, Pa. I do remember you telling me that before."

Matthias reached in his pocket and pulled out a hanky that he wiped across his forehead, folded in half and then wiped across his top lip. "Well, of course you know it is talking about your affections—what you are choosing to set your eyes on."

Marigold nodded.

"If you look and someone and they look back at you," said Matthias, "and the conditions are just right, you can see the reflection of each other in your eyes."

"I understand what you are saying Pa," said Marigold, "but I am not sure if I am getting your meaning."

"What I am trying to say is that what you focus on will become the object of your affection, even if it might not be what you should be looking at. Eyes—both our natural eyes and our minds' eyes with our thoughts—are gateways right into our souls."

"That is according to Hoyle," said Marigold, "but I am a bit at sea as to why you are telling me this."

Matthias paused and scrutinized his daughter's expression. A loud silence hung between them broken only by the sound of the stream bubbling over the rocks at the perimeter of the property.

"I will leave it to you to ponder then, daughter."

CHAPTER 22

"I think it is coming along nicely," said Penny, "and it is such a pleasure to have you here at my place for a change."

"We do seem to congregate more at the original Johnson homestead," said Rosalie. She looked up from her sewing and smiled at the ladies gathered in Penny Mayfield's parlor. They were scattered about the well-appointed room, working and chatting.

Penny sat in her favorite cushioned rocking chair next to the carved walnut fireplace mantle. "I know we don't really have a lot of extra time for a quilting bee, but since we all live so close together, it is not too challenging to steal an hour here or there."

"It is a pleasant diversion from our daily duties," said Millicent as she poured steaming tea from a delicate porcelain pot into a matching cup. "And I am so enjoying watching the quilt come together."

Pansy Joy stitched a completed yoyo to a growing strip of vibrant circles. "I don't think any quilt has been churned out of Briar Hollow any faster," she said.

The ladies had been working on their circles at home in the evening hours, sewing running stitches through their folded edges and then pulling the threads tight to draw in the fabric. These formed gathered pouches that were flattened and formed into discs that were then being sewn together in strips with no rhyme or reason. The result would be a colorful non-pattern when all the strips were united to form a one-of-a-kind quilt.

"What is Marigold doing?" asked Penny.

"She has been helping Pa with the apple picking and sorting," said Rosalie. "Pa says there is a bumper crop this year."

"That is good news," said Millicent. "It seems all the ventures around Briar Hollow are thriving this year."

"Thank the good Lord," said Penny.

"Speaking of thanking the good Lord," said Pansy Joy, "I am so thankful for Abby's progress."

"Me, too." Rosalie ran her thread through the eye of her needle and knotted the ends together. "I have to say, I was worried for her, but Doctor Byerly thinks she will most likely pull through just fine."

"What are they doing for the poor little one?" asked Millicent.

"Not too much right now," said Rosalie. "They are giving her white willow bark for pain. She is not her lively self, of course, but since she woke up the doctor said she could do what she felt like doing as far as moving around and eating. They just don't want her to be jostled around."

"Poor baby," said Penny.

"I know," said Rosalie, "but I have to tell you, when I saw that fluid draining from her ear, I was praying hard. That can be an indication of a serious injury."

Tsk. Tsk. Millicent settled herself in a chair and reached for two yoyos from the community basket on the dining table. "Is there any permanent damage?"

Rosalie shook her head. "We don't know yet," she said, "but she will have to be watched carefully the next few days. She really can't be left alone at all."

"Oh, no." Pansy Joy thrust out her full lips in a pout. "That means they can't come to the harvest party."

Rosalie nodded, but offered a slight smile. "We could be planning a funeral," she said. "I am just grateful she is improving. There will be plenty of times for parties and picnics and hayrides in the future."

"So true," Millicent nodded.

Marigold looked at the basket of apples on the table. Of course, they did not have lips, but they sure enough seemed to be talking to her. *Take me to town*, they cried over and over.

What am I thinking? Marigold scolded herself as she pulled the pot of ham and beans forward on the cast iron cook stove and gave the contents a stir with a sturdy wooden spoon. *I can't just be skipping off to town without a good reason.*

She checked the johnny cake in the oven. It needed a few more minutes before the top turned golden brown the way her father liked it. *I wonder if Eli likes johnny cake?*

Awareness began to dawn in Marigold's reality. It started small, like the light of a new day peeking across the horizon and then radiating from that tiny beginning to thoroughly enlighten the day. Her father had been right. She was "focusing" on Eli Thalman more and more, and the more she thought about him, the more she wanted to think about him—and see him. She had not been guarding her affections at all. She had allowed her emotions to take control of her thoughts and even her footsteps.

I have been so distracted. Marigold reached inside the cupboard for plates and began setting the table for supper. As she did, her eyes fell on the brown wrapping paper that contained the kaleidoscope she had purchased for Balim's family, especially Abby and Abram.

Guilt stabbed at Marigold. She had planned to give the gift earlier, but had not made time to do so. Once Abby got hurt, it had not seemed to be the right time, so she had brought it home from Rosalie's. And there it sat.

God, help me get my thoughts where they should be. I don't want to miss opportunities to do good because I am being scatterbrained by thoughts of a good-looking man. Besides, Eli has just been a gentleman, and I have been making far too much of his kindness and good manners.

Marigold determined to deliver the kaleidoscope the next day. Since Balim and his family could not go to the harvest party, it might be a nice distraction for them.

Fred McGhee and Burke Calhoun stood at the bar of Drake's Tavern in downtown Washington.

"Hey, Fletch," said McGhee, "Give us another round."

"Whatever you say." Fletcher Drake turned to retrieve a bottle from the counter behind the bar and filled the short glasses in front of the men with copper-colored liquid.

"I am buying," said Calhoun. "I will be getting my money's worth in labor from ol' McGhee here tomorrow night."

"One drink would hardly be fair payment for removing that whopping, oversized stump in your yard, Calhoun." McGhee picked up the glass and swigged its contents in one quick motion. "But that is what friends are for, right Fletch?"

"Whatever you say, McGhee." The bartender wiped the counter with a towel and moved down to tend to his other customers.

Burke shot down his drink, placed the cup on the bar and wiped his mouth with his sleeve. "I have got to get going."

"Me, too," said Fred. The two men donned their hats and headed out the tavern door.

"Well, that was easy enough," said Calhoun. "Our alibis are set for sure. Now it is all done but the lynching."

"Not quite," said Fred McGhee. He grasped the horn of his saddle, and slipped his left foot into a stirrup. He hoisted himself up and threw his right leg across the saddle. "Follow me."

Calhoun climbed into his saddle, and the two rode through town accompanied by the *ba da rump ba da rump ba da rump* of the horses' hooves as they struck against the flagstone street.

"Whoa." McGhee reined in his horse at Calhoun's place a mile out of town.

"What are we doing here?" Calhoun asked.

"I thought you lived here." McGhee swung down from the saddle and ground tied his horse.

"I reckon I do at that," said Calhoun. He dismounted and adjusted his hat on his head.

"We need to get to work on that stump," said McGhee, "at least enough to make it look like we put in a great effort on it."

"Right," said Calhoun, nodding, " the alibi."

"Right," said Fred. "You got a pickaxe?"

"Yeah, in the barn."

"And chain?"

"That too."

Calhoun disappeared inside a small but serviceable building just large enough to store hay, grain, a few tools, and house one horse. He quickly returned with chain and pickaxe in hand.

"You ever removed a stump before?" asked McGhee.

"Not one as big as this," said Burke as he dropped the chain to the ground and leaned against the handle of the pickaxe.

"Well, I don't want to spend too much time here, but we need to show some effort. Start digging around the stump with that pickaxe and pop the small roots. I brought a maul to work on the bigger ones.

"Once we get things loosened up, we will wrap the chain around it, team up the horses, and see if we can pull it out."

"That sounds like a lot of work," said Calhoun.

"We don't have to work at it too long," said McGhee, "but it does need to look like we spent some time, so be right messy with your digging."

"Mules would be better for the job," said Calhoun. He swung the pickaxe at a root.

"That is true," said McGhee as he walked around his horse and slid a heavy maul from the back of the saddle.

Burke struck at the smaller roots on one side of the stump while Fred hammered his maul into the larger roots on the opposite side of the stump.

"Hey," said Burke, "what do you think about burning it?"

"Calhoun, I think you might have something there." McGhee stood and wiped his forehead with his sleeve. "Let's keep working these roots and leave the chain here, but we can set this stump up for burning, and then you can light it tomorrow right after the lynching. It will still be hot in the morning and make for an even stronger alibi."

The men roughed up the perimeter around the tree and then McGhee took control of the pickaxe. With a mighty swing, he stuck the implement into the stump with a thud and then picked up his maul. Using the pickaxe as a wedge, he swung the heavy hammer against its flat side, forcing the pickaxe into the stump. He repeated the action several more times until a hole was created about ten inches deep.

"Here," said McGhee as he withdrew the pickaxe and positioned it near the first hole. "Your turn."

McGhee pulled a quirley from his shirt pocket, struck a match against his fingernail and lit the hand-rolled cigarette. "You keep working at them holes," he said as he lifted his horse's reins and mounted.

"Where are you going?" Calhoun straightened and glared at Fred McGhee. "This is *our* alibi. Remember?"

"Oh, I remember, all right," said Fred. "You just get those holes ready, and I will be back with some saltpeter I got over in Clay County at the Saltpeter Hollow Cave. That will get your fire going and keep it going better than anything I am guessing you have got sitting around here."

Calhoun contracted his lips into a pucker and gave a quick nod. "Well, you are right about that," he conceded.

By the time Fred McGhee returned, Burke Calhoun had completed a ring of holes around the stump.

"Clean the rubble out of those holes, and then we can scoop some of this in them," said McGhee.

Once the holes were emptied, McGhee scooped some saltpeter into each of them with a trowel. "There, now," he said with a short, quick nod. "Come tomorrow night, we will come back here and put some hot water in the holes. That will dissolve the saltpeter. You got some scrap wood?"

"I can get some," said Calhoun. "What do you need it for?"

"Once the saltpeter is dissolved, we put the scrap on top like a teepee, light it, and step back. Then we just watch it smolder until that ol' stump turns to ash."

"That is a great idea," said Calhoun. "With all the preliminaries done, it won't take no time at all to get this burning."

"That is right." McGhee lowered his eyelids in a squint and lifted his chin. "We are gonna need tomorrow's time for tomorrow's special engagement."

"That big ox won't be thinking he is a high muckamuck when he is swinging from that tree over at the Corbin place."

CHAPTER 23

Marigold lifted a diaper from the bleaching ground and folded it. Rosalie had done double duty washing both Mattie's and Abby's diapers this week. While Monday was regular laundry day, clean diapers would not wait.

Rosalie stood by the stretch of land set aside as a drying ground in a grassy corner by the wildflower garden. It was well open to the sun, but sheltered from the attention of any wandering farm critters that might soil, tear or even eat the clothes bleaching in the sunlight. She folded the diaper in her hand and placed it in the basket on the ground beside her.

Daisy barked announcing Pansy Joy's arrival in the Hollow.

"Good afternoon, my sisters," said Pansy Joy.

"So formal now, aren't we?" Marigold cast a look at her petite, curly-headed sibling.

"There is nothing wrong with being polite now, is there?" Pansy Joy settled both of her hands on her hips and made a face at Marigold.

"Well, that is a mixed message," said Rosalie, "sweet words and a sour expression."

"Come on," said Marigold. "What do you want to borrow now?"

Hmph. Pansy Joy raised a booted foot and gave an indignant stomp. "Marigold Johnson, why would you ask such a question?"

"Well?"

Pansy Joy lifted her chin in defiance to Marigold, but then changed her expression and smiled sweetly at Rosalie. She reached for a diaper and began folding it. "Rosalie," she said in a lilting, melodious tone, "I was wondering if you might have some apples you could spare."

Marigold threw her head back and howled. "See there! What did I tell you?"

"I did not come to borrow anything from you at all," said Pansy Joy glaring at her roaring sister.

"Well, just who do you think picked the apples?" Marigold's brown eyes danced with merriment.

Pansy Joy turned her shoulder on Marigold and faced Rosalie. "Like I was saying, Rosalie, do *you* have any apples you could spare? I want to try a new recipe for the baking contest."

"I could probably help you out," said Rosalie with a grin that traveled up her face and into her green eyes. "What are you making?"

"Well, I have made some wonderful cheese that would be a perfect complement to some apples. I was thinking about an apple cake with a creamed cheese filling and praline frosting."

"Mm. That sounds delicious," said Rosalie, "and yes, I can definitely spare some apples for you. Lucas brought over a whole bin of windfall apples today and you can have all you need."

"Thank you." Pansy Joy lifted the edge of her skirt with one hand and curtsied. "I appreciate your kindness ever so much."

"You are welcome," she said. "I can't wait to try your cake."

"Are you making something for the baking contest?" Rosalie asked Marigold.

"I think I would make a better judge than contestant," Marigold grinned.

"I have just about decided to do something with pumpkin," said Rosalie. "I am tired of looking at apples."

"You and me both," said Marigold as she bent to pick up another diaper. "I wonder if the Thalmans will participate in the contest. Eli says his mom and sister are both bang up cooks."

"Did he now?" Rosalie smiled while Pansy Joy turned to study her younger sister's face. "When did you talk to him?"

"Yesterday. We did some bartering, and I went in to pay my debt with some honey."

Pansy Joy's eyebrows lifted in a high arch. "Marigold Johnson," she drawled out the words and shook her head slowly from side to side, "what are you saying? Just what did Eli Thalman give you in exchange for some . . . *honey*?"

Taken aback by her sister's insinuations, Marigold stammered as she tried to collect her hijacked thoughts. In quick succession, her contemplations advanced from confusion to full blown indignation.

"Mrs. Pansy Joy Eldridge," said Marigold waggling her head in a way that sent her braids bobbing, "you should know better than to even hint at anything improper between me and Eli Thalman. We had a business deal, and that is all."

Rosalie chuckled but then came to her sister's defense. "It is true," she said. "We needed some safety pins for squirmy Mattie's diapers, and the mercantile was out."

Marigold threw her shoulders back and looked Pansy Joy straight in the eyes, "That's right. And Eli would not let me pay for them, so I brought him some honey as a thank you."

"I see" Pansy Joy nodded. "You seem to be making lots of trips to town these days—and they seem to find you in the tailor's shop more often than not."

Marigold's brown eyes grew wide. "For your information, Eli Thalman happens to be a gentleman, and he would never do anything inappropriate. Neither would I, for that matter."

"So just how well do you know this Eli?" Pansy Joy prodded.

Color climbed Marigold's neck and then made its way up her freckled cheeks. She reined in her emotions, composed herself in the most dignified way possible, and spoke in a calm, measured tone.

"Rosalie," she said, "if you will excuse me please, I have work to do back at the cabin."

Without waiting for a reply, Marigold spun on her heel and promenaded behind the cabin. She disappeared from view on the path that led from Briar Hollow to the Johnson cabin on the other side of the orchard.

"Pansy Joy," Rosalie shook her head at her sister. "What was that all about? I have never seen the two of you act like that."

"Well, if you are noticing things that have not happened before, have you observed the way Marigold seems to be smitten with Eli Thalman?"

Rosalie sighed and tightened her thin pink lips into a straight line.

"Have you?" pressed Pansy Joy.

Rosalie remained silent.

"While you think about it," said Pansy Joy, "let me tell you, she has about admitted as much to me that they have some kind of feelings for each other."

Rosalie looked her sister square in the face. "When did this happen?"

"A couple of weeks ago when we delivered Pa's old clothes to the Thalman's so they could use them to pattern his new suit."

"What did she say?"

"She confirmed that she noticed the tender looks he throws her way. She was quiet in the most unusual way, and then she started making excuses about why things couldn't work out and how she did not want to get trapped with a fellow and things not turn out for the good."

Rosalie shook her head slowly from one side to the other. "Oh, dear."

Pansy Joy quieted at her sister's response.

"I have noticed," said Rosalie. "I was hoping it was just her being friendly and neighborly like Marigold is to most folks. Eli has been out to Briar Hollow more than once the last couple of weeks, and Marigold has certainly found reasons to go to town. She has been in town more this month than she has been in the entire year past."

"I know I was abrupt with Marigold," said Pansy Joy. "Part of it was just getting her back for teasing me, but I do think she is hiding some feelings that need to be dealt with."

"I don't know what to say," said Rosalie. "Scripture is as clear as it can be about marrying a non-believer."

"I know," said Pansy Joy. "The Thalmans are faithful people; and we do believe in the same God, but they aren't Christians."

"It is not enough to believe in one Creator. We have to have faith in the redemption work of Jesus. It was His sacrifice that makes us right with God." Rosalie lifted her eyes to the sky but did not see the puffy white clouds drifting before them. "They don't know that the God they worship came to earth as a man and went to Calvary to pay the price for their sins."

The sun shone down on the girls, each absorbed in her own reflections.

"Then that is what we will have to pray," said Pansy Joy.

"What?" Rosalie turned her gaze from the sky and refocused on her sister.

"We need to pray that the Thalmans will have a divine disclosure straight from Jesus Himself," said Pansy Joy with a smile. "He died for them, too. He doesn't want them to be lost."

Rosalie nodded and a tender expression filled her heart-shaped face.

"You are right," she said. "That is just what we will do."

Marigold tromped down the orchard path, made a quick left at the tree line, and continued right past the cabin onto the macadamized road to Washington.

That Pansy Joy has got some kind of game.

Marigold knew she was inordinately upset, but she was having a hard time reconciling her heart with her head.

Like I would give "honey" to Eli Thalman.

But wouldn't you like to? Her heart betrayed her overdramatic indignation.

Oh, dear Jesus. Help me. It is no use trying to hide my secrets from You.

By the time Marigold reached town she had simmered down from a full boil to a more subdued frame of mind. Without conscious consideration, her feet led her in front of the store with the picture window that read "Thalman and Sons Clothiers."

Now what to do? she wondered.

A closed sign hung on the door. It was late afternoon, and the Thalmans had completed *seudah shlishit*, a lite meal taken near the close of their Sabbath. The sounds of singing drifted from the upper quarters of the shop. The melodies were slow and mournful, but beautiful at the same time. They reflected the sadness that Sabbath was drawing to a close.

Eden, seated near the window of the sitting room, stood and looked out the glass. Without missing a note she turned and signaled to Eli who rose to join her.

The last note of the song was still hanging in the air when Eli spoke to his father.

"Abba, may I be excused to take a walk? It is a beautiful evening, and I will not go far."

Hiram studied his son. He was an astute man and had perceived for some time that Eli had been searching, studying and seeking after God for his life. "Just be back for *Havdalah*," he said.

Eli grabbed his straw hat, opened the door and walked as fast as he dared down the steps. The bells on the shop door tinkled a pleasant song as he pulled it open and stepped out into the pre-evening gloam.

Marigold stood on the rope walk with her back to the door. The sound of the bells made her catch her breath, and her heart leapt to full attention. With great concentration of effort, she turned ever so slowly to see who had opened the door.

Eli.

A slow smile lifted the corner of her lips, but though her mouth indicated pleasure at seeing him, her eyes held a more complex message.

"Miss Johnson." Eli nodded and returned his gaze to her magnificent brown eyes.

"Mr. Thalman."

"Shalom," he breathed out in barely more than a whisper.

"Oh, yes," Marigold responded in echoing hushed tones, "shalom."

Face to face the couple stood a foot apart from each other in silence for what seemed like hours to both of them. Unable to translate the signals he was receiving from this mystery of a girl before him, Eli prayed for the right words to say.

"I was just out for a short walk before the close of Sabbath," said Eli. "Do you have a few minutes to join me?"

Marigold pondered the invitation only a moment before agreeing. "Which way?"

Eli placed his hand on her elbow, steered her in the direction away from her return path home, and then let his hand drop to his side. The couple walked together, but with a proper distance between them.

"Do you know what *shalom* means, Miss Johnson?"

"Yes." Marigold nodded. "It means 'peace,' right?"

"For a small word, it has many meanings," said Eli. "Not only does it mean peace, but also wholeness and completeness."

"That all sounds good to me." Marigold lifted her shoulders and let out a sigh.

"To me, too," said Eli.

The couple walked past Cooper's blacksmith and the livery. The sound of a horse whinnied from within, punctuating the silence.

"I have been reading the writings of Isaiah," said Eli.

"That is a beautiful book," said Marigold. "Some of my favorite passages are in Isaiah."

"All my life I have prayed and asked Elohim to help me understand His Word," said Eli. "As I was reading from Isaiah, I took special note of a passage that said He would 'make thy officers peace, and righteousness thy magistrates.'"

"I know the passage," said Marigold. "The King James version of the Bible uses different words, but they have the same meaning."

"I was thinking about Elohim's promise to make peace my officer," Eli paused for a moment. "I must confess I have not been very peaceful of late. So I prayed to understand this passage."

Marigold stopped in front of the feed store and turned to give Eli her full attention. "And do you? Understand it better, I mean?"

Eli drank in the features of the face that had become so dear to him. He never tired of looking at her, and he had imagined many times that he never would.

"I think so."

"Oh, please share." Marigold clasped her hands in front of her. "I could use a fresh dose of peace myself."

"Would you like to sit?" Eli motioned to the bench in front of the feed store.

"Sure." Marigold sat on the bench and smoothed her dress down at the sides. She turned so she could see Eli's face when he spoke.

"An officer has many responsibilities," said Eli. "He has the care and oversight of those in his custody. He also has all the provision and the authority to exact punishment if necessary."

"That doesn't sound too peaceful," Marigold chuckled.

"But you see, peace *is* the officer."

Marigold considered his words. "I think I am understanding. Peace is actually like the big boss, the decision maker."

"Exactly." Eli nodded. "You are seeing it as I have come to."

"And if I am not feeling peace, would that be like being corrected?"

"I think correction is a good way to think of it," said Eli. "If we lack peace, it could be a divine hand at work to place us on the path we were meant to take."

"And when we are on the right path, in God's will for our lives, we should have peace about it. Right?"

"That is my belief." Eli stood. "I must get back before candle lighting and blessing. Are you ready, my dear?"

CHAPTER 24

66 I would be pleased if you would join my family for *Havdalah*," said Eli as he reached to open the door of the shop.

"Would that be acceptable?" asked Marigold. "I mean, I am not Jewish."

"Judaism is not for Jewish bloodlines alone," said Eli. "Surely you have read in the Scriptures how strangers and converts joined the Children of Israel."

"That is true." Marigold brightened with understanding, but then remembered that darkness was fast approaching.

"I would like to," she said, "very much, but I am concerned Pa will be worried about me coming home in the dark by myself."

"I will be happy to escort you home, should you decide to stay."

A warm sensation flooded through Marigold. She felt God's peace, and it was almost audible with its welcome guidance.

"In that case, I would be happy to accept."

Marigold slipped through the door Eli held open for her and climbed the stairs to the Thalman's living quarters.

"Abba, Ema," Eli greeted his parents, "we have a guest for *Havdalah*."

Hiram stood to his feet and welcomed Marigold. "Come in. Come in. We were just getting ready to start."

"I will get a chair for you," said Asher. He disappeared into a room and returned with a chair. Motioning to Marigold to sit, he slid the seat beneath her.

Hiram filled the cup with grape juice until liquid overflowed on the plate beneath it and then lit a braided, two-wick candle. He lifted the cup in the palm of his right hand and prayed.

"Behold, God is my salvation, I will trust and not be afraid. Indeed, God is my strength and my song and He has become my salvation. You shall draw water with joy from the wells of salvation. Salvation belongs to God; may Your blessings be upon Your people, Selah. The Lord of Hosts is with us, the God of Jacob is a refuge for us, Selah. Lord of Hosts, happy is the man who trusts in You. God, save us; may the King answer us on the day we call. 'The Jews had radiance and happiness, joy and honor.' So may it be for us. I will raise the cup of salvations and invoke the name of God."

Hiram continued: "Blessed are You, God, King of the Universe, Creator of the fruit of the vine."

The Thalmans answered as one, "Amen." Marigold nodded and offered her amen, as well.

Hiram moved the cup from his right hand to his left and held it while he picked up a decorated spice box with his right. The scent of cloves and bay leaves filled the room.

"Blessed are You, God, King of the Universe, Creator of various kinds of spices," said Hiram, followed again by a chorus of amens. He lifted the box to smell the spices and then passed it around for all to enjoy.

"Blessed are You, God, King of the Universe, Creator of the lights of fire." The room again filled with amens and the Thalmans extended their hands to the flames to see their fingernails in the light of the candle. Not knowing the significance of the ritual, Marigold kept her hands folded on her lap.

"Blessed are You, God, King of the Universe, who makes a distinction between sacred and mundane, between light and darkness, between Israel and the nations, between the seventh day and the six working days. Blessed are You, God, Who makes a distinction between sacred and mundane."

Hiram sat, lifted the cup to his lips and took a long drink from it. He then took the candle and dipped the double wicks in the excess grape juice that had been purposely spilled over in the plate at the beginning of the ceremony.

A pleasant smile filled Hiram's face. "And now you have experienced *Havdalah,* our neighbor."

Marigold returned the tailor's warm expression with a broad smile. "It was more than lovely," she said. "I especially enjoyed the verses you quoted from Isaiah. Eli and I were just discussing Isaiah a few minutes ago."

"What brings you to town so late in the day?" asked Judith.

"Oh my." Marigold broke from her revelry and realized the time. "I was just taking a walk, and ended up in town, but I better get going. Pa will be worried about me."

"Abba, I offered to see Miss Johnson home. I did not think you would mind given the lateness of the day."

"You were right to do so," said Hiram. "Asher, would you go to the livery and get the carriage, please?"

"Yes, Abba." Asher headed out the door.

While Eli and Marigold waited for his return Hiram explained some of the elements of the ceremony before discussion turned to the harvest party.

"I can't wait for the hay ride," said Eden, bubbling with joy.

"It is quite the fandango," said Marigold.

"Fandango?" Judith wore a puzzled look on her face.

"Oh, that is just a saying for a lot of excitement," said Marigold.

The door opened and Asher popped his head inside the frame. "Ready to go?"

"I sure am." Marigold beamed a gracious smile around the room. "Thank you for including me. It was a blessing to share part of your Sabbath with you."

"Come on, Eden," said Asher. "A drive sounds nice, doesn't it?"

"Let me get my wrap," Eden opened a chest and pulled out a crocheted shawl.

"Take one for Miss Johnson," said Judith. "I am sure it is much cooler now that the sun has gone down."

The entourage made their way down the steps and outside the shop. "Do you want to drive, or shall I?" Asher asked.

"I will." Eli motioned Marigold to the front seat and assisted her inside the surrey while Asher helped his sister in the back seat.

Once the young men were inside and moving down the road, Marigold turned to Eden with a question. "Are you making something for the bake-off?"

"Oh, yes," said Eden. "I had a hard time choosing. Of course, I thought of an apple cake, but I thought that someone else might bring one, so I decided to make *kugel*."

"What's that?" asked Marigold.

"Hm. How do I explain *kugel*?" Eden placed a finger on her chin. "It is made from noodles, but it is like a baked pudding. I am making it with apples, of course."

"It is delicious," said Asher, "very hearty with a sweetness that is so mild I can eat far more than I should."

Marigold laughed. "Come tomorrow night I am thinking we will all be feeling like we ate more than we should."

"It is hard to resist so many temptations," said Eli.

"I am looking forward to the corn maze," said Marigold.

"I have never been in one," Eden's excitement caused her voice to lilt in a melodious tune.

"Oh, they're dreadful fun," said Marigold. "My Ma and Pa actually started their courting days at a corn maze."

"Is that right?" Asher grinned. "Are corn mazes for courting purposes then?"

"Oh, no." Marigold's hand flew over her mouth. Heat rushed up her cheeks. She gave silent thanks for the darkness and realized she had blushed more the last month than she had her entire life. "It is just a labyrinth cut in the corn fields. They make a different design every year. It is like walking through a puzzle, and you have to choose different paths and directions."

"That does sound fun," said Eden.

"The Eldridges have a bang up time designing and cutting them every year. Sometimes they will have special puzzles, and you have to find hidden clues, checkpoints, and such along the paths. I remember one year they did a 'no left turn' maze. It took me quite awhile to find my way out."

Light from two oil lamps flanking the front of the surrey shone on the road, and all too soon for the riders, onto the turn-in to the Johnson place. Eli signaled the horse to a stop, and when the wheels stopped turning, he leapt out of his seat to assist Marigold.

The door to the cabin swung open and a silhouette of Matthias Johnson's 6 foot 5 inch frame, gun in hand, filled the opening. Light streamed in from behind, but darkness cloaked his facial features.

Eli startled when he saw the gun pointed his direction.

"It is me, Pa." Marigold called to her father. "I am so sorry I am late. I did not plan to be out this late, or I sure would have told you."

Matthias slowly dropped his rifle, leaned it on a wall inside the cabin, and retrieved his cane. "We can talk about that later, I reckon," he said as he stepped out into the dimly lit night.

The gruffness in Matthias's voice masked his relief at seeing his daughter safe and sound. He had been minutes away from gathering a search party.

"I apologize, Mr. Johnson," said Eli. "When I saw your daughter in town I invited her in to share the closing of the Sabbath. Of course, I could not let her walk home alone in the dark."

"I appreciate that." Matthias approached the surrey and observed the passengers in the back seat.

"May I introduce my brother Asher and my sister Eden?" Eli motioned to his siblings.

"Matthias Johnson." Marigold's father nodded.

"Pleased to meet you," said Asher.

"Me, too," said Eden.

"I would ask you in, but it is a might late." Matthias leaned on his cane.

"That it is," said Eli. "We need to get back ourselves and get the surrey returned to the livery. Good evening, Mr. Johnson, Miss Johnson."

"Thank you for the ride," said Marigold. She watched Eli walk around the surrey and hoist himself in. He drove the horse forward to the turnaround and circled along the path to reposition the surrey to reenter on the road back to town.

"Goodnight." Marigold smiled and waved as the horse and carriage disappeared into the darkness.

Once inside the cabin, the expression on Matthias Johnson's face let his daughter know she would not be heading off to bed any time soon.

"Sit down, girl."

"Yes, Pa," Marigold seated herself in a chair at the kitchen table while Matthias eased himself into a cushioned rocking chair.

"What is the meaning of these shenanigans, girl?" Matthias stared at his daughter and then shook his head. "You know what kind of goings on we've been having around here. Why, you could have been dry gulched and left for dead, gone up the flume for good."

"Oh, Pa." Marigold was dismayed when she realized her father had been so concerned for her wellbeing. "I owe you an apology."

"You done apologized," said Matthias. "What I would like to know is what you were thinking? And what were you doing?"

Marigold hung her head. Remorse flooded her senses like the creek in the springtime running rapid and overflowing its banks. "I knew I was late in getting home," said Marigold, "but I never put two and two together that you would be so powerful worried about my safety."

"I was, daughter." Matthias nodded his head. "That I was."

"It was promiscuous of me, Pa." Marigold lifted glistening eyes to meet her father's gaze. "And it all happened because I let my emotions get the better of me. Please forgive me."

"What got you so riled up?"

"It wasn't anything worthy of making you worry like I did." Marigold shook her head. "I just had a run in with Pansy Joy that got my hackles up. I thought a walk would help, and before I knew it I was in town."

"I am sorry you can't find refuge in your own homestead these days," Matthias spoke with a mix of compassion and grit.

"Oh, Pa, you know I love it here. I just wanted to walk off some steam, and I did not realize how late it was getting to be."

Matthias rocked back and forth. Tense silence filled the usually homey cabin. "Well, you told me some of the why, how about the what? What were you doing all this time?"

"It is like Mr. Thalman said," Marigold answered. "He came out of his father's shop as I happened to be going by. He only had a few minutes, but we walked just down to the feed store and back. He had to get inside to his family for the close of the Sabbath, and he asked me to join him."

Matthias continued rocking and nodded his head. "Go on."

Marigold's anxiety eased somewhat as she shared the details with her father. "Actually, Pa, it was quite interesting. Why, Eli and I were talking about passages from Isaiah when we were walking, and then right smack dab in the middle of the Sabbath blessings, his Pa recited Isaiah talking about drawing water with joy from the wells of salvation."

Matthias ran a hand through his hair and then dropped it with a plunk on his knee. His mind was full, and his nerves had been rattled. He needed some of that water from the well of salvation for his own soul.

"We can talk more tomorrow," said Matthias. "Lucas has been in bed for an hour, and I am ready to turn in myself."

"Sure, Pa." Marigold stood and looked at her father seated in his favorite chair. He was a big man, and had been a scrapper in his youth, but he was kind, and she sincerely regretted adding a moment of worry to his day.

With a soft tread, Marigold padded the few steps to Matthias' side and pecked a soft kiss on his bearded cheek.

CHAPTER 25

Rosalie lifted a wooden spoon in the air and winced before slamming the back of it on the top of a newly made pumpkin pie.

Crack.

"What are you doing, woman?" Zion shook his head at his wife. "And what did that poor pie ever do to you?"

"It did not do anything to me," Rosalie laughed. "It is a new recipe for the baking contest this afternoon." Rosalie had covered a traditional pumpkin pie with a cracked caramel topping she had made by cooking water, corn syrup, and sugar in a small saucepan until it came to a hard-crack stage. She then poured it over the pie, spread it out evenly, and let it thoroughly cool before cracking the top.

"It is a cracked caramel pumpkin pie," she said, "but I confess I was a bit nervous hitting it with the spoon."

"Sometimes a good smack with a spoon is needful," Zion grinned.

"Speaking of needful," said Rosalie, "I hate to say it, but we really need to deal with the outhouse. Have you decided if you want to clean it or move it?"

"Well, now, darlin'," said Zion, scrunching his nose, "I don't *want* to do either one."

Rosalie chuckled. "I don't blame you."

"Can't we just stir in some more ashes and lime for awhile?"

"That is the problem," said Rosalie. "You were so busy with your horse farming it did not get cleaned out in the spring. We have to do something before winter sets in, or we are going to have a serious problem."

"Ok, ok." Zion hung his head and closed his eyes. "I will ask your Pa what he recommends. I suppose it is always better to clean it out, if possible. It is a lot of work to move an outhouse."

"You can talk to him after church." Rosalie turned to her daughter who had made a tower of dominoes on the kitchen table. "Dahlia, it is time to put those away."

"I will help her while you get Mattie," said Zion. "The team is hitched and ready to go."

Rosalie disappeared inside her bedroom and returned with Mattie wrapped in a knit blanket. "I wish Balim and Minnie could come," she said. "It would be so good for them to get out of the house."

"I know."

Dahlia put the last domino in the tin, and Zion put the lid in place.

"But I know they can't," said Rosalie with a sigh. "Abby is not ready for such excitement."

"She is doing remarkably well." Zion reached for his hat and opened the door. "We will just have to be thankful for that, I suppose."

"I suppose," said Rosalie. "Let's go, Dahlia."

"Coming, Ma."

Zion placed a big hand on his daughter's mahogany-covered head. "You want a ride, little bit?"

The girl's hazel eyes sparkled with adoration for her father. "You bet, Pa," said Dahlia. She scurried into a kitchen chair and then on to Zion's back.

Outside the cabin, the horse and wagon stood waiting to take the family to Sunday service. Rosalie watched smoke curl out the chimney of Balim and Minnie's residence and then billow out into the beautiful fall sky. "Should we check on them before we go?"

"How about we check in on them after church?" said Zion. "That way we can share the pastor's message with them."

"That is a wonderful idea," said Rosalie.

Zion's tanned cheek dimpled with his smile. "What else would you expect from your wonderful husband?"

"In today's text," Reverend Dryfus addressed the congregation from the pulpit, "the psalmist prayed that God would unite his heart. What he was asking for was to have an undivided will— that God would knit his whole heart to Himself and deliver him from any inconsistencies or wavering. He was asking God to keep him from corrupt worship and from loving and pursuing lusts and vanities in this present world.

"My friends, having a united heart means that we walk in the ways Jesus taught, without error in doctrine, or deviating from righteous living. We must believe all the things God has revealed, and do what He has commanded. When the affections of your heart are not divided between God and the world or your own desires, you will have a heart that is single in its views and purposes. What prayer could be more appropriate than to ask the Lord to unite your heart with His supreme purpose?

"Let us pray."

Marigold closed her eyes and bowed her head for the closing prayer, but her mind lingered on the words her pastor had preached so eloquently.

"Dear Jesus," she prayed, "I need You to put me together. I am as scattered as Easter eggs on the lawn, and I could sure use some help collecting myself together."

Matthias had been less than warm at the breakfast table, and it was clear to Marigold her father was still ruminating on the happenings of the night before. Even young Lucas had noted Matthias' detachment from the usual banter around the breakfast table.

"I hope he warms up before the party," Lucas had said to Marigold when Matthias had stepped outside to hitch the horse to the buckboard. Throughout the ride to church, the single seat on their simple, four-wheeled wagon had seemed smaller than usual. With concentrated effort, Marigold had worked to keep herself still on the wagon seat next to her father, but the bumps on the road and springs on the bottom of the seat teamed against her attempts to keep from brushing against him.

For some unexplainable reason, her father's bristly demeanor had reminded Marigold of the time she put a cocklebur under West's saddle with the full intention of seeing Zion's fine stallion buck Logan off when he attempted to ride him the first time. A giggle escaped Marigold's lips, unbidden and unwelcome.

Wordless, Matthias had given his daughter a sideways glance that spoke volumes.

Relief swept through Marigold when she noted the change in her father's disposition following church.

Thank You, Lord! She offered silent praise for Matthias' relaxed expression and the return of his usual smile. She thought long and hard about bringing up the subject again, not wanting his mood to revert to its earlier melancholy, but her tender heart would not allow her to leave things unsettled.

"I want you to know I am sorry for being out late, Pa." Marigold placed her left hand on her father's right forearm as he drove the family home after service. "I won't do it again."

Matthias nodded and continued to look at the road in front of the wagon. He was thankful for the peace he felt after being in the Lord's presence in the worship service and hearing Reverend Dryfus break open the Word.

He had reflected on the previous evening's happenings, and he knew two things for sure. The first was that Marigold had never done anything like that before. Yes, she was ornery playful at times, but she was an obedient, thoughtful daughter. She would never have purposely done anything to put herself in a compromising position, make her pa worry, or show him even the slightest inkling of disrespect.

The second thing he admitted after consideration was that he had allowed himself to get worked up in a way that was unequal to the circumstances. He had stewed and worried in a way he would not have done just a month ago. The fact was that the recent goings on with Balim and Abby had him on high alert.

Ever since he and his beloved Sharon had moved to Briar Hollow decades before, Matthias had always found Washington to generally be a peaceful and safe settlement. Masked men riding in the night, threatening good people, and the revelation that the goat cart accident had not really been an accident at all—these things had struck a bit too close to home for Matthias.

With his free hand he rubbed his injured leg. The bullet still lodged inside after so many years was an ever-present reminder that Matthias Johnson was the kind of man a person could ride the river with. As a boy serving as a fife player at the Battle of San Jacincto, he had taken a bullet from a Mexican soldier in his efforts to protect Sam Houston.

Matthias turned his head to look at Marigold and gave her a slight smile. "I know, daughter." The horse pulled the wagon a few yards down the road before he spoke again, "I know you did not mean no harm. I was just plumb worried. That I was."

"I understand," Marigold said as she straightened on the buckboard seat. "Things have sure been balled up around here lately, but we can't throw up the sponge on life. There are still heaps more good people than bad."

"That is sound on the goose, daughter." Matthias nodded.

"And we have a harvest party to go to today." Marigold lifted her shoulders and drew in a deep breath. Her freckled face broke out in a broad smile that lit her countenance and brightened the atmosphere in general.

"I was thinking I would take the kaleidoscope over to Balim since Abby is able to sit up and play with it now."

"Fine by me," said Matthias.

"I'm hungry." Lucas rubbed his stomach with one hand.

"Me, too, Lukey," said Marigold, threading her right arm through brother's. "We will have some ham and biscuit sandwiches when we get home. That will tide us over until the picnic."

Eden looked in the mirror for the third time in as many minutes. "Do I look ok?"

Asher held his chin between his thumb and forefinger and studied his sister. "Hm," he said, "I don't know if that will do at all."

Eden spun and stared at her brother with a worried look on her dark features. "I knew it," she said. "What should I do?"

"I was thinking we could whip up something out of some feed sacks," said Asher. His sober expression morphed into mirth. "It is a harvest party, after all."

"Oh, you *shtunk!*" Eden glowered at her brother, spun around on her heel, and looked in the mirror again. She smoothed her lavender cotton skirt that fell to the floor in an even hem over a coordinating dainty floral calico shirtwaist with a white rounded collar. Her glossy black hair was tied out of her face in a neat bow of white satin ribbon.

Eli shook his head at his brother. "Oh, Eden," he said, "Asher knows you have never looked prettier. That is why he feels at liberty to tease you."

Eden threw her arms around Eli and gave him a tight squeeze. "Thank you, Eli!" she said, and then drew her lips together in a tight line. As she walked past Asher, she worked to keep from sticking her tongue out at him.

"If stupidity was a tree, you would have been a forest," she whispered in his ear on the way to the kitchen.

"Come now," said Judith. "No whispering."

"Yes, Ema." Eden smiled sweetly at her mother and then turned her attention to the dish on the counter. "Do you think they will like the *kugel?*"

Hiram leaned over the creamy baked noodles and breathed in its medley of nutmeg, apples and brown sugar. "If they don't, I will have to suffer and eat the entire dish."

CHAPTER 26

Judith admired the grounds of Comfort Lodge with appreciation. Living in town over the shop was certainly convenient, but there was a peaceful beauty here that captured the soul.

A weeping willow waved the Thalmans onto the property. Beneath the graceful giant's wispy, sweeping branches, two benches beckoned the visitors to rest and enjoy the quiet surroundings. Across from the willow tree, a cattail-lined pond hosted a green goose house trimmed in white. Down the lane on the left, stood a large barn painted a cheery red with white trim. A big white X was painted on the door attached to the adjacent corral. The barn's black roof arched over a haymow with a crane, and a henhouse and springhouse completed the outbuildings. Across the path, Comfort Lodge nestled in the shade of tall timbers.

Painted a deep green, the vastness of the lodge blended into the lovely scene. A large wrap-around porch swung across the front and both sides of the first floor. Four ladder-backed rocking chairs wore the same floral cushions as the bench swing suspended from the porch ceiling. The black-shingled roof donned eight gables, four facing front and four looking into the woods. Clusters of black-eyed Susans lined the flagstone path to the porch. Their bright, yellow-gold petals lured a hummingbird to a pollen-laden center cone.

"What a beautiful place," said Eden.

In front of the lodge, planks on sawhorses created makeshift tables covered in red-and-white checkered cloths. Ladies buzzed around them setting the food out while the men stood around talking.

"You got those horseshoes ready, Erlanger?" Zion stood next to his neighbor James Erlanger who, along with his wife Florence, was the proprietor of Comfort Inn.

"If you are ready to get whipped," said James.

Zion threw his head back and guffawed at his friend, "Listen to you trying to bulldoze the horseshoe champion of Mason County. You will be backed down before we are halfway through the first game."

"Right," said James. He shook his head and nodded towards the Thalman's surrey. "Who have we got here?"

"Have you met the Thalman's?" Logan waved to the surrey.

"Not directly," said James, "but I have seen their shop in town, of course."

"Hiram Thalman is the best tailor I have ever known," said Logan.

"Is that who fixed you up with those new duds you've been sporting?" James asked. "You sure have been cutting a swell around this berg."

"Looks like a regular politician," said Zion.

"Let's go greet the new arrivals," said Logan, and he led the procession to the surrey that had just come to a stop.

"Welcome to Comfort Lodge. I'm James Erlanger."

"And I am Hiram Thalman," said the tailor, nodding at his host. He motioned to his wife on the seat next to him. "This is my wife, Judith, and these are my sons, Eli and Asher, and my daughter Eden."

"We are pleased as punch to have you," said James.

"Thank you for the invitation." Hiram stepped out of the fringe-topped surrey and circled around the front to help his wife.

"Can you take this?" Judith handed him a covered dish of potato *latkes*.

"I can get that for you," said James. He stepped forward and took the dish from Hiram.

"And this?" Judith lifted a towel-encircled pot from the bench beside her. It was filled with fragrant beef brisket, onions and root vegetables.

"Allow me," said Zion. "Just smell that, fellas."

"And this?" Eden called from the back seat.

"I'll be," said Logan as he accepted the dish of *kugel* from Eden. "Did you bring the whole kit and caboodle?"

"We are five," said Hiram, "and we like to eat."

"Well, I don't think anyone is going to leave here hungry," said Zion. "Let's put this on the table, and then we can visit some more."

"Oh, you look so pretty, Eden," said Pansy Joy, admiring the younger girl's lavender outfit. "That color with your dark hair is quite fetching."

"Thank you, Mrs. Eldridge." Eden's slight shoulders swayed as she inclined from side to side.

"You can call me Pansy Joy."

"What is that dish?" Penny lifted the covering off the *kugel*.

"It is for the contest," said Eden, turning sparkling dark eyes to Penny. "I will tell the judges all about it then."

"Oh, ho," said Pansy Joy with a chuckle. "I see we have a competitor among us."

A sweet smile played across Eden's face. It had been a long time since she had enjoyed a companionable conversation with someone besides her family. "Where is Marigold?" she asked.

"I am a bit surprised to say it, because she is usually one to stay outdoors as much as possible," said Rosalie, "but she is inside helping Mrs. Erlanger with refreshments."

"I will take you inside," said Pansy Joy. "Would you like to come, Mrs. Thalman?"

"Yes, of course," said Judith.

"I used to work here from time to time," Pansy Joy's lilting tone matched her buoyant steps, "before I got married, that is."

Judith and Eden both admired the coordinating rocking chairs and bench swing as they stepped across the porch and into the front door of Comfort Lodge. To their left a massive parlor stretched across a good portion of the lower level.

"This is where I got married," said Pansy Joy. "Actually, we have lots of special events here."

She pointed up the stairs that led to a narrow hall. "The guests stay upstairs," she said, "and over here is the dining hall and the Erlanger's living quarters." Pansy Joy motioned to a large dining room to the right of the parlor. It abutted the kitchen, washroom, two bedrooms and a private sitting room.

In the dining room that smelled as sweet as the funnel cake booth at the fairground, four matching tables with walnut balloon-backed chairs stood atop a gleaming wood floor. Cream-colored basket-weave cloths covered each table, all with red and cream cross-stitched embroidery sewn around their fringed perimeters. Paned windows capped with ecru lace valances marched along the front wall that overlooked the porch.

In the corner of the dining room, the flat lid of a dormant wood stove held a crockery pitcher of burnt-red coneflowers and Queen Ann's lace, a colorful complement to the cheery tablecloths. A functional sideboard crafted in a simple rectangular style with a rich walnut finish was positioned next to the wood stove.

"Hey, Marigold," Pansy Joy announced her coming before entering the kitchen. "The Thalmans are here."

Marigold wiped her hands on a towel and greeted Judith and Eden warmly. "Mrs. Florence Erlanger, these are my friends Eden and Mrs. Judith Thalman."

"We're so glad you could come," said Florence.

"Thank you for having us," said Judith.

"Yes, thank you," echoed Eden.

"Let's say we get a wiggle on with these drinks." Marigold lifted a glass pitcher of lemonade and handed it to Pansy Joy. "It has got to be close to eating time."

"I think it is," said Pansy Joy.

"Eden, would you mind carrying this?" Marigold lifted a pitcher of tea with fresh mint leaves floating on top.

"Not at all."

"I can help, too," said Judith. She reached for the second pitcher of lemonade, while Florence took the second container of tea.

"Marigold," Florence called, "we did not get the ice yet. Can you have one of the men help you with that, then we will say grace and eat."

"No problem, Mrs. E."

Back out in the sunshine, the ladies placed the handled pitchers filled with drinks on the make-shift tables, and Marigold headed to the barn.

"Miss Johnson," said Eli as he diverted from the group of men gathered on the lawn talking horseshoes and sack races.

"Well, hello, Mr. Thalman," Marigold greeted Eli with a beaming smile. "How are you this lovely fall day?"

"Second to none," said Eli, matching his gate to Marigold's. "Where are we going?"

"To get ice."

"In the barn?"

"Yes," said Marigold. "The Erlangers have an ice house built right into their barn."

"That is convenient," said Eli.

"What is convenient is that you are here, and I need help." Marigold smiled up into Eli's dark eyes.

The construction of the ice house was simple. It was a building within a building made partially underground of two walls fourteen inches apart. The walls were filled with sawdust and a block of ice rested on a bed of sawdust over a floor of poles that allowed for drainage below. On one side a double door facilitated putting in ice and ventilation, and a foot of sawdust topped the ice.

Marigold grabbed a bucket that held an ice shaver and pick. "Have you ever shaved ice?"

"Not until today," said Eli. He reached in the bucket and drew out the cast iron scraper. The tool was about eight inches long and had a bowl about three and a half inches deep. At the bottom of the bowl was a slot with a toothed edge; and on the top, a hinged cap closed over the ice captured in the tool as it was scraped over the surface of the block creating thin shavings.

"Should I scrape it right off the big block?"

"We don't want to leave the doors open too long," said Marigold. "It is best to pick out a block and then do the shaving."

Eli set to work hewing out a smaller cube from the large block with a hammer and chisel. Ambient cold diffused into the air immediately in front of the open doors, and a shiver raced down Marigold's back.

"Cold?"

"Surprisingly." Marigold smiled. "I have been warm all day. It is pretty amazing how one minute a girl can be flush as a peach pie right out of the oven, and then shivering in just a few shakes of a lamb's tail."

"I guess the difference is what you are standing next to." Eli turned to look Marigold squarely in the eyes.

"I guess so." Marigold watched in silence as Eli finished cutting out the block. She reached for a set of single-hand tongs hanging from a peg on the interior wall of the barn. "Use these to pull it out," she said and handed him the tongs. "Then we will move over to the workbench for the shaving."

Eli opened the tongs and allowed the legs to close around the cube. Their pointed ends embedded into the surface of the block, and he pulled, freeing the cube. "There we go," said Eli. "A successful delivery."

Marigold smiled and closed the double doors of the ice house before following Eli to the workbench with the bucket. Eli stood at the table, while Marigold pulled up a stool to watch his first attempt at shaving ice.

With a tailor's nimble dexterity, Eli grasped the handle of the cast iron implement and worked the shaver down the block. He lifted and shaved down repeatedly in a rhythm that reminded Marigold of the needle in Hiram's treadle sewing machine.

Marigold smiled and nodded. "Nice work, Mr. Thalman."

"Thank you." Eli paused before speaking again. "I would be pleased if you would call me by my given name."

Marigold sucked in a deep breath and slowly let it out.

"All right . . . Eli."

His name danced off her tongue and flung through her lips into the barn making the most delightful sound to her ears.

"Then you should call me Marigold."

"Then I will . . . Marigold."

Eli turned to look into Marigold's sweet freckled face. Her honey braids rested across her shoulders, and he longed to lift one—to caress the silky tresses between his fingers and feel their texture for himself.

He knew this girl had gotten under his skin. She was such a delightful mosaic of confidence and playfulness augmented with a fragment of shy vulnerability lost to all but the most careful observer, and Eli had been carefully observing.

With her head tipped to one side, the expression in her big brown eyes spoke volumes. Undoubtedly, the tomes included many unanswered questions.

"What is the hold up in here?" Zion bellowed into the barn. "Don't you know there are hungry folks just waiting to eat all this good food heaped up on the tables out here?"

Marigold laughed. "I guess we have enough ice to get things started," she said and turned to answer her brother-in-law. "Mrs. Erlanger asked me to get some ice, and Eli offered to help."

"Well let's go then, girl."

Eli made a final dump in the bucket and placed the shaver on the workbench. "Let's go."

CHAPTER 27

The afternoon progressed handsomely, beginning with prayer, and then on to an incredible miscellany of foods. Lawn games followed. The younger ones played Blind Man's Bluff, and held an egg-in-the-spoon race, while the men conducted a horseshoe tournament and sack race. A lively contest of shuttlecock transpired as ladies took turns with the rackets.

"All right, friends," James stood on the porch steps and called through cupped hands, "It is time for the corn maze. Everybody on the wagons for a hay ride over to the Eldrige Farm. We will come back to see who has won the bake-off and have dessert and coffee before the singing."

With an orderly chaos, the partygoers climbed into two wagons chattering like a company of black-billed magpies. The wagon beds were lined with bales of hay that formed seats around the perimeters. Ladies sat on the bales with children on their laps. There was room for some of the men on the bales as well, but others joined the drivers on the wagon seats or sat cross-legged in the middle of the wagon beds.

James Erlanger and Angus Carver each drove a team down the lane, across the road, and down the short way to the Eldridge place.

Burke Calhoun pulled a silver flask from an interior vest pocket, took a swig, and wiped his mouth with the back of his hand. "Do we wait for dark?"

"I have been thinking about that," said Trigg Simon. "There is a chance folks will be returning home before nightfall."

"True." Fred McGhee nodded his agreement. "Some of them have little ones."

"I say we go now," said Simon.

"So you think it is just the black folks in the hollow?" asked Calhoun.

"I reckon so," said Simon. "I just happened to be by the good doctor's office this week making small talk, and he confirmed that girl of theirs is housebound for at least a few more days."

"Well, let's ride then," said McGhee.

"You got your hoods?" asked Simon.

McGhee and Calhoun nodded.

"When we get to Briar Hollow we will slip into the woods across the road and put the hoods on there," said Simon. "We don't want to be too long in public in the light of day."

Once the wagons came to a stop and the partygoers stepped back on terra firma, Lowell Eldridge took charge.

"Everybody listen up," Lowell cried out loudly. "If you rode with James, your number is one. If you rode with Angus, your number is two."

"What's he doing?" asked Rosalie.

"I am not sure." Marigold shrugged her shoulders.

"He doesn't want us to go in all in a herd," said Pansy Joy. "He came up with this plan to mix things up."

"If you are a one, line up to my right; and if you are a two, line up on the left," said Lowell. He stood with arms outstretched as his friends and guests formed two lines.

Marigold lined up with her sisters at the beginning of line one. Eli stood across from her in line two with his family.

"To make this a bit more interesting, I will give you a hint on the shape of the maze this year. I am sending you in two by two." Lowell Eldridge grinned as he saw some of the people connect the dots.

"It must be an ark," Pansy Joy whispered.

"How fun," said Rosalie.

"I knew that," Marigold chuckled. "I helped with the cutting of it. But I did not know he was sending us in two by two."

"I am not just sending you in two by two," barked Lowell. "I am sending you in two by two by two."

"Explain yourself, granger!" Zion called from the back of line one.

"I am taking one from each line and giving each a two-minute lead into the maze," said Lowell. "You won't be able to lean on the crowd this year. No bilking, either."

"You got booby traps in there this year?" James asked.

"Some dead ends, for sure," said Lowell with a hearty laugh, "but I will let you figure out if there are any booby traps on your own."

"Call the roll, then, Farmer Eldridge," Garth hollered at his father.

"All right." Lowell pulled out his pocket watch and checked the time. "Rosalie and Eden, you go first."

The girls smiled at each other, clasped hands and disappeared inside the maze.

"Booby traps?" Hiram turned to Florence Erlanger, a concerned look on his face.

"It is nothing to worry about, Mr. Thalman," said Florence. "Lowell just sometimes puts obstacles in the paths, and we have to figure out how to move them or get around them."

"I see." Hiram nodded his understanding.

"Asher and Pansy Joy, you are up next."

A flutter of excitement made its way into Marigold's heart. The two minutes seemed longer as she waited for Lowell Eldridge to call her name.

"Eli and Marigold."

Eli grinned. *I like the sound of that*, he thought, and then turned a full smile to Marigold as they entered the maze together.

"What a nice surprise," said Eli.

"I love a good surprise myself," said Marigold. A jolt from her memory banks shifted her thoughts to her forgotten surprise—the kaleidoscope. Distress etched across her face.

"Is something wrong?" Eli asked.

"Oh, Marigold Johnson, you coffee boiler, you."

"Coffee boiler?"

"Yeah, a coffee boiler," she said and then poked her lips out in a full pout. "I have had a surprise planned for Balim for days. Well, it is mostly for Abby and Abram, but I forgot to give it to them. I especially wanted them to have it since they couldn't come to the party today."

"Does this have anything to do with the package you were carrying from town the other day when you were caught in the rain."

"Yeah."

Marigold's spring bounced away, and her light steps turned to what looked more like a death march than a fun trek through a corn maze.

Marigold took her right hand and ran it along the labyrinth wall. She knew the trick to finding her way through the maze was to keep a right hand on the wall and keep walking until eventually she reached the exit. It worked because most mazes were like strings laid out on the ground. You just "grab ahold" and follow it to the end.

As her thoughts raced, she realized she knew the exact place on the perimeter of Eldridge's agricultural ark that would let her out near the property line shared by the Edridge farm and Briar Hollow.

Eli watched her in silence, and when she lifted her head, possibilities filled her brown eyes.

"What are you thinking?" asked Eli.

"I am thinking that I know just how to slip out of this maze and over to Briar Hollow," she said with a smile. "I could deliver the kaleidoscope and be back before the last couple makes their way out."

"Are you sure you know the way?"

"For sure and for certain." Marigold's brown eyes sparkled. "Would you like to come with me or continue on in the maze without me?"

Eli's dark eyes softened in a way that made Marigold's stomach tighten.

"I don't want to continue on without you, Marigold."

Marigold reached for Eli's hand, "Well, come on then," she said. "We will have to hurry or we will be late for the desserts."

With pleasure, Eli allowed himself to be led through the maze of field corn.

Under the shelter of the woodland across from Briar Hollow, the trio of men donned their masks. The rope was ready. The time was right.

"Move out," Simon barked, and he led the charge across the road and into the juniper-lined lane.

Inside their home, Balim and Minnie looked up from their supper and locked eyes over the table. The sound of hooves thundering down the lane was unmistakable.

"What's that?" Minnie asked, her eyes growing wider by the second as the shouts of the riders broke forth in expletives and threatenings.

"I am guessing we is fixin' to find out." Balim stood, walked to the door and reached for the handle.

"What are you doing, Balim?" Minnie cried out in alarm.

"I am going outside, woman." Balim turned the handle and looked back at his wife. "You stay in here with the kids now, ya hear me?"

"Balim, Balim," Minnie sobbed as she watched her husband walk out the door. "Don't go."

"We are almost there," said Marigold. "See the horse barn?"

"I do," said Eli. "I have never seen a round one like that close up."

"Oh, Logan and Zion worked together on that," said Marigold. "They have been partnered up since Logan and Penny got hitched."

"It must be nice to have such a close family all working together."

"You should know." Marigold smiled. "Yours seems to do right nice working at the shop together."

"For the most part," said Eli. "We do have our moments. Asher loves to tease Eden."

"I guess I have done some teasing myself," said Marigold, "and the truth is things were not always in apple pie order around here."

"What do you mean?" Eli asked.

"I mean Penny and Logan Mayfield used to agree like cat and dog. You should have seen them spar."

"Really?" Eli shook his head in surprise. "I can't imagine that at all."

"Oh, it is true, for sure and for certain." Marigold snickered. "And if you want the whole truth, I wasn't any too happy with Mr. Logan Fancypants Mayfield myself when I first met him."

"I find that hard to believe," said Eli.

"I will tell you a secret," Marigold lowered her tone, although there was no one other than Eli around to hear her disclosure. "When Logan first got here, things were so balled up, I did something awful."

"You?" Eli lifted his brows, causing his eyes to grow wider behind his wire-rimmed spectacles. "I can't believe you would do something awful."

"I did." Marigold hung her head, but her lips turned upward in a smile as she replayed the scene in her memory. "I got me a cocklebur—a big one covered with stiff, hooked spines and stuck it under West's blanket right under the saddle's gullet. Poor Logan did not know what happened when he mounted and got thrown in the dirt."

Eli pursed his lips to keep back a laugh. "So in other words, I better behave myself, or I might find myself in danger of a prank?"

"Oh, no," said Marigold. "I wouldn't do that to someone I like."

The couple approached the round barn and began to circle around it.

"And you like me?"

Marigold grinned.

The rapid fall of horses' hooves pounding against the lane released a sound that cut off Marigold's answer.

Men shouted words—they were ugly and frightening. Rattled, Marigold's brown eyes searched Eli's for answers. Finding none, she reached for his hand. Slowly, with her heart racing, she edged enough around the barn to see the scene playing out on in her beloved hollow.

Her family's refuge was being intruded upon by hooded, vulgar men, and Marigold felt both violated and terrified.

Repulsive words.

Angry threats.

Marigold's hand flew over her mouth. "Balim," she whispered behind her fingers when she saw her dear friend step out of his home and approach the riders.

CHAPTER 28

Time stood still.

With a sadness in his eyes that bellied his confident posture, Balim waited in silence for the hooded men to reveal their intentions.

"We have come to take care of a problem that has been escalating around these parts," said Trigg Simon, sneering behind his mask.

Balim nodded, but remained silent.

"That would be you," said Calhoun as he used his gun to point at Balim.

Marigold prayed for wisdom, "Dear Jesus, what should we do?"

A girl and an unarmed man pitted against three men with guns on horseback was not an even match, even with Balim on their side. With only three pulls of three triggers, this confrontation could come to a tragic end.

"We can't just stand here," Marigold whispered. Love for Balim overwhelmed the terror in her heart. She released her grip on Eli's hand and started running.

"Hey! Hey!" she yelled and flapped her arms as she rushed toward the altercation.

It only took a moment for an astonished Eli to grasp what was happening. He ran after Marigold, valiantly trying to keep himself between her and the armed men, but she kept moving about like a jackrabbit with a bobcat on its tail.

"What is this?" Fred McGhee was the first to hear Marigold's howling and turned to see the oncoming couple.

"You." Trigg motioned to Balim. "Get on my horse now or I shoot every living thing on this property—starting with that girl."

Without hesitation, Balim accepted Trigg's hand-up and mounted behind him on his silver Gypsy Vanner.

Trigg signaled the horse to make a quick exit. McGhee and Calhoun followed his lead and disappeared in the tree-lined lane before Eli and Marigold reached the corral.

Marigold stopped. She dropped both arms and her jaw simultaneously. There was no way she and Eli could catch up with the men on horseback. She felt helpless and sick to her stomach. A pervasive sense of evil lingered behind the riders and enveloped her in its darkness.

"Marigold," said Eli as he cupped the girl's face in his hand, "we should check on Balim's family. They could be injured."

Distraught, it took a few moments for Eli's words to penetrate Marigold's swirling thoughts. She shook her head to rattle her brain back into reality and looked Eli in the eye. "Yes," she said and grabbed his hand. The two ran towards the cabin.

When they reached the door, Marigold abruptly rapped on it and called out at the same time, "Minnie! Minnie! It is Marigold. Are you ok?"

Minnie bustled to the door, opened it, and fell into Marigold's arms. "Oh, Miss Mar'gold. What's done happened to my Balim?"

Marigold glanced around the room. A half-eaten supper was still on the table, and a wide-eyed, paralyzed Abram remained in his seat. Little Abby slept in a make-shift bed Balim had made for her to use during her convalescence.

"I don't know, Minnie," Marigold answered, "but are you or the kids hurt?"

"No," said Minnie shaking her dark head. "No. We ain't hurt none, but oh—what are they gwanna do with my man?"

"Minnie, I am going to go for help," said Marigold, and then she turned to Eli. "I think it is best you stay here for now—unless you can ride bareback."

Eli nodded his understanding. "Can I do anything here while you go?"

Marigold's big brown eyes glistened. A solitary tear eked out one corner and slid down a freckled cheek. "Just pray, Eli. Pray."

"Whoa." Trigg reined in Pied Piper in front of the barn at the old Corbin place and shoved Balim off the back of his horse.

Umph.

Balim landed hard on the ground.

Calhoun dismounted and kicked Balim in the side. "Should we have a little fun before the hanging?"

"No time for that," said McGhee. "With those kids showing up like they did, we better get down to business."

Balim roused himself and stood to his feet.

"We could put him in ol' Corbin's slave jail," said Calhoun with a snigger. "I seen some rings still attached to the floor. We could tie him up and come back when there is more time."

The dilapidated barn loomed behind. In years past, slaves had been imprisoned inside, or "stored" according to those who claimed to own them. Men had been chained, tethered two-by-two to a central chain on the straw-covered floor. The close quarters and unsanitary conditions often led to outbreaks of cholera.

It was a slave ship turned upside down and planted in Kentucky's fertile soil.

Throughout Mason County, dozens more of these slave holding cells were hidden inside tobacco barns, shrouded from public view.

Marigold rushed into the horse barn and went immediately to Balim's horse. Star was low-withered, wide backed and short enough for Marigold to get on with the mounting block—the perfect choice for a bareback ride.

With one foot on the mounting block, she lifted her full skirt and reached the opposite leg over.

"Good boy, Star."

Marigold balanced herself on the horse's back and allowed her legs to hang naturally.

She directed the horse out of the barn and then from a walk to a trot. Galloping would be a risk. She had never ridden Balim's horse bareback, and she did not know if he had ever carried a rider without a saddle. Still, given the urgency of the situation, she breathed a silent prayer, squeezed both legs, and leaned slightly forward. Star responded with a four-beat thump, thump, thump, thump; and Marigold reached the Eldridge Farm in two minutes flat.

Lowell stood at the entrance of the corn maze with his pocket watch in hand ready to send the last of the party-goers inside.

"Oh, thank God," Marigold huffed out the words.

Zion and Logan were the last participants still standing outside Lowell Eldridge's corn maze. Relief washed over her as she saw them.

"Marigold." Zion rushed to his sister-in-law's side. "What's going on? And how did you get here?"

Marigold exhaled deeply, her shoulders rising and then falling in a great heave. "Hooded men . . . at Briar Hollow . . . they took Balim."

"Dear Jesus."

"We better get this done and then ride on to our alibis," said McGhee.

Trigg nodded and pulled a rope from the strap attached to the horn of his saddle. He made an S shape with the rope and then pinched it together. Using a middle loop, he wrapped the pinched place from the right side to the left leaving a short piece of rope that he poked through the top of the loop.

Pinching the coiled part, he used his thumb to hold down the short piece he put through the loop on the left side, bent it and then pulled it on the right side until it closed the loop on the left. With a nod of satisfaction, he adjusted the coils and tightened the opening to the right size.

Dropping the noose to his side, Simon began to swing the rope back and forth. After a few swings, he sent the noosed end sailing over the largest branch of the 60-foot ash tree.

"Hold this," said Trigg. He threw the loose end at Calhoun and then turned to Balim with a sneer on his hate-filled face. "Are you ready for your last ride?"

"All that book reading and proud ways of yours ain't done you no good at all, have they?" Burke mocked Balim as Trigg slipped the hangman's halter around his neck.

"And when we finish here," said Trigg, "that message is going to ring loud and clear around Mason County."

Simon stared Balim in the eye. "Mount up."

"There is no time to waste," said Zion as he sprung to action. "We would have heard them if they rode past here, so they either went north or into the woods."

Zion swung himself onto Star's bare back. "Logan, follow me in the wagon. Mr. Eldridge, see who you can round up from the maze."

"Giddup, Star!" Zion and the horse exited the Eldrige Farm and made a sharp right towards Briar Hollow.

"Help me, Jesus," he prayed. "Help me find Balim. Protect him from the plots of evil men like you have done so many times before for Your people."

The broken branches across the road from Briar Hollow gave Zion a clear path to follow. The kidnappers must have been in a hurry to leave such an obvious trail.

Logan saw Zion pull off the road in front of him and turn into the woods. When he reached the spot, he reigned in the draft horse pulling the wagon, ground tied it, and then ran into the woods.

Balim sat calmly on Trigg's silver horse. The noose was already around his neck, and as Calhoun finished tying the end of the rope to the tree trunk, he prepared his mind to enter eternity. He had readied his soul long before when he had repented of his sins, gone into the river to be baptized in Jesus' name, and come up out the water speaking in a heavenly language. He had walked closely with his Savior ever since.

Thank ya for saving me, Lawd. Keep a watch over Minnie and the chilluns, Jesus. I ask you to have mercy on these poor sinners. They don't know what they is doin'.

The sound of a rider approaching set things moving double time.

"Someone's coming," said McGhee. He placed his foot in a stirrup and hoisted himself into his saddle. Calhoun followed suit.

Trigg slapped Pied Piper on the thigh.

The horse whinnied and jolted forward.

Balim surged forward with the animal, but only for a moment as the rope pulled at his neck scraping him off the horse's back.

Without taking time to watch Balim swing, Trigg mounted Pied Piper and took off into the woods after his cohorts.

Unlike gallows executions that dropped a person to a quick, almost instantaneous death, Balim faced a slower death by strangulation.

Zion burst through the tree line horrified at what he found. In his peripheral vision he caught a glimpse of a man riding off on a horse, but his focus was on his dear friend hanging at the end of a rope.

Crunch. Crack.

Before Zion had time to process what was happening, the branch Balim was hanging from broke off the old ash tree.

Balim fell three feet to the ground and the large branch crashed beside him only inches from his head.

"Dear God!" Zion dismounted and rushed to his side. He loosened the noose around Balim's neck and checked for breathing.

"Balim, Balim!" Zion clasped both hands around his friend's dear face.

Whoo.

Hope flooded Zion's face when he heard the faint intake of air.

"Oh, Balim. I am so sorry this happened. You don't deserve this." Zion gently pulled the rope from around Balim's neck and over his head.

"You are going to be ok, buddy."

CHAPTER 29

Logan crashed through the woods, the dried leaves under his feet amplifying the sounds of his arrival.

"Over here," Zion called.

When he broke through the trees onto the scene, Logan froze in his tracks. "Oh, dear Lord, what happened?"

"He was hanging from the branch when I got here, but it broke and he fell to the ground," said Zion. "He is alive."

"Thank God!" Logan shook his head in disbelief.

"Can you help me move him to the wagon?"

"I will do my best."

Logan looked over Balim's sturdy form. Considering his slight build, he worried that dropping him might do more damage to the already traumatized man.

"Do you think we could lay him over Star's back and walk him through woods?" he asked. "I would sure hate to drop him after all he has been through."

"Good idea," said Zion.

Eli cleared the supper dishes off the table and sat down next to Abram and Minnie. With all that was going on, it did not seem appropriate to move to the comfortable padded rocking chairs in the sitting area.

No words could help.

Nothing he could do would change what had happened.

They would sit.

They would wait.

Compassion stirred deep inside Eli. His family had experienced a measure of prejudice, but nothing like this poor woman was undergoing this very moment.

He wanted to pray with her, but she was a Christian and he was a Jew. Would Elohim even hear his prayer? Would Jesus?

Minnie sat in her chair twisting a bandana in her hands, her son silent at her side. With dark eyes brimming with compassion, he reached for Minnie's hand.

It occurred to him as he did that it was the first time he had ever touched black skin. It felt no different than his, except for the calluses Minnie wore in testimony to her years of physical labor.

She is just like me—just like my own mother.

Eli closed his eyes and willed the deep sympathy he felt inside to be somehow transferred to the woman beside him. In the stillness it was almost as if he heard a whisper in his spirit that impressed him to speak aloud a favorite passage of Scripture.

"The LORD is my shepherd; I shall not want. He maketh me to lie down in green pastures; He leadeth me beside the still waters. He restoreth my soul; He guideth me in straight paths for His name's sake. Yea, though I walk through the valley of the shadow of death, I will fear no evil, for Thou art with me; Thy rod and Thy staff, they comfort me. Thou preparest a table before me in the presence of mine enemies; Thou has anointed my head with oil; my cup runneth over. Surely goodness and mercy shall follow me all the days of my life: and I shall dwell in the house of the LORD forever."

Minnie squeezed Eli's hand. "Yes, Jesus," she said. "Yes, Jesus."

An extraordinary sensation coursed through Eli. It was as if some sort of power transferred from Minnie's hand and surged into his. A sweet and welcome warmth swept through his spirit.

Jesus? His lips dared not say the name that echoed in his soul.

Marigold arrived at the wagon as Zion led Star out of the woods. Logan kept a firm hand on Balim's motionless body draped over the horse's back.

"No!" Marigold's hands flew over her mouth and her eyes grew wide.

"He is alive, Marigold," said Zion. "Here, stand by Star and keep him steady while we transfer him to the wagon."

"What happened?" Marigold implored Zion for an answer.

"A lynching gone bad," said Zion as he climbed into the wagon and motioned for Logan to bring the horse near. He broke open a bale of hay and spread it across the wagon floor. Grasping Balim's upper body, Zion waited for Logan to climb in the wagon and help him swing Balim's body around and down onto the hay.

Balim stirred, uttered a pitiful moan, and reached a hand to his neck. He was having difficulty breathing, but he was alive.

Zion climbed onto the wagon seat and Marigold handed him the reins. "I am taking him to Doc Byerly's" he said, "Logan, you stop by the Eldridge place and let folks know what's going."

"I will go tell Minnie," Marigold called over her shoulder as she hurried across the street and on to the lane leading to the hollow.

"Sweet Lawd a mercy." Minnie clasped Marigold in a ferocious hug. "You sho he is alive, girl? You sho?"

"I saw him myself," said Marigold.

Abram, still seated at the table, dropped his head and let out a mournful cry. "Mammy, Mammy," he wailed repeatedly.

"Hush now, boy," said Minnie. She scurried to her young son's side, "You is all right, and so is yo Pappy." She stroked his tight black curls with the palm of her hand and whispered in soothing tones. "King Jesus is still on His throne, and you is all right, now, ain't ya? Yes, you is, Abram Coldwell. Yes, you is. Thank Ya, Jesus. Hallelujah."

What words came next, Eli did not understand, but he felt a warm presence fill the room with a peace that made no logical sense, but somehow seemed just right.

Wagon wheels turning and hooves clip clopping on the lane drew Eli's attention to the window. "It is Garth," he said. "He is here with Rosalie and a wagon."

Eli opened the door and Rosalie and Garth stepped inside the small cabin.

Rosalie stretched her arms around Minnie and Abram in a consoling huddle. "I am so sorry," she spoke in a soothing tone. "I have come to stay with Abby and Abram so you can go to Balim. Grant is here to take you in the wagon."

"Oh, thank ya, Miss Rozlee. Thank ya." Minnie cupped Abram's chin in her plump hand. "I will be back before ya know it, baby. Now don' you worry none. Miss Rozlee will stay with ya 'til I get back."

Minnie gathered her skirts and followed Garth outside and into the wagon.

Marigold exhaled a deep breath and offered a weak smile at Eli.

"Did you want to go with Garth?" asked Rosalie.

Marigold shook her head. "No. I wouldn't be much use sitting around Doc Byerly's place." She scanned the small cabin and suddenly felt closed in. "Actually, if you don't mind, I'd like to get some fresh air."

Rosalie studied her sister's face. Tension and worry had written a strong message in her features that a bit of fresh air might ease.

"Of course," said Rosalie. "Why don't you walk down to the Lodge? After Logan stopped by with the news, people started heading back to the Erlanger's. Comfort Lodge is much more accommodating."

"I will walk with you," said Eli. He rose and opened the door.

When the couple reached the road, Marigold stopped and stared into the woods where only a few short minutes ago Zion had stepped through with Balim.

The sun was beginning its journey to the horizon, but there was still plenty of light, and with a vulnerable supplication in her brown eyes, Marigold turned to Eli.

"I, I need . . . I want to go in there," she said.

Eli watched as she struggled for words. "I will go with you."

It was easy to follow the path the horses had made, and in just a couple of minutes Marigold and Eli arrived at the old Corbin place. Marigold surveyed the site and found the dilapidated barn creepy, and a general eeriness pervading the atmosphere.

"I have been here a hundred times," she told Eli. "I have walked in these woods since I was a little girl."

"Sometimes one moment, one experience can change the way we think about things forever."

"That is for sure and for certain."

Marigold stood by the tree and lifted her eyes to the broken branch. "I hate that Balim had to go through such a horrible struggle," she said, "but it seems the Lord was looking out for him."

Eli followed her gaze and then looked at the branch on the ground. The rope still looped around it, and one end was yet tied to the trunk of the big tree. "I can't believe such a large branch would just break off like that."

"It wouldn't," said Marigold with a smile on her freckled face.

Eli carefully considered the expression on Marigold's face. It was not reconciling with her words, and it puzzled him. "What do you mean?"

"See that hole?" Marigold pointed to a large cavity in the fallen branch.

Eli nodded.

"That hole is telling me two things. One, there is rot inside that tree. And two," Marigold bent both knees to stoop beside the branch, "see these wax moth cocoons?"

"I do."

"These wax moths move into abandoned hives and eat up all the wax. They destroy the old combs, but this was sure enough a hive at one time."

"Did the hive damage the tree?" Eli asked. "Is that what made the branch fall?"

"No, something else did that. It could have been a lightning strike, a bug, a fungus or something else that wounded the tree. But what I do know is that branch is hollow quite a ways inside."

"So when Balim's weight pulled on the limb, it broke off."

"Yep." Marigold nodded. "You might not know this, but one hive can hold thousands and thousands of bees that can make up to one hundred pounds of honey in a year."

"That would have to be a pretty big hole to hold all that."

Trigg pulled ahead of the other riders and signaled them to stop. He yanked the hood off his head. Calhoun and McGhee followed suit.

"I am headed to Goose Creek," said Trigg. "You two better ride on over to Burke's place and start that stump to burning."

"There ain't nothing to worry about," said Calhoun. "The deed is done and no one saw us. I'd rather go to Drake's and get a drink."

"Who do you think you are fooling?" Trigg sneered at Burke Calhoun with contempt in his eyes. "We all know you've got plenty of drink at your place. Now go on and make that alibi tight. I will check in with you when I get back."

Burke and Fred avoided the roads as they headed back to Calhoun's place just outside of town. Once they arrived, it only took a few minutes to warm the small amount of water needed and pour it into the stumps. They piled the shavings on top and added a few sticks in teepee fashion for good measure. Fred lit the shavings, and faster than either of them had ever seen before, the stump started burning from the inside out.

McGhee pulled a log a safe distance from the fire and set it on end. "Calhoun, why don't you go in and get us something to drink. I will get you a seat."

When Burke returned with a half-filled amber bottle and two short glasses, he found Fred sitting on a stump smoking and staring into the fire. Burke poured a shot into a glass and handed it to McGhee. Fred tossed the contents of the glass in his mouth in one motion, and then squeezed his eyes together and shook his head.

"Where did you get that rotgut, Calhoun?" McGhee squished his lips around his face.

"Made it myself," said Burke with a nefarious grin.

"You don't say?" McGhee spit on the ground, and then dragged on his quirley.

"I wonder what it feels like to hang to death," said Calhoun.

"One of these days you just might find out."

CHAPTER 30

"It hurts to swallow," Balim croaked out in a hoarse whisper. "I'm feeling a might dizzy, but at least I ain't seeing stars no more."

"That is all normal," said Doctor Byerly, "and you are doing well, but I am going to want you to stay here with me for a few days."

Balim gave the doctor a sideways glance. "If I am doing so *well*, why you want me to stay here fo?"

"In cases of strangulation, there is always a small chance the cartilage and bones in the throat were damaged, even if there is no external evidence. If they break or collapse, that could finish up the job those fellows started on you. We don't want that, now do we?"

"No, suh," Balim whispered and closed his eyes.

"But just look at you," said the doctor. "Your brain is fine."

"That is debatable," said Zion, grinning at his friend. "That assumes it was fine to begin with."

"Well, assuming that," said the doctor. "But you are breathing well, and these abrasions and scratches on your neck will heal up in no time."

"And he will be as ugly as before," said Zion.

"I think our patient needs to rest now, Mr. Coldwell," said Doctor Byerly, "without your compassionate nursing assistance."

"All right. All right," said Zion. "I can see where I am not wanted. I'll head back now and fill everyone in."

Balim opened his dark eyes and lifted the corners of his full lips in a quasi smile.

"You caused quite a stir tonight, my friend," Zion placed a hand on Balim's shoulder.

"'Twere not me with the stirring stick, Massa Zion."

"I will be back to check on you soon."

Garth brought the wagon to a stop in front of the doctor's office just as Zion was coming out the door.

"Massa Zion," Minnie called as she jumped out of the wagon without waiting for help, "how is he?"

"The doctor said he is doing fine," said Zion, "and he will be as ugly as ever in no time."

By the time Zion returned to Comfort Lodge, Marigold and Eli had been back for some time. The gathering, though not as lively as before, had turned from somber to reservedly calm. No one felt much like judging the baked goods, but the guests were willing to eat them and wash them down with cups of Florence's hot coffee.

"Do you have any idea who would have done such a thing?" James Erlanger asked Zion around a mouthful of Rosalie's cracked caramel pumpkin pie.

"Not yet," said Zion, "but you can be sure Sheriff Nash will be looking into it." He took the cup of coffee his wife handed to him. "I stopped by his office on the way back from town, and he said he had some suspicions about who was behind some of the other shenanigans going on around Washington."

"Zion," Marigold waited for her brother-in-law to acknowledge her call.

"Yes?"

"I just remembered something."

"Well, tell us," said Zion. "You saw more than anyone, and anything you remember could be very important."

"When Eli and I got to Briar Hollow and saw those hooded men, I was too surprised and scared to pay much attention to figuring out who those deadbeat curly wolves were." Marigold closed her eyes to bring her mental picture into better focus. "I don't know for sure," she said, "but I recognized one of their horses."

"Are you sure?" Logan asked.

"Oh, I am sure," said Marigold, nodding her head up and down several times. "I would recognize that silver pied horse anywhere."

"Pied Piper?" Zion could hardly believe his ears.

"Have you seen any other silver horse in these parts with star-shaped dapples, long feathers, and a white mane and tail?"

"No," said Zion. "I definitely have not, and I definitely would have noticed. I have had my eye on that Gypsy Vanner since he arrived in town."

"Trigg Simon," Garth spat the words out of his mouth. "I should have figured."

Marigold's disclosure caused Zion to have a memory flash of his own, and he recalled seeing the rump of a silver horse racing into the woods at the Corbin place.

"I think we need to take this news to Sheriff Nash right away," said Zion.

"My Pa's gone over to the salt works on business," said River, Simon, barely hiding his contempt at the sheriff's inquiries. "He has been in Goose Creek all day."

"I see," said the sheriff. "Well, thank you for your time."

"What do you think about that?" Zion asked Eudell Nash as they walked away from Simon's big house.

"Don't know what to think yet," said the sheriff, "but you can bet I will be verifying that bit of information."

The men mounted their horses. "I have been noticing Simon's been running with Fred McGhee and Burke Calhoun lately."

"That makes a neat and tidy threesome," said Zion. "And that is what we're looking for."

"I think I will take a ride out to Burke's place. It's just outside of town."

"I will come with," said Zion. He adjusted his hat and signaled his horse. "Giddup, West."

"I missed the singing," said Pansy Joy, "but at the same time, I did not feel like singing."

"It reminds me of that Scripture about the Israelites hanging their harps in the trees," said Penny.

"Hanging?" said Marigold. "Let's talk about something else."

"Oh. I am sorry." Penny cast her eyes to the ground. "I didn't mean it that way. I was just referring to how they lost their desire to sing because of their circumstances."

"I know," said Marigold. "It's ok."

Eli reined in the horse in front of the picnic tables and the Thalman's surrey came to a stop. "Here we are," he called to his family and then stepped down from the carriage to help them collect their dishes and say goodnight.

Florence and James joined the little group. "We are so glad you came," said Florence. "I hope to see you more often now that we're friends."

"I hope the same," said Judith. She smiled and extended her hand for a warm shake.

"That *kugel* was Ace high, Eden," said Marigold. "I thought I had tried every apple dish known to mankind, but you showed up with that receipt and sure made a mash."

Eden's dark eyes danced with pleasure and she threw her arms around Marigold for a happy hug.

His sister's outburst of emotion amused Eli, but as he watched the exchange, he wished he could know the pleasure of Marigold's embrace.

Marigold placed her hands on Eden's shoulders and looked her in the eye. "You come on out to the orchard any time," she said. "There is always something going on and folks around doing something."

Rosalie smiled and nodded. "Right now we're working on a yoyo quilt in our free time," she said. "If you like to sew you can come by after lunch. We try to steal an hour or so in the afternoon when the little ones are napping to work on it together. It is a great time to visit."

Eden looked to her mother, not knowing how she should respond.

"Oh, Mrs. Thalman," said Rosalie, "you are certainly welcome, as well."

"But what if I don't like to sew?" Judith chuckled. "I did not marry a tailor for no good reason."

"Well then," Rosalie laughed, "you can come and pour the coffee."

The sun had dipped in the sky, and the moon arisen. Its crescent glow, Eli noticed, was kind to Marigold's profile. He enjoyed watching her. Daylight. Twilight. Dark. It did not matter to him. Deep inside he knew that he would never tire of looking at her expressive, freckled face.

Marigold sensed his eyes upon her and slowly turned to offer him a nod and a smile. She wanted to thank him for being with her today. He had been such a strength to her, but it did not seem to be the right time and place for such a conversation.

She thought back to the times she had reached for his hand. Of course, she had held hands with her father and her brother, but this was an entirely different sensation. It rather reminded her of *Goldilocks and the Three Bears*. Pa's hand was too big. Lucas' hand was too little, but Eli's seemed just right.

The fact that he had placed himself between her and the hooded men made Marigold feel special in a way she had never experienced before. A man would not risk his safety for someone he did not care for, she reasoned. While Marigold never envisioned herself as a princess in need of a knight in shining armor, it warmed her heart to think that Eli would put himself in harm's way to protect her.

The Thalmans loaded themselves and their belongings in their conveyance. Marigold walked to the back seat where Eli sat next to his brother and sister.

It had been quite a day and her emotions were stumped, but she had a sweet peace in her heart that displayed itself on her countenance. The corners of her mouth lifted in a pleasant curve.

"Thank you for everything today." Marigold tipped her head to see Eli's face in his elevated position on the surrey seat.

Perhaps everyone might not find Eli Thalman show-stopping handsome, she thought. He did have a prominent nose and wore those wire-rimmed glasses, but Marigold did not focus on one feature over another. The combination of his dark curly hair, obsidian eyes and short beard on his elongated face all worked together to make a presentation she quite enjoyed looking at.

Marigold had become accustomed to having him near, and it was an effort to keep her hand from reaching up to touch his arm or take his hand. With a deep breath she checked her impulses and clasped her hands together in front of her calico skirt.

"Good night, Eli."

"Good night."

Stars twinkled in their navy canopy as Sheriff Eudell Nash and Zion Coldwell made their trip through town on horseback.

"I don't like to think of any of our locals doing such an abominable thing to another human being," said Zion, "but the truth is, three someones did."

"There will always be evil in the world," said Sheriff Nash. He sat tall in the saddle, his body moving in perfect rhythm with his horse's gait.

"That is true enough," said Zion, "but I don't like it in my little part of the world."

"Briar Hollow has always had a sense of sanctuary about it," said Nash.

"That is has." Zion nodded his agreement. "I remember the first time I rode in there. It got under my skin, I tell you."

"Briar Hollow? Or a certain red-headed Johnson girl?"

"Both, I guess," Zion chuckled. "And I want to keep both of them as safe and peaceful as I possibly can."

"You got any information on Calhoun or McGhee that could be useful?" asked Eudell. "All I have got is they have been running with Simon here lately. And as slippery as old Simon is, that won't be enough."

"Nothing that I can think of, Sheriff. And all we have on Simon is that Marigold thinks she saw his horse today. I have to admit, when she said that, I recalled seeing a flash of silver rump and a white tail out of the corner of my eye when I came up on Balim hanging in the tree at the old Corbin place."

"That is not much, but maybe we can flush something out of these croakers."

In front of Calhoun's ramshackle shed of a house, Burke and Fred sat on logs near a burning tree stump. An empty bottle and glasses lay on the ground between them.

"Hello, fellas," Sheriff Nash greeted the men as he dismounted.

"It is the law," slurred Calhoun with lolling head and bleary eyes that he turned towards McGhee. "Better look out now. Maybe they know something."

Fred stood to his feet and stuck out his hand for a shake. He teetered but caught himself from stumbling. "Howdy, Sheriff. What brings you out this late?"

"You know us peace officers like to make patrols now and again," said Nash. "Everything harmonious in your neck of the woods?"

"No disturbances here," said McGhee, "except we about wore ourselves out trying to get this stump out of Calhoun's yard."

Nash surveyed the site: Tools, chains, a burning stump and two drunk men seemed to corroborate McGhee's story.

"Where's your buddy tonight?"

"What buddy would that be?" McGhee answered the sheriff's question with one of his own. He wanted to keep Calhoun out of the conversation as much as possible. He was so liquored up there was no telling what he might say.

"Trigg Simon, of course," said the sheriff. "I have noticed you three have been running pretty tight here lately."

"Simon ain't nobody's buddy," Calhoun guffawed and lifted himself off the stump on wobbly legs. "Why he would up and run off on a body to save his own hide. Yes, he would."

"What do you mean?" Zion asked.

"Ole Calhoun has had one too many snorts of low-grade oh-be-joyful," said McGhee. "He ain't making no sense at all."

"Do you happen to know where Trigg Simon is this evening?" asked the sheriff.

"Should I?" McGhee asked, a blank expression on his face.

"Not necessarily," said Nash. "Just wondering."

"Why all the questions, Sheriff?" McGhee shifted his weight from one booted foot to the other.

"We did have an incident today, and I am just making some rounds about town doing a little investigating."

"If you want to investigate that tree stump, I'll pull you up a log," said McGhee. "If you want to talk to Trigg Simon, I suggest you go to his house."

"But he run off to Garrards in Goose Creek," said Calhoun. "Don't you remember?"

CHAPTER 31

Sitting up in his bed, Eli glanced across the room. Asher's breathing was slow and steady, but he was wide awake. The events of the day whirled in his mind like dancers at a wedding, and he was finding it hard to settle down for the night. A picnic. A girl. A hanging. A girl. A prayer. A girl. Around and around they spun.

The lamp flickered at his bedside casting a glow on the books stacked on the small table. He picked up the *Tanakh* that rested on the top of the pile and turned to where he had left off reading in Isaiah.

Eli longed for more of God. What he had felt in the little cabin when he and Minnie held hands at the table had captured his spirit and he yearned for more.

Speak to me from Your Word, Elohim, HaShem, Adonai. You are the Eternal One—and that means today—right now You are alive and here with me in this little room.

Eli had read through Isaiah many times. Although he was not well versed in the teachings of what Christians called the New Testament, he knew enough to connect some of the tenets of the Christian faith with his own.

Isaiah had written prophetic words about the Messiah that was to come, and they seemed more and more to pair with what he had heard of Jesus.

Isaiah spoke prophetically that the Messiah would be born of a virgin and have a ministry in Galilee. An heir to the throne of David, he would be both exalted and spat upon, even disfigured by suffering. Isaiah wrote that Messiah's wounds were for mankind's transgressions, and his bruises for iniquities—that peace and healing came through his undeserved punishment and the stripes he took on his body.

The things he read in Isaiah did not reconcile with the Jewish teaching that Messiah would be a great political leader who would win battles for Israel, and that Messiah would be a man, not a God-man. His redemption would be to restore Jerusalem and establish a government in Israel that would be the center of world government for both Jews and gentiles.

Eli recalled reading how the Messiah would be rejected, and he was pricked in his conscience. How could Elohim lay on the Messiah the iniquity of all the world and then suffer their rejection?

Show me Your truth, Elohim. I long to know You more.

Eli moved the ribbon marker out of the way and began reading in Chapter 9. His finger trailed the precious words, but then stopped abruptly.

"For a child is born unto us, a son is given unto us; and the government is upon his shoulder; and his name is called Pele-joez-el-gibbor-Abi-ad-sar-shalom."

The child that is born is a gift for the children of Israel? The son will have all the government upon one shoulder? His name is called Pele-joez-el-gibbor-Abi-ad-sar-shalom? Wonderful? Counselor? Mighty God? Everlasting Father? Prince of Peace?

How can a man be all these things? Both the son and the Everlasting Father?

Eli closed the book and pondered what he read. If the Messiah was born of a virgin, impregnated by the Spirit of the Creator God, that would make Him fully human and fully God.

He recalled the teachings he had received since he was a young man. In the *Midrash*, a book of rabbinic literature, the Tabernacle of Moses was compared to a cave near the sea. When the sea roars and floods the cave, the cave fills with water, but the sea is not missing anything. Eli had been taught that in the same way, an outward materialization of God's presence filled the Tabernacle in the wilderness while His Spirit was yet ever present and radiating over all the world.

He wondered if this analogy applied to the Christian view of Messiah. Did they believe Messiah to be man and God at the same time? Made by the uniting of a maiden's egg with God's Spirit, wouldn't that give the God-man all the character, power and authority of deity—while at the same time Almighty God continued to rule and reign over the universe?

Oy vey. So much to think about, but I have got to get some sleep.

Eli turned down the wick. Darkness closed in around him.

You know my heart, Elohim. It is only You—Your truth that I seek.

"Something is definitely not sitting right in my gizzard," said Zion.

"I know what you mean," said Nash. "I guess I will be riding out to Goose Creek tomorrow. If this threesome is involved like I am suspecting they are, I need something to get their alibies nailed to the wall."

"Want some company?"

"If you are free." Nash turned to look at Zion. "Is horse farming slow these days?"

Zion laughed. "No, sir. I just have competent hands. Angus is a pro, and Logan is doing a bang up job with bookwork and promotions. Coldwell Farms is prospering under the blessings and favor of the Good Lord."

"You are right about that," said Nash, "but you are down one of those good hands right now."

"That is true," said Zion, "I guess I am anxious to do anything I can to help figure out this quandary."

"If we can't stop the low lifes who did this, it might spur them on to more lynchings in the future," said Eudell. "They have been increasing in the state here lately, in Frankfurt, Louisville, Owensboro, and two in Paris."

Zion nodded. "And if we can't find and stop them, they just might feel brazen enough to come back and try to finish the job on Balim."

Marigold peered out the small window of her loft bedroom and stared at the stars in the indigo sky. She wondered if Eli was looking at the same stars. Was he having as a hard a time drifting off to dreamland as she was?

Who am I kidding, Marigold scolded herself. *I have been living in dreamland.*

What has gotten ahold of me, Lord?

I have been trying to let Your peace be my guide, but sometimes I get to wondering if my natural desires haven't been shouting a bit louder than that peace seems to be a whispering. All the girls my age have done married off and set up housekeeping on their own, and here I am still with Pa and nary a prospect for a husband—before now.

Visions of Eli sprang forth from her memory and paraded before her—his kindness, his courteous regard, his fine handsomeness. He seemed to show up right when she needed rescuing or a friend.

Marigold knew she was in a dilemma of her own making, but she did not know how she was going to make things right. She had let her emotions have their fun, and now she was likely going to have to pay a high price for her carelessness.

Oh, Jesus. I know I can't yoke up with a non-Christian and be in Your perfect will. The truth is sometimes I think settling somewhere "close enough" to Your will could work out right fine. But I know that is some kind of namby-pamby, airy-fairy thinking.

How can I have made such a mess of things?

Rosalie stood at the end of her bed in a cotton chemise running a boar bristle brush through her auburn hair. "It is hard to be excited about Pa's birthday with everything that is been happening around here," she said.

"That is the truth," said Zion as he watched his wife prepare for bed. Every night she braided her waist-length auburn hair to keep it from tangling while she slept. Tonight it made a pretty picture at the end of an especially hard day.

"I hope the suit will be ready on time," said Rosalie.

"Mr. Thalman assured me he was just putting on the finishing touches." Zion patted the bed and flipped the corner of the Rose of Sharon quilt for his wife to slip in beside him. "How are those fancy socks coming?"

Rosalie smiled. "They have been a bit of a challenge, but I have to say, I like the way they are turning out. They have . . . personality."

"Well, so does your pa."

Rosalie rolled on her side, laid her head on Zion's chest and cuddled under his strong arm. "Abby is doing well," she said.

"That is something to be thankful for." Zion yawned.

"I can't believe she slept through everything this afternoon," said Rosalie, "but when she got up, she was bright eyed and ate well."

"Mmhmmm." Zion closed his eyes.

"The gash on her head is starting to close up on the ends and the swelling is all but gone."

"All but gone."

Zion drew in a breath with a soft snort and then transitioned to even, quiet breathing.

Rosalie grinned.

Well, it is just You and me, Lord.

Thank You for watching over Balim today. Where would we be without Your hand of protection upon us? Bring a quick healing to him so he can come home to Briar Hollow where he belongs.

Thank You for the work of healing You are doing in little Abby. Oh, how we have needed You these last trying days.

I pray You would let Your peace settle into Briar Hollow and comfort Minnie and Abram— comfort all those who have been wounded in body or soul.

And, Lord, I don't know why You have put such a burden in my heart for the Thalman family, but I pray You will continue to bring us together with opportunities to share the love of Jesus with them. They are good people with a strong faith, and it hurts my heart that they have not yet come to know You for who You really are—Emmanuel, God with us.

And Lord, it is impossible to miss the looks that pass between Eli and Marigold, so I ask You to accomplish Your will in this situation. I know it is Your heart's desire to see every soul saved, so I pray You will reveal Yourself to Eli somehow. His heart is so tender.

I know it's hard to wait for the right person to marry, but it has got to be harder to be married to the wrong one for the rest of a person's life. So if needs be, I ask You to help Marigold back out of any attachments she has made in her heart to Eli Thalman that are outside of Your purpose and plan.

CHAPTER 32

Pansy Joy leaned over the fence and scratched Blossom's chest. The goat rubbed her head against her arm in approval. "I am planning to go to town for Pa's suit tomorrow," she said.

Marigold lifted the top off a covered bin and thrust a tin scoop into the grain. Billy beat the does to the feeder before Marigold dumped the tin's contents and went back for another scoop. Bleating their way to Billy's side, Blossom and Blondie nudged their way in, and before Marigold returned with a second scoop, the three goats were chewing away, their bottom lips circling around the top with each chomp.

"That is nice," said Marigold. She lifted the tin scoop and tipped it over the feeder. With fastened scrutiny, Marigold watched the feed slowly, slowly spill out in the receptacle below. The sound of grain falling on grain made a pleasant crackling noise.

"You want to come with me?" Pansy Joy grabbed a flake of hay from a nearby bale and reaching across the fence, pitched it in the goats' manger.

Marigold shook her head, her focus still on the goat feeder. "No," she said. "I have things to do around here."

"Oh, come on," said Pansy Joy. "We have been in on this together since the beginning. You should come with me to pick it up."

A dull ache swelled inside Marigold. The fact was she wanted to go to town right now, but she had to be honest with herself and God. If a body was not honest with themselves and the Good Lord, they were heading up the flume, for sure and for certain.

No. She had determined to rein in her runaway heart and trust the Lord to bring His will to pass without her help.

With a blank expression on her face, Marigold looked her cajoling sister in the eye. "I have been to town enough lately, PJ. I am staying home for awhile."

"Are you worried something might happen to Minnie or the kids?" Pansy Joy fished for some reason that would keep her sister home when she knew she wanted to go.

"No."

"Did something happen between you and Eli?"

Marigold snapped her head at her sister, a look of bewilderment on her features. "What would make you say a fool thing like that?"

"Excuse me." Pansy Joy backed up a step. "Don't bite my head off."

Marigold heaved a long sigh through pursed lips. The tension had been building in her all morning, and she hoped to release some with her long exhale.

"Did you know there was a dead chicken in the run this morning?" Marigold asked.

"Oh, no," said Pansy Joy. Concern filled her bright eyes. "Has that got you upset?"

"Well, yes and no." Marigold hung the tin scoop on a nail in the wall and smoothed her calico skirts. "I know animals die. It is just a shame, because this was one of our best layers and it did not have to happen."

"Do you know why it died then?"

Marigold turned her gaze to the ground. "Beans."

"Beans?" A look of confusion furrowed Pansy Joy's brow. "What are you talking about? I feed beans to our chickens all the time."

"Not dried ones."

Silence hung for a minute while Pansy Joy processed the information. "Did you feed a chicken dried beans on purpose?"

Marigold forcefully shook her head, sending her honey-colored braids swinging back and forth across her shoulders. "Do you think I would do that?"

"I did not," said Pansy Joy. "That is why I asked. Tell me what happened?"

"Yesterday before the picnic, while I was watching Dahlia and Mattie, I sewed up some bean bags for Abby and Abram out of some of Rosalie's scraps."

"That was a sweet thing to do." Pansy Joy smiled at her sister.

"Yeah," Marigold sighed. "Sweet."

"Go on."

"I was on my way to deliver them, but I tripped on a root in the yard and dropped one. It split open like a watermelon falling from a two-story building."

"Oh, no!" Pansy Joy's hands flew over her open mouth. "I am so sorry."

"I realized I better not give them to the kids to play with or Minnie might not be too happy with me, so I pitched them in the trash. I knew I did not get all the beans, but I was in a hurry, and planned to go back for them later, but I forgot."

"Oh, Marigold. Are you sure that is what happened to the chicken?"

"If you put two and two together, you get four." Marigold shrugged. "The beans were gone and the chicken was dead. That equals four to me."

"I guess it is chicken for supper tonight then?"

"Oh, you." Marigold waved a finger at Pansy Joy.

"Well, that is better now," said Pansy Joy placing her hands on her hips. "There is a bit of the old Marigold spark."

Marigold wagged her head and chuckled.

"So are you coming to town with me tomorrow or not?" Pansy Joy asked. "The chicken won't care one way or the other."

Asher rose early, dressed for the day and headed to the kitchen for coffee and hopefully something tasty to go with it.

The closing of the bedroom door roused Eli from his dream. He sat up in bed and rubbed his gritty eyes with his fists.

"Jesus?"

Perplexed, Eli shook his head and tried to collect his thoughts.

The dream had been so vivid. It replayed before his closed eyes in stunning detail.

One moment he had been reading from the book of Isaiah in his bed, pondering the Scriptures and what the prophet had foretold of the coming Messiah.

In a flash, he was in Minnie's kitchen holding her hand in his. The same sensation he had experienced at her table swept over him in his dream.

From there the scene flashed to the Corbin place, the site of Balim's hanging. Everything was as he had left it yesterday afternoon, yet there was something ethereal, something supernatural filling the atmosphere. Eli sensed the presence of angels. It was as if he could almost hear them singing *holy, holy, holy*.

Eli dropped to his knees beside the fallen branch. He wanted to pray, but he was not sure how.

Pray to the God of Abraham, Isaac and Jacob.

The impression was so strong Eli dared not deny it. He lifted his hands and threw back his head. With a desperate cry, he called out, "Oh, God of Abraham, Isaac and Jacob, help me."

Eli lowered his head, closed his eyes and waited for he knew not what.

Suddenly he felt a strong presence in front of him and slowly opened his eyes. Before him stood the glowing form of a man in a long white robe.

He was too frightened to look up, but there was no mistaking the identity of this man.

There were holes in His feet.

Tenderly, He reached out to Eli with nail-scarred hands.

"I AM that I AM."

"His alibi is tight," said Nash. "Garrard is backing Simon up 100 percent. I am not sure we are going to be able to pin anything on him or his cohorts."

"Something will turn up," said Zion. He adjusted his hat on his head. His body swayed effortlessly with the motion of the horse beneath him.

"You are probably right." The sheriff nodded. "These arrogant types usually get cocky and overplay their hands."

"What do you think of Calhoun?" Zion asked.

"I think he is the weak link, especially with a little who-hit john in his system, but there is something about McGhee, too.

I think he has a stronger streak of conscience. I may try to tap into that."

The miles from Goose Creek to Washington were long, but well spent. Zion enjoyed the time with Sheriff Nash and the two had the opportunity to discuss several concerns in the area.

By the time Zion arrived in Briar Hollow, he was ready to trade his saddle in for a feather mattress.

"How is Balim today?" Zion asked Rosalie. He sat in a ladder back chair beside the kitchen table, his elbows on his knees.

"Very well." Rosalie wore a broad smile on her heart-shaped face. "I took some supper down earlier, and his appetite was voracious. He hardly left enough for Minnie."

"That is not like Balim." Zion used both hands to lift a booted foot over one knee.

"Oh, he did not know Minnie had not had supper. Besides she was more than happy to see him sitting up and eating with such enthusiasm. It was encouraging, I have to say."

Zion tugged at his boot, but it did not budge. Sensing his weariness, Rosalie positioned herself in front of him on the floor. "Let me help."

"Woman," Zion mustered some strength in his voice, "if there comes a time I can't take off my own boots, I will be happy to let you. For now, I am just glad I can do it for myself."

With an unexpected adrenalin rally, Zion pulled off one boot and then the next.

"Did I miss anything else today?"

"We did lose a chicken," said Rosalie. "Marigold took it pretty hard."

"Loosing a chicken happens regular enough. Why did it bother Marigold?"

"Because it was one of our best layers, and she felt to blame. It got ahold of some dried beans she had dropped outside, and you know they have to be cooked or they are poisonous to chickens."

Zion pinched his lips into a line and shook his head. "Poor Marigold. She did not need that on top of everything else that has been going on around here."

Rosalie circled around the chair and kneaded the taut muscles in Zion's broad shoulders. "It got me to thinking."

"Mmmm. Can you think and rub at the same time?"

"I think so. As I was saying, that bird dying because it ate something it should not have eaten got me to thinking that maybe that is how prejudice works."

"How so?"

"A person can't be born prejudice, can they?" Rosalie asked.

"It doesn't seem so to me," said Zion. "The young-uns around here did not come out that way, and still aren't."

"Exactly my point." Rosalie slipped around the chair again and this time slid sideways onto Zion's lap. He wrapped his arms around her as much to enjoy her closeness as to keep her steady.

"Somebody has to 'feed' prejudice—to teach it. It is just not natural in a loving environment."

"I see what you mean." Zion buried his nose in his wife's hair and drank in the fresh scent of lavender.

"Or maybe it is because people are hurt and don't feel good enough so they put others down."

"Or use them," said Zion. "Some folks try to make others feel lesser so they can use them for selfish purposes."

"It is sad," said Rosalie, "but it all goes back to my point. Prejudice is not a natural result in a loving environment. If everyone felt loved, accepted and appreciated for who they were, they would not have hostile or unreasonable opinions of others."

"So if we feed love and acceptance, that should grow," said Zion.

"And if we don't, then hatefulness and exclusion can grow where love and acceptance should have been all along."

CHAPTER 33

E li finished pressing the seam in Matthias Johnson's navy suit jacket while Asher stood at the counter cutting out varying sizes of denim dungarees.

"You are awfully quiet today, brother." Asher usually enjoyed quite the banter with Eli in the workroom of Thalman and Sons Clothiers, but today he could almost hear the crickets outside.

"When you are quiet, you can hear more," said Eli. He pushed his glasses in place with both hands and offered a negligible smile.

While Eli had a tremendous levity in his spirit this morning, it was married to a very real apprehension. Instinctively knowing he was on the edge of a precipice, Eli did not want to say anything wrong or make any wrong moves.

"You usually talk my ear off, brother," said Asher. "Is everything all right?"

"Words should be weighed and not counted," said Hiram. He lifted his head from his work at the sewing machine. "And no one is as deaf as the one who will not listen."

The bells on the door of the shop announced an incoming customer in the receiving area. "Well, I hear the bells," said Eli. "I will see who is here."

"Good morning, Mr. Thalman," Pansy Joy greeted Eli with a bright smile. She watched his countenance contort ever so slightly as he looked first to her and then to Penny at her side. He cast a quick glance out the shop window to their buggy parked outside, and then composed himself when he realized Marigold had not come.

Eli had wanted so much to see Marigold this morning of all mornings. When his father had told him Matthias Johnson's suit needed pressing because it was being picked up today, he was certain providence had played a part in ordering his circumstances.

His heart had taken wing when he saw the first Johnson daughter, but then sank when he realized her sister-in-law had come instead of the honey-haired, freckle-faced girl who filled his thoughts.

"Mrs. Eldridge," Eli nodded. "I was just ironing your father's suit. I have only the lapels left to finish. Would you like to sit while I ready everything for you?"

Eli motioned the girls to the carved table in the corner and pulled out one of the upholstered Belter chairs.

"Thank you," said Pansy Joy. She sat in the chair offered.

Eli pulled a second chair out for Penny. "Would you like coffee?" he asked.

"Oh, no thank you," said Penny with a shake of her head, "not if you are only going to be a few minutes."

"All right then. I will be back with your order shortly."

True to his word, Eli returned in less than five minutes with the navy ditto suit in hand. Hiram and Asher followed him out of the workroom.

"Oh, it is lovely," said Penny.

"I can't wait to see him in it," said Pansy Joy with a smile.

"Have the other items come in?" asked Penny.

Hiram nodded to Asher who stepped behind the counter and retrieved a box containing the ordered accouterments: a top hat, cane and pocket watch.

Pansy Joy reached inside the basket she had brought in from the buggy and pulled out a crisply folded sheet. "I brought this to carry the suit home," she said. "It will keep it clean and covered, just in case Pa should show up at Rosalie's."

"I have a little something to add," said Eli. He laid the matching pants and jacket on the table revealing his surprise: a double-breasted, shawl-collared vest in a burgundy, cream and fawn brocade draped over his arm.

"It is exquisite," Penny gasped her pleasure. "How very kind and thoughtful of you."

"I love it," said Pansy Joy. "The colors and pattern are perfect."

"And when he wears this," Penny slipped the fold of the shawl collar between her delicate fingers, "it will be like having a second suit altogether."

"I am glad you like it." Eli's obsidian eyes twinkled behind his wire-rimmed glasses.

"Very nice, son," said Hiram.

"I wish you could be there when he opens it," said Pansy Joy, "but we are keeping things small—just family. Pa does not like to be fussed over, even on his birthday."

"That is understandable," said Eli. "He should certainly feel appreciated and cared for with all your family has done to honor him."

"It speaks to his character," said Hiram.

"Oh, he is a character all right," said Pansy Joy with a toothy grin, and then her countenance softened with loving thoughts of her father. "He is a right wonderful Pa, too."

At the tan yard, Fred McGhee used a sturdy pole to pull a hide from the vat where it had been soaking in a mixture of water and lime. The smell was strong as he agitated the contents in the odorous vat, but the hide looked ready. The lime had eaten away the top hair-bearing layers of skin.

Wearing a well-worn leather apron with robust leather straps reinforced with copper rivets, McGhee spread the hide over a large log that was tilted at a 45 degree pitch angle to the floor. The curve of the log would protect the hide from nicks and cuts during the scraping, but first it had to dry before he scraped away any remaining hair on the top and then flipped it to remove residual fat or tissue from the underside.

Across the tan yard were several works in process. Some had already received their first soaking and stripping and had been returned to the vats with tannin made from tree bark added for a final soaking. Other hides of elk and deer hung over drying lines carefully positioned to keep the sides of the hides from touching.

Tools of the trade: a buffer, fleshing knife, sleeker, and un-hairing knife, hung from pegs on the wall of the workshop. In the yard stood a large circular stone mill with a huge grinding stone where a horse walked in circles around the mill grinding oak-tree bark for tannin.

The clip clop of horses' hooves on the road slowed as they approached the tan yard. Without looking up from his work, McGhee knew who it was. Trigg Simon.

"How was Goose Creek?" Fred threw the question over his shoulder.

"Long ride." Trigg dismounted. "Garrard is ornery as ever, but he covered for me."

"The law came by Calhoun's place Sunday night," said McGhee. He turned to look at Simon.

"And?" Trigg glared at McGhee.

"And Calhoun is a pathetic drunk," he said. "I am not so sure it was wise to bring him in on precarious matters."

"Oh, Calhoun is all right," said Trigg. "He didn't shoot his mouth off, did he?"

"With some intervention on my part, I was able to deflect the sheriff's attention away from his roostered up remarks. If his brains were in a bird, I swear it would start flying backwards."

McGhee stepped to the workbench and drew a dipper full of water out of a bucket. "So have you heard how things played out?"

"Played out?" Trigg spread his legs slightly apart and hooked his thumbs in his belt. "What do you mean?"

Fred took a long drink from the dipper. "He survived the lynching."

"Is that a bluff, or do you mean it for real play?" Trigg could not believe what he had just heard.

"Genuine fact." McGhee gave a decisive nod. "Simon pure."

Trigg pulled his hat off his head and ruffled his hair with his fingers. "I will have to give this some thought."

"You do that," said Fred.

"Did you finish the socks?" Marigold asked Rosalie.

"All but the ribbing on one." Rosalie pinned the last fold of Mattie's diaper with a safety pin.

Marigold's mind raced back to Thalman and Sons Clothiers and the day she went into town for the pins. In particular, she remembered Eli standing in front of her studying her with those dark eyes of his that seemed to penetrate her to the very core of her being. She had fidgeted beneath his gaze, but delighted in it, as well.

"Neighbors and friends help each other out in emergencies," he had said.

Neighbors and friends.

Neighbors and friends.

The words echoed through her dampened heart and lit a glimmer of possibility where there had been only desolation moments before. She did not have to write Eli out of her life. Why, that was not even the Christian thing to do, after all. The Bible said plain and clear that believers were to be hospitable to strangers—even entertain them.

Though she yearned for a more intimate relationship with Eli, Marigold realized in a moment that if she kept her emotions in check, there was no reason not to be a good neighbor and friend to Eli and all the Thalmans.

Pansy Joy opened the door to the Coldwell cabin and practically bounced inside with the suit lifted high off the ground. "We're here," she said. Penny followed her inside carrying a rectangular box.

"Oh, good." Rosalie set the baby on a blanket on the floor. "I can't wait to see it."

"It is handsome, indeed," said Penny, "and you should see what Eli made for your Pa. He is such a nice young man."

Marigold smiled and stayed out of the way while Pansy Joy laid out the wrapped suit on the table and pulled the sheet back. It was fine craftsmanship and quality fabric, and it was sure to fit Matthias Johnson to perfection since it was custom made using some of his old work clothes for a pattern.

"Mine will be a surprise," said Penny. "Can I keep these here, Rosalie?"

"Sure," she said. "There is room in the chest at the end of my bed. Just put them in there."

While Penny tucked the gifts in their hiding place Rosalie pulled out the basket of calico yoyos. "Are you going to join us for the quilting today, Marigold?"

"I think I better head back home and look to supper."

"You would rather cook than quilt?" asked Pansy Joy.

"I would rather clean deep litter out of the chicken coop after a long winter than quilt," Marigold chuckled. "My last sewing efforts proved fatal."

Lucas stood outside the Johnson cabin, his thin pink lips bent in a toothy smile that stretched across his baby face.

"I got it, Marigold," his green eyes beamed.

"Got what, Lukey?" Marigold ruffled his saddle brown hair.

"The Man on the Flying Trapeze!"

"Really? That is great," said Marigold. "Well, let it fly."

"Wait," said Lucas, "I have to get the tension out of the string first. That was my biggest problem all along."

He took the yoyo off his hand and starting at the top, pulled the string all the way down. When it completely untangled, he put it back on his finger. Starting with the yoyo above his shoulder, Lucas threw it out and did a quick release that sent the yoyo swinging. With a quick maneuver, the yoyo hopped over his left index finger and landed on the string.

"Bully for you!" Marigold grinned. "Did you beat Ben Dryfus in figuring it out?"

"I can't say for sure, but I think so."

"Say," Marigold surveyed the grounds, "where is Pa?"

"Taking a siesta."

"Worked himself to exhaustion, huh?"

"He said he was played out."

"So you are out here just killing time until he wakes up?"

"Pretty much," said Lucas, "and getting my trick down pat before I meet up with Ben."

Marigold leaned in to her brother and whispered, "I barely escaped a quilting bee. I better find something to do with myself or I will be hearing some squawking from the hens."

The kaleidoscope!

With a plan in place, Marigold gently opened the cabin door thankful when she saw her father's closed bedroom door. With careful steps she padded across the room, retrieved the wrapped kaleidoscope, and then exited back in the yard.

"Lucas," she said, "I have been holding on to this for some time now, and I think it is time to make a delivery. I am going to town to see Balim. If Pa wakes up, tell him I have supper all planned and I will be back in plenty of time to put it all together."

"All right," said Lucas. "Tell Balim hey for me, and I am glad he is feeling better."

"I will." Marigold strode across the property and turned left on the road to town. It felt good to be out walking in the sunshine on a crisp fall day. She felt lighter than she had in a long time, and she wanted to savor every moment.

She passed the orchard, and then Briar Hollow, whistling as she continued on her way. Comfort Lodge marked the halfway point, and before she knew it, she was in town. She could hardly believe it when she saw Eli walking her way, smiling and waving.

"Marigold," he called out and hurried towards her, the tape measure around his neck swinging back and forth. "I am so glad to see you."

Marigold smiled the bright bold smile Eli had come to love. "I am glad to see you, too."

"I was worried when you did not come for the suit today with your sister. Are you all right?"

"Oh, I am fine." Marigold was touched by his thoughtful concern, but she refused to let her heart go soft. She was determined to be the best friend, neighbor and Christian witness she could be to this young man who had come to mean so much.

"I just came to town to make a delivery."

Eli spied the package in her hands. "Is that the same package you carried from town not too long ago?"

Marigold's nose crinkled over her smile and she waggled her head back and forth. "It is at that, my friend. And I am bound and determined I am going to deliver this today by hook or by crook."

"Are you taking it to Balim?"

"I sure am," said Marigold. "He is just laying around the doc's office. Maybe it will help him pass the time. He can share it with the little ones when he goes home—hopefully soon."

"I won't keep you," said Eli, "but I was hoping to have a chance to speak with you. Something incredible happened early this morning."

"Really?" Marigold's brows arched in surprise. "Do you want to talk now? I have some time."

Eli looked down the street. Duty called. "I should get back to work now. We are pushing to make the denim dungarees before Rueben returns. Could I come see you tonight after supper?"

God, what are You doing to me? Everything in Marigold wanted to throw herself in his arms, but she had made a commitment to the Lord, and she knew she could not back down. Still, there was something different in Eli's eyes. His request seemed recklessly urgent, but could she trust herself to meet with him?

Eli noted the bewildered look in Marigold's brown eyes. He sensed her hesitancy, but his need to talk to her pressed him on. Things were changing so fast for him. He longed to share them with her, but she looked almost frightened.

With resolve, he pushed past his concerns and clasped a hand around her forearm. "Marigold, I had a dream. I need to talk to someone about it. Please say yes."

Eli's out-of-character behavior captured Marigold's curiosity. Of course she wanted to see him, too, as long as it was a "friendly" visit, and she was definitely interested in hearing what had moved him with such passion.

"Neighbors and friends help each other out," said Marigold with a smile.

Relief flooded Eli's features. "Yes," he said. "Yes, they do."

CHAPTER 34

M r. Jenkins waved Eli off the street and into the post office. The log building was the first post office to open west of the Appalachian Mountains in 1789, and served not only Kentucky, but also Ohio, Indiana, Illinois, Wisconsin, and Minnesota.

"Did you need me?" Eli asked the clerk.

"Got a package for you," said the clerk. "It came on the coach this afternoon from Auburn."

"Thank you, Mr. Jenkins." Eli accepted the package addressed to his father and hurried back to the shop.

"Abba," Eli called over the ringing of the doorbells, "you have a package."

Hiram stood from the sewing machine and walked to the table where Eli had placed the package. He opened it and found inside a pair of soft burgundy dress gloves.

"I had forgotten all about these," Hiram said. "The family ordered them separately, so they did not come in with the other items."

"Are those for Mr. Johnson?" asked Asher.

"Yes, they are."

"The party is tomorrow," said Eli. "Would you like me to deliver them later?"

"Thank you," said Hiram. "It would be nice to have the entire ensemble there for the celebration."

"I will go after supper."

Eli hummed and lined up the sides of a front piece and a back piece of a pants leg, right sides facing in. He handed it to his father, and Hiram ran the seam down the leg with the sewing machine while Eli assembled the next two pieces.

Hiram handed the leg to Asher who pressed the seam open and then turned the leg inside out. From there, it would be slipped into the right-side-out leg when it was sewn and pressed, and then the legs would be sewn together at the crotch. The Thalman men were on a roll, cranking out pair after pair of denim dungarees in no time flat.

Eli worked with care and precision, but with one eye on the clock. When Eden called down the stairs announcing that supper was ready, he was the first to lay aside his work and head out of the workroom. He gave a valiant effort at the table, trying to measure the pace he consumed his meal and be attentive to the conversation.

Finally, Hiram closed out the meal with prayer.

"For all this, Lord our God, we give thanks to You and bless You. May Your Name be blessed by the mouth of every living being, constantly and forever, as it is written: When you have eaten and are satiated, you shall bless the Lord your God for the good land which He has given you. Blessed are You, Lord, for the land and for the sustenance."

"Amen. Thank you for dinner, Ema." Eli pushed back from the table. "Is it all right if I take the surrey, Abba?"

Hiram nodded his approval.

"Where are you going?" asked Eden.

"To Briar Hollow," said Eli as he slipped on his jacket. "A package came in for Mr. Johnson's birthday. I want to make sure they get the rest of his gift on time for the party tomorrow."

"I could take it out tomorrow while you are working," Eden offered.

Eli shook his head. "Oh, no, thank you, Eden. I have been looking forward to getting some fresh air all day."

"You should see how many dungarees we made today," said Asher, scooting his chair back from the table. He rubbed his left shoulder with his right hand. "Fresh air sounds good, but I am ready to sit for awhile."

Eli started for the door.

"Eli," Hiram called to his son.

"Yes, Abba?"

"You forgot the gloves."

"Oh," Eli stuttered and picked up the gloves from the counter. "Right." He offered a sheepish smile, and then disappeared out the door.

"So what did Balim think of the kaleidoscope?" Matthias asked Marigold at the supper table.

"He studied it a long while before he said anything." Marigold scooped some applesauce on top of a thick slice of ham. "He seemed pretty fascinated with it, but then they are pretty captivating to most folks.

"He looked in the glass, and turned it, and looked some more," said Marigold. "Then he said the patterns and colors shifting reminded him of the days and seasons that keep changing and painting new pictures for folks to look at."

"That sounds like Balim." Matthias stabbed a forkful of greens. "Things have certainly been changing in the last few years. I never thought we would have a civil war, and then when we did, I wondered if the nation would survive it. But here we are now learning to live life from a new perspective."

"I think that is what Balim was getting at," said Marigold.

"Guess what?" Lucas grinned up at his big sister with sparkling eyes.

"What, Lukey?"

"I beat ole Ben Dryfus learning the yoyo trick," he said. "It sure felt good when he told me."

"I'll bet," said Marigold. She stood and walked to the stove for the coffeepot.

A knock sounded on the door.

Lucas jumped to his feet and ran to the door. "I'll get it."

"Oh, hey, Eli." Lucas smiled and opened the door wide. "I was just telling Pa and Marigold I beat Ben Dryfus learning the Man on the Flying Trapeze. You were right. I just had to make sure I had the tension out of the rope. Once I did, it just came with a little practice."

"I am glad to hear that, Lucas." Eli smiled at the boy and then looked around the room. "May I come in?"

"Sure thing, young man." Matthias nodded. "We were just getting ready for some coffee. Would you like some?"

"That would be fine as cream gravy," said Eli with a grin.

Marigold blushed.

"I see you have been picking up some of my daughter's vernacular," said Matthias.

"That and more," said Eli, "and hopefully more to come."

Marigold could hardly believe Eli's boldness. What could he be talking about? And right to her pa, no less?

Matthias studied the young man in front of him. *What's going on, Lord? I have got Holy Ghost gooseflesh running up and down my arms like ants on a picnic blanket.*

"Mr. Johnson, I would like to speak to your daughter, but can we talk first?"

"You mean just you and me, son?"

"Maybe later," said Eli with a peculiar expression on his face, "but for now, together is fine."

Marigold handed Eli a mug of coffee. Wonder swam in her big brown eyes. *What has gotten into you, Eli Thalman?*

"If you are wondering what has gotten into me tonight," said Eli, "I have the answer."

Eyes wide, Marigold coughed and threw a hand over her mouth.

For a moment Eli could not speak. His dark eyes glistened with unshed tears.

"He came to me."

Eli pinched his lips together and shook his head.

"Jesus," he said, "He came to me last night."

Marigold gasped. Her chest heaved in a silent sob, and a tear slid from one eye down a freckled cheek.

"Oh, Eli," she said. "Tell us what happened."

"I have been searching the Scriptures for some time now, but lately I have been repeatedly drawn to the writings of Isaiah."

Matthias's lips curved upward in a smile, and a wave of peace swept over his spirit. He nodded his head, encouraging Eli to go on with his story.

"Yesterday, when I was with Minnie, I felt so helpless. I wanted to comfort her, but I did not know how to pray—with her being a Christian and me a Jew. But she was so still and her sorrow so deep I just had to do something. I took her hand and recited one of King David's writings, what you call the twenty-third psalm.

"As I spoke the words, a peaceful presence seemed to enter the room. When she said, 'Yes, Jesus,' I felt a power surge from her hand into mine. It was an amazing experience."

"Holy Ghost fire," said Matthias with a nod.

"Anyway, right before I went to bed last night I picked up my reading in Isaiah. When I got to the part about the Son being born, and He would be called Wonderful, Counselor, the Mighty God, the Everlasting Father . . . well, I could not read any further. I prayed and then fell asleep.

"Early in the morning, I had a dream, but it was more than a dream. I know it was, because it changed me from the inside.

"In the dream I went from reading Scripture, to praying with Minnie and feeling that powerful presence, to the place where Balim was hung. It seemed like there were angels all around, and I dropped to my knees to pray, but I did not know how. That is when I felt impressed to pray to the God of Abraham, Isaac and Jacob. So that is what I did.

"I cried out to the God of Abraham, Isaac and Jacob to help me, and when I did I felt a strong presence in front of me. It was a man. He was glowing. I did not dare look at His face, but I saw His feet and hands, and they had holes in them."

"Hooey," Matthias let out a deep breath.

"Did He say anything?" Marigold asked in barely over a whisper.

"He touched me." Eli dropped his head and shook it from side to side remembering the holy moment. "And then He said 'I AM that I AM.'"

"Great God Almighty." Matthias slapped his knee with one hand. "The favor of God is upon you to have received such a visitation from God."

"I know there are steps I need to take and much to learn, but I assure you, Mr. Johnson, my faith is in Jesus. He is God. And He came to me. He came to me."

Matthias pulled a bandana out of his dungaree pocket and blew his nose with a loud trumpeting sound. "That is just what He does, son. He comes to those who seek Him."

"Oh, I have been, Mr. Johnson, for so long." Eli nodded. "I don't know what I will say yet to my parents or how they will take the news, but I know that this is the way I have been called to walk."

"Do you know what the name Jesus means?" Marigold looked at Eli with tear trails on her freckled face.

"No," said Eli, "not exactly."

"It means 'Jehovah is Salvation,'" said Marigold.

"This is all too much," said Eli beaming a tremendous smile, "but I want more. I know there is more."

"There is, son, and I am happy to talk to you about getting baptized in Jesus' name and filled with that power you felt coming from Minnie. God wants you to have that, too."

"Hallelujah!"

CHAPTER 35

Marigold grinned at Eli. He was practically glowing. "That was some prayer meeting," she said.

"I'll say. God is so real."

"I will be praying things go well with your family."

"Thank you." Eli reached for Marigold's hand as the couple walked to the surrey.

The stars were bright in the clear navy sky. A warbler sang along with the brook's bubbling melody.

When they reached the surrey Eli saw the package in the front seat and laughed. "Oh, yeah," he said, "I came to Briar Hollow tonight to deliver this package."

Marigold chuckled. "Right," she said, "the package."

"Really," said Eli. "These are the gloves for your father's birthday. They arrived at the post office this afternoon, and I wanted to make sure you had them for the party."

Marigold shook her head jostling her braids in a way that made Eli smile. "And you brought them here? For Pa to see?"

"Oh," Eli chuckled, "I guess maybe I should have taken them to the Coldwells."

"I guess," said Marigold, "but I am glad you didn't."

Eli placed his hands on both of Marigold's shoulders and turned her to face him. The moonlight was kind to her features and she looked angelic standing there in front of him.

"Marigold Johnson," he said, "from the first day you walked into the shop, I knew you were something special."

Marigold tried to relax—to let the tension out like Lucas had done to his yoyo string. If the peace was there, she would know she was on the right track. Like learning the yoyo trick, there would be lessons to learn, but everything would work out by the grace and help of God.

She drew in a deep breath, let it out slowly, and willed herself to relax and enjoy this moment for what it was—this moment. If the Lord chose to spin her kaleidoscope and make a new beautiful picture for her life with Eli in it, she was ready. If not, she had already given God the reins, and she chose to trust Him, come what may.

"From the first moment I met you, things were set in motion that brought me to this day. I am so thankful for all God is doing in my life."

"I am, too." Marigold smiled. "I have been praying for you—for your whole family."

"I know, and I thank you."

"I feel like my life is a book, and I have turned the page on a new chapter. I don't know what the Lord will write on the coming pages, but I know I want each page to have your name on it."

Marigold could hardly believe what was happening. Could this be real? She felt like she could fly if only she would take a running start and leap with the joy that flooded her soul. She had trusted God and look what He had done—a miracle—a miracle of salvation that had come to Eli, and so much more.

Her heart felt free and light, and at the same time heavy with sweetness, like a honeycomb full to the brim and ready to be harvested.

"Marigold Johnson," Eli spoke in a husky voice as he lowered himself on one bended knee, "I love you, and I want to marry you. Will you say yes?"

EPILOGUE

B alim and Abby Coldwell made full recoveries from their injuries. Sheriff Nash, with Zion's help, was able to get a confession out of Burke Calhoun and charged him, Trigg Simon, and Fred McGhee with attempted murder. With their arrest, peace returned to Briar Hollow, and they lived happily ever after.

Other Affirming Faith Resources
by Lori Wagner

Fiction
The Briar Hollow Series, Book 1: The Rose of Sharon
The Briar Hollow Series, Book 2: Buttercup
Gateway of the Sun

Discipleship/Christian Growth
Holy Intimacy: Dwelling with God in the Secret Place
Gates & Fences: Straight Talk in a Crooked World
Christian 101: Biblical Basics for New Believers and Youth

Inspirational/Devotional
Quilting Patches of Life
A Patchwork of Freedom
The 8 Days of Christmas

Board Game
*Orbis: The Fun Family Game You Win by
Blessing Your World*

LOOKING FOR A SPEAKER?

Based out of Clarkston, Michigan, Lori Wagner speaks internationally at a variety of events, from church services to conferences to banquets of all sizes and denominations.

For more information, or to schedule Lori Wagner at your event, visit the website:

WWW.AFFIRMINGFAITH.COM